LOST LUSTRE:
A NEW YORK MEMOIR

LOST LUSTRE:
A NEW YORK MEMOIR

Josh Karlen

TATRA PRESS LLC

Lost Lustre: A New York Memoir
Copyright © 2010 by Josh Karlen
All rights reserved. Printed in the United States of America. No part of this
book may be used or reproduced in any way without written permission from
the publisher, except in cases of brief quotations in reviews.

Library of Congress Control Number: TK

Contact Chris Sulavik
Tatra Press LLC
292 Spook Rock Road
Suffern, NY 10901
www.tatrapress.com

Jacket design by Kathleen Lynch, Black Kat Design.

Book design by Isabella Piestrzynska, Umbrella Graphics.

ISBN: 0-9819321-1-8

For Lorraine
and for Arno

Preface

THIS MEMOIR IS ABOUT A BOY, LATER A YOUNG MAN, GROWING UP IN MANHATTAN during a time that, while not so long ago, already has for me the dream-like quality of remotest memory.

Childhood and youth often feel remote, but the disconcerting sense I have of revisiting a far-away place in these pages also derives from the many changes—economic, societal, technological—that have reshaped the city since the late sixties. The Washington Square Park where as a boy I watched hippies strumming guitars in a late-afternoon haze of pot-smoke seems as lost to time as the Washington Square of Henry James. The ruinous tenements of Alphabet City, where I grew up, have been gentrified. The rowdy dens of my adolescence in the eighties—clubs like CBGB and Max's Kansas City—have been shuttered. The crime-ridden, graffiti-covered subways have been replaced, repaired, policed—even air-conditioned. Times Square is now safe for families. The city is, in short, far more tidy and, in many ways, more civilized.

Nevertheless, there remained, when I was growing up, vestiges of a more prosperous and elegant Manhattan: the big Checkered taxis with twin jump-seats that we piled into as teenagers, and the majestic movie theaters we visited on Saturday nights. Street corners still had glass phone-booths which, when they weren't vandalized or serving as homes for vagrants, provided shelter from the elements and privacy during a phone call. These gracious, if worn, relics co-existed with the bankrupt, trash-strewn mess the city had become, and were as integral to its atmosphere as the blare of transistor radios and, later,

boom-boxes. Their absence today—along with the more recent proliferation of hand-held computerized gadgets—contributes to the feeling
I have of looking back across a great distance.

Not all has disappeared, of course. Many Manhattan streets,
parks, and landmarks are remarkably unaltered. Even the newspapers I grew up with—the *Post*, the *Daily News* the *Times*, the *Village
Voice*—have, somehow, all survived and still chronicle the city. And
New York still hustles and dazzles and flings people into crazy orbits
as it always has and as no other city quite does.

Still, this book was not originally intended to be primarily about
Manhattan. I began to write it a few years ago, when I learned of the
death of the closest friend of my childhood and adolescence, after
many years of being out of touch. It was to be a sort of eulogy. But, as
more memories surfaced, I found myself writing about other facets
and periods of my early life in New York. Although I am a Manhat-
tanite almost since birth, I had not returned to my schools or many
other places I once knew—even on this narrow island, our routines
keep us in our own neighborhoods, work and families keep us busy,
and I had not felt sentimental about my earlier years. Now, though,
I was prompted to go back. And as I did, the book expanded. I hope
the reader will view these pages as I do—as the reflections of a New
Yorker who has reached his forties and paused to look backward
at an earlier city and an earlier self. For those who knew that city
in their youth, this book may bring back a piece of their own lives;
for those who did not, it may hold other interest. The pieces are
arranged in a roughly chronological sequence but are also intended
to stand alone.

This book describes little of my life after I left New York for college,
and so I must add here that, since I met my wife, Lorraine, twenty
years ago—at the time where this book leaves off—she has been
the greatest blessing of my life. Her understanding, patience,

intelligence, and humor, her dignity and generosity of spirit have helped guide me through these last two decades and, more recently, to complete this book.

I also must express my sincere gratitude to my family, to all of those whom I quote in the book and to many others whom I don't mention but who were invaluable in so many ways during the process of writing: Leslie Anders, Fred Burwell, Cynthia Cotts, David Ginsborg, Adam Hyman, Elisa Koff, Jonathan Lethem, David Marcus, Neil Martinson, Josh Milder, Paul Muryani, Yolanda Porventud, Jacob Saulig, Matthew Sharff, Gisell Torres, and Gloria Williams.

Table of Contents

1. My Sixties

My Sixties

I CAN PINPOINT EASILY ENOUGH THE DAY THE 1960s LAUNCHED FOR ME: October 20, 1964. On that date, my mother pushed me into this world at Madame Kladaki's Psychoprophylactic Maternity Home, at No. 26 Bouboulinas Street, in Athens, Greece.

My parents had been criss-crossing Europe for several months in a small, dusty, blue, two-horsepower Citroen, while my father wrote articles for *Holiday* magazine, where he worked as an editor, based in New York. They ended up settling in Athens just before I was born.

But by the time my sixties began, that fall of 1964, my parents' sixties were already nearly ten years old, reaching back deep into the fifties—if the decade is framed not primarily by boundaries of the calendar but by personal points of reference. And I have found that by considering the sixties in this way, I can mark the day when the decade ended for me—as much as it ever can be said to end.

The magazine hadn't sent my father to Europe on assignment; he and my mother had yearned to go abroad, particularly to Greece. They had been inspired by Laurence Durrell's writings about the country and by the late-night music at the Greek cafes that in the early sixties lined Eighth Avenue, and at the Café Feenjon, on MacDougal Street. And Greek music was in the air: the 1960 hit film *Never on Sunday*, in which an American tourist in Greece tries to reform a prostitute, had unleashed a fad for Greek music throughout the United States.

My parents had planned to live in Sphakia, a traditional village on Crete, where my father would write a novel and my mother would care for me and wash grapes in the sea.

2

They lived in Greece for nearly a year, but they never made it to Sphakia: my father was asked to return to the magazine offices in New York. And daily life in congested, alien, difficult Athens was not the idyll they had sought and expected. They returned to the States in wry disillusionment and carrying me, bundled in blankets, aged three months. They were both twenty-seven years old when our plane hit the tarmac at J.F.K. on the evening of January 27, 1965.

It was one thing to be twenty-seven then, but in 1967, my parents were thirty, a particularly awkward age to be amid the intensifying tumult of that time. I, for one, would not wish to be exactly age thirty when the slogan "don't trust anyone over thirty" appeared. My parents were caught in the crossfire of the country's generational war.

Still, many thirty-year-olds did experiment with LSD and pot, went to rock concerts like that at Monterey, in 1967, and Woodstock, in 1969. (My step-father, who was a year younger than my mother, did go to Woodstock at thirty.) But rock concerts, drugs—these weren't my parent's *bag*, to use a term of the day. They didn't wear far-out clothing—sandals, bellbottom jeans, peace medallions—although my father did grow his hair and sideburns longer. He was forced by his magazine job to discard his army-surplus clothes for suits—he wore the hip styles—wide lapels, broad, colorful ties. My mother wore the mod-but-mainstream fashions—long hair, short skirts.

Both my parents came from families with Old Left and bohemian traditions. They met in the mid-fifties, at Antioch College, a liberal campus in Yellow Springs, Ohio.

My mother generally cast a slightly amused and easy-going eye on life. At Antioch, she hung around with student actors, social outcasts, folkies. She considered herself a writer from a young age.

My father also was a writer—fiction, journalism, poetry, criticism, non-fiction. In the fifties, he grew a goatee (a serious statement during the era of the gray-flannel suit), lived in the Village, hitchhiked and drove jalopies across the country, worked odd jobs, froze in garrets, spent a year at the Sorbonne. He was a radical, fought for civil rights in the Deep South. But he, like my mother, could not relate to the drug- and music-based youth culture that later emerged. My parents considered the hippies muddle-headed kids they couldn't quite understand, even if they shared certain causes. As an old-school bohemian, my father scorned the hippies for lacking true intellectual seriousness and passion. He said that in the Village in the fifties you could identify people by the books they read in the cafes, not the drugs or music they were into. (*"Were you reading Bakunin or Rimbaud?"*) He saw the 130-year-old, European bohemian tradition fade in Greenwich Village during the years 1957 to 1959, and he once remarked that those years were when *his* sixties began. But then, just when does an era begin and end?

◇

For those people older than I am, it may seem too facile to say my sixties opened the day I was born. For millions of Americans, the sixties began, grievously, shockingly, on November 22, 1963—the day President Kennedy was assassinated. But the date of my birth is the point here, because my birth, in late 1964, wedges me into an unusual position among Americans, just as my parents were in an unusual position forty years ago. While I am just too young to remember the sixties with any real clarity, I am just old enough to remember fragments of representative scenes beyond the crib and playground, and, more generally, to have deeply absorbed, largely through popular culture—records, films, television—the charged atmosphere of the period.

Most people I've met who are only a few years younger lack such specific memories and the more amorphous feeling for the mood of the late sixties, which make those years an integral part of who I am, even now. And those who are even only a few years older than I retain more detailed memories of the decade, which bind them more completely to that time. Like my parents, I am by birth caught between generations, but for me, the decades are the Technicolor sixties and the gray seventies.

One friend, born in 1963, clearly recalls his mother telling him that the Beatles had broken up, an event I don't remember. Still, the Beatles—and through their conduit, so much of late-sixties popular culture—occupy an enormous part of the terrain of my early memories.

After my parents separated, in 1968, my mother brought me and my brother, who is two years younger (and who lacks memories of the sixties), to live in a housing development on the Lower East Side, where she played *Abbey Road* on the turn-

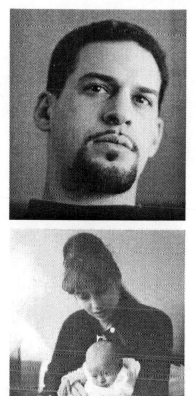

Top: The author's father as a young bohemian in the 1950s; bottom: The author and his mother in Athens a week after his birth, in 1964.

table until I had each of its lush, baroque, gracefully fluid melodies memorized. I also memorized the *Sgt. Pepper* and *Magical Mystery*

Tour albums. The haunting, mellotron-laden psychedelia of "Lucy in the Sky with Diamonds" and the disorienting "I Am the Walrus," with its upside-down horns, inside-out cellos, and sexual, surreal, mysterious lyrics, opened the door, prematurely, to the dark side of the adult world—LSD, rock music, sex—which I could only partly comprehend: I was still singing "If I had Hammer" in school and was only a little beyond books like *Peter Goes to School* and *Mr. Pine's Purple House.*

I saw the psychedelic animated Beatles film *Yellow Submarine* and owned a toy metal yellow submarine. On my bedroom wall for many years were Scotch-taped the four Richard Avedon photo-portraits of the Beatles and the jagged, photo-collage poster that was folded inside the 1968 *White Album.*

The Beatles were so omnipresent in my life they were still current to me long past 1970. They followed me to Ohio each summer. In suburban Cleveland, during the long afternoons, with the perfect lawns and homes of Beachwood outside the window stretching away under the August sun, I would lie on my older cousin's bed in the attic room and listen to his eight-track tapes of the Beatles, entranced by the harmonies and melodies of songs like "Penny Lane," while reading comic books. It felt like 1967, could have *been* 1967, even though that annual ritual did not begin until 1969.

My older cousins were not quite hippies, but they grew their hair long, smoked pot openly, wore colorful clothes, listened to psychedelic music—all of which their parents (my mother's family) tolerated in an easy-going way. In that big house in Beachwood, Ohio, of all places, the sixties persisted for me well into the seventies.

It was my step-father who had first brought us the Beatles. He was far more a part of, or at least receptive to, the sixties youth culture than was my father. He also brought to our apartment an acoustic guitar, bellbottoms, wild hair and groovy clothes. He drove a sporty orange Fiat convertible, which a couple of years later he replaced with the car that I grew up with: a 1966 navy-blue Bonneville Pontiac— a very sixties sort of machine: a massive cruise-liner of a car with a ferocious engine, no air-conditioning and hand-cranked windows. There were no laws yet requiring seatbelts. Our Bonneville carted us around the country during our summer road trips throughout the seventies like a time-capsule on wheels.

My step-father also brought, in addition to his Beatles albums, records like Janis Joplin's *Cheap Thrills* (with its grotesque and explicit cover artwork by R. Crumb), Jimi Hendrix, The Doors, and a lot of blues and jazz. These were added to my mother's folk albums of the Kingston Trio, the Weavers, and the music recorded live at the Greek nightclubs.

From the albums that lined our shelves, I internalized most of the popular-music fads from the previous two decades: the flavor of the Greek music, the working-class rage and laments of the Old Left, the sex, drugs, and love gospel of rock—though the

Three albums of the sixties: Top to bottom: "Cheap Thrills" (1968); "String Along with the Kingston Trio" (1960); "Recorded Live at Menachem Dworman's Café Feenjon" (1966).

messages were often bewildering or only partially understood. And of course, I learned from the Beatles that all you need is love.

I spent much of my childhood in New York's epicenter of counter-culture, St. Mark's Place, with my friend Jack, who lived there on the top floor of a tenement with his divorced mother and older sister. St. Mark's Place was New York's rough equivalent of Haight-Ashbury, with its gritty mix of hippies, drifters, artists, musicians, writers, counter-culture celebrities, derelicts and lost souls. Just down the block from Jack's tenement was the Fillmore East, where Jimi Hendrix, The Grateful Dead, and Jefferson Airplane had performed just a couple of years earlier. There were little bars and shops that sold peace buttons and beads and used-clothing. Among those who had lived within a block or so from Jack in the sixties were Lenny Bruce, Abbie Hoffman, and Diane Arbus.

The sixties films, like pop songs, also sent complex messages for a young boy, and Jack and I saw many films at the St. Marks Cinema—a decaying venue that showed second-run double-features, with a long gash down the screen, bums snoring in the chairs and blue clouds of pot smoke swirling across the flickering light-beams of the projector. We saw all kinds of films that we shouldn't have seen; the ticket-takers never stopped us at the entrance. We saw the 1968 film *I Love You, Alice B. Toklas* a couple of years after it came out. That film plunged me prematurely into the adult world of flower children, drugs, and sex, just as the Beatles' music and the album cover of *Cheap Thrills* had. I remember sitting in the dark theater and being disoriented, fascinated and frightened.

That film probably was, along with *Easy Rider* (which I believe we also saw at the St. Marks Cinema), one of the quintessential sixties films, replete with pot-filled brownies, a white-clad guru, and a plot about a square lawyer who falls for a hippie girl in California and becomes a hippie himself, wearing a headband and beads. The film was, in fact, mildly skeptical of both hippies and squares, but such subtleties were lost on me. I only perceived that adults were projected on an enormous screen dressed as hippies—and if adults wore love beads and danced amid lava lamps, it all must be what adults properly did—and I assumed that I would, too, someday. Even forty years later, some part of me can't completely reject those love beads and lava lamps.

◇

It's frequently been observed that centuries and decades don't begin and end when they properly should: the 20th century, it's been suggested, began on June 28, 1914, the date of the assassination of Archduke Franz Ferdinand, and ended on November 9, 1989, when the Berlin Wall fell. The sixties, for many, began on November 22, 1963, and ended on various dates: for some it was August 9, 1969, the day of the Charles Manson murders; for others it was December 6, 1969, at the Altamont music festival; for still others, it was January 23, 1973, the day President Nixon announced the agreement to end the Vietnam War. Another symbolic date: April 10, 1970—the day Paul McCartney publicly announced he'd broken with the Beatles. (Their final recorded album, *Abbey Road*, closes with a song titled, almost too neatly, "The End.")

The point is that we know the atmosphere that characterizes a period cannot be neatly contained within the dates that mark our centuries and decades, and so we seek to impose order on, and gain insight into, history, by identifying cultural milestones or certain meaningful personal memories as the "true" start or end of an era.

To be sure, the spirit and the pivotal events of certain decades, such as the twenties (boom) and thirties (bust), do seem, somewhat unnervingly, to fit within their proper periods. But, far more commonly, fixing decades on a zeitgeist is like trying to contain smoke in a wire cage. We know that the cultural and political upheavals and the atmosphere of the sixties did not begin on the morning of January 1, 1960, and end on December 31, 1969. They continued into the seventies, faded and changed as the seventies gradually took its own shape.

During the early seventies, the mood of the sixties remained thick in Greenwich Village—I think of the bearded kids in sandals lounging on the grass in Washington Square Park or strumming guitars in Tompkins Square Park, and I remember the tenement apartments and SoHo lofts where my school friends lived with divorced mothers and their boyfriends, and which always seemed cluttered with pot plants and psychedelic wall-hangings and bongo drums and the scent of burning incense.

In 1970, I started first grade at a school in the West Village, a few blocks from my father's apartment. The school was, if not quite a hippie school, very nearly so. It was "experimental," with "open" classrooms. We called our teachers by their first names, in true sixties' style. Our teacher's name was Lucy, and I always associated her with "Lucy in the Sky with Diamonds." My classmates were, of course, children of Greenwich Village parents, and in our class photograph we all have an abundance of hair. In 1972, a school friend brought me with his family in their Volkswagen bus to a patch of grass by a highway outside Manhattan, where his blond parents—*real* hippies— decked out with headbands and bellbottoms, got high, a dog nosed around, and the song "American Pie"—dreamlike, grieving, angry, soaring—blared from a radio.

One pop-culture example of how the flavor of the sixties persisted into the seventies is *Rowan & Martin's Laugh-In*, a comedy television program as emblematic of the sixties as any, with its flower children and girls painted with peace signs on their bellies, and its tag-line, "sock it to me." The show's name itself was a play on the then-current term "love-in." The program, which NBC launched in prime-time in January, 1968, was among the most popular in America for a few years, but viewership dwindled after 1970, and it went off the air on May 14, 1973. (One could say the sixties ended on *that* date.) Jokes about flower-power had become passé, but, nevertheless, three years had passed since the end of the previous decade. (NBC's *Saturday Night Live*, which premiered in October, 1975, has been described, rightly, as the seventies' version of *Laugh-In*, with the sixties program's zaniness weighted by post-Watergate cynicism and carrying a political explicitness that had not yet appeared on TV.)

When I attended college in the Midwest, in the early and mid-eighties, there were still discussions on campus about how the sixties spirit was finally fading. There, too, it might be said, the sixties didn't quite begin and end when the decade should have, but, rather, ran from 1964 to 1978, the dates of the college's experimental educational plan.

As late as 1980, the sixties could suddenly resurge across America (and the world) as a potent cultural force—recall the intense grief that exploded following the murder of John Lennon, in New York, on December 8 of that year. I had spent so many hours communing with the Beatles at home and in that attic room in Beachwood, that Lennon's death felt like the loss of a companion of my childhood. Again, it could be said that the sixties ended on December 8, 1980, just as the decade started with another murder, on November 22, 1963. But, finally, searches for symbolic boundaries for the spirit of a decade such as the sixties are futile exercises, since such periods never truly begin or end. The passions, beliefs, political issues, and cultural shifts continue to reverberate through subsequent generations, just as the Great Depression persists through the parsimony of survivors, or as the fifties persisted in our home through my mother's folk records. Like MacArthur's old soldiers, eras like the sixties never die, they just fade away. Even now, people gather to sing Beatles songs in Central Park across from the Dakota, where Lennon was shot.

◇

The atmosphere of the sixties—the street protests, race riots, civil rights marches, rock music, drugs—which I absorbed in the vague, yet astute and thorough way that young children always absorb their surroundings, is intertwined with the political issues of the period. And while I was far too young to properly understand politics, I already knew, in 1972, that I was a Democrat and that I supported George McGovern's campaign for president. I even wore a McGovern button.

All adults, from my child's perspective, considered McGovern to be Good and Nixon to be Evil. This was Truth, because my parents, and seemingly all the adults in my world, said it was Truth. A child cannot distinguish among such fine concepts as the "lesser of two evils," which many voters considered the Democratic candidate. So I believed that everyone was emphatically "for" McGovern. But while the election was held in 1972, it was still in many ways a late-sixties-era political contest, and it was the foundation of my identity as a Democrat.

With McGovern as my first childhood political hero, how could I *not* be a Democrat when I reached voting age? Like our religion and our sports teams, our political affiliations are usually passed down through family. These affiliations are bound up with deep tribal feelings of loyalty, affection, sentimentality and, often, of inertia: to switch alliances in religion and politics requires a conscious effort of the will and often demands careful, logical, difficult thought about what are, at least partly, emotional issues. I never had a need, though, to rebel against my parent's liberalism. I like to think that I have thoughtfully examined the political issues and have come to a reasoned conclusion that I agree with many ideals of the Democrats and the sixties. After all, as the (seventies) song asks: what's so funny about peace, love and understanding?

But I do know that to hold an allegiance to the Democratic Party solely because it was my parents' party would be absurd; to hold an allegiance to the Democrats decades later because of what it was in 1972 would also be nonsensical. Almost everything has changed— the candidates, many of the political issues, the world itself. Such an allegiance to the Democratic Party would ignore the complexities of the issues not only of the present but also of the sixties. In a sense, I am not an Obama democrat, or a Carter democrat or even an LBJ democrat. I am by sentiment a McGovern democrat, who remains in the party admittedly, in part, for sentimental reasons.

◇

Yet, despite all of this, I cannot fully embrace the ideals and culture of the sixties, and I attribute my ambivalence, like my attachment, to my awkward birth-year, 1964. The date puts me on the border between the youngest of the Baby Boomers and oldest of so-called Generation X'ers, or Baby Busters, the generation that came of age in the seventies and eighties, disillusioned by the economic and cultural bleakness of those years in America. Like a citizen of two warring countries, I hold a dual allegiance. The sixties youth were rebelling against a post-war America I had not known. As a boy among the hippies of the Village, I knew only the late rebellion, not its cause; knew only the strange and raucous new world created on the wreckage of an America I had not lived in. I was a little bundle just starting to be formed by the sixties when it all began to recede. And in truth, most of my clear memories begin at the precise end of that decade: 1970. As the pot smoke and the guitar strumming began to disappear from Washington Square Park, I sensed, although with only a half-conscious puzzlement, that the grown-up world around me was changing, was even rejecting the values I had been taught to embrace.

As an adolescent, I certainly did not consider myself a sixties' child; in high school, in the late seventies, my friends and I scorned the small group of second-generation hippies who smoked pot in the nearby park, wore sandals and long hair. Their loyalty to sixties' ideals seemed pitiably naive, comically outdated. We had embraced the angry nihilism of punk rock. Yet, even then, I intuited that my condemnation was a betrayal of a part of myself. The directly opposed outlooks of these two groups within the adjacent generations—love and peace; hate and violence—co-existed within me uneasily as I grew up. But at some fundamental level, my deepest affection was, and remains, for the world I knew in my earliest years, and my deepest identity is as a child of the sixties.

◇

Today, the sixties are ancient history. Hippies are senior citizens, or nearly so. Generation X has given way to Generation Y and beyond. Adults in their twenties see the sixties as "History" in same way that I see the fifties as "History": they lack that childhood feeling for the period that makes it alive for you, part of you. And sometimes I sense the sixties are more intimately a part of me than even I can know. In addition to the memory fragments that fasten me to the decade, there are also so many memories that lie submerged until something prods them to the surface. During a recent visit to the New York Transit Museum, I saw a city bus from the sixties, the same model that I had taken each day to and from elementary school, with the primitive fare-collection machine that let passengers' coins fall on a tray that the driver opened by pushing a lever, and which filled the bus with a *chank-a-chank* rhythm that always made me think of "Pick a

Bale of Cotton," a song I knew from my mother's folk albums. I had forgotten, or thought I had forgotten, about that machine, that *chank-a-chank* rhythm, that old folk song. I've wondered how many such buried memories fasten me to that time like invisible cords. And I am bound by still older memories, memories so lost in earliest childhood that they will never fully resurface as specific images, will provide only vague and perplexing feelings of recognition for certain objects that I inexplicably associate with the sixties. These feelings are stirred up by the most mundane and unlikely objects, noticed in the briefest of glances—a wooden salad bowl on a wood table; a row of plants along a window sill; a hammock in a yard; a black-and-white television discarded on a curb; a typeface on a shop sign. On a fall day last year, I saw, in a side-street in the Village, a sun-faded sign propped in a dry cleaner's window, with a drawing of a young couple wearing fashions and hair styles that clearly dated from the sixties and which had apparently been sitting in that window for forty years. That image resonated within me the moment I saw it—possibly, I had seen it decades before, perhaps even in that same window.

Nevertheless, in looking back through my personal history, I find I can pinpoint the moment the sixties did, in a sense, end for me. It was, in fact, a day in the early seventies, though I don't recall the date or even the year, and I did not fully grasp the larger societal changes at work. It was not Watergate, or any other headline-making event, but as is so often the case, it was a small and very personal incident that indicated something profound had altered in the world. One morning, my father emerged from the bathroom and as I looked at him I noticed something was different. I studied his profile as he stood at a table and went through some papers, and then I realized what it was.

"Why did you shave your sideburns short?" I asked.

My father thought a moment, then shrugged. "Fashions change," he said.

2. Farewell, Avenue C

Farewell, Avenue C

One day I was walkin' 'n'
Finally came upon a series of alphabet streets
A-B-C and D, but I went for "C"
The most of the hard-to-forget streets
                    —"Avenue C," Lambert, Hendricks & Ross (1957)

In the winter of 1968, when I was four years old, my mother brought my infant brother and me to a new housing development that had risen among the tenements of Avenue C, to start our new life.

She had separated from my father, who had moved to Greenwich Village, and whom we would thereafter visit on weekends.

Our family, until that winter, had lived near Gramercy Park, one of Manhattan's most pleasant middle-class neighborhoods. Our apartment building faced a row of four-story, Italianate and Greek Revival houses—the sort of sturdy yet graceful homes built in the 19th century by merchants and financiers for their sprawling families. There was a vest-pocket park nearby, with green wood benches and sylvan sculptures, where in the afternoons black nannies brought white children—and where our own nanny, a large-bosomed old southern lady we called Mike, brought us, wheeling my brother in a carriage.

As calculated by the map—that is, as measured horizontally—we had moved a distance of only about one mile: four long avenues and twelve short streets. But calculated vertically, we had plunged through the Heavens to a street somewhere in Hell.

In those days, the stretch of ruined tenements along Avenue C between Houston Street and Fourteenth Street was becoming the heroin capital not only for New York City but for the entire United States.

One former Ninth Precinct officer, Edward D. Reuss, who began to patrol the neighborhood about a dozen years later, wrote:

The neighborhood had been given the notorious name "Alphabet City." Drug trafficking was out of control. The rubble of the empty buildings provided excellent cover for the sale of narcotics. The dealers had created a labyrinth of connecting tunnels through the walls and floors of the dilapidated tenements. They had placed booby traps in doorways and staircases designed to cause injury...There were so many junkies and coke addicts walking around...Drug dealers would often conceal sawed-off shotguns with shoulder slings under those coats. Under the street conditions in the 9th Precinct, the six-shot revolver just didn't cut the mustard. Backup guns were a must and most cops carried them. Double layers of Kevlar bulletproof vests were also commonly worn.... The presence of a marked police car made no difference to those legions of drug users who actually lined up on the burned out stairwells to make their buys...The area was later described in an official NYPD training bulletin as an "open air drug market."

So what on earth were *we* doing there?

◇

My mother always said, through all the years we demanded an answer to this question, that she had brought us with the expectation that the neighborhood was on the verge of being "gentrified." She clung to this belief for the fifteen years I lived there, despite all glaring evidence to the contrary. To my brother and me, any move to clean up Avenue C would be as futile as sending the NYPD to try to gentrify Hell itself. Still, in the long—the very long—view, her prediction proved prescient: the neighborhood *did* gentrify, though with excruciating slowness. We were in the vanguard of the forty-year gentrification process that is still going on: gentrification was what those towering housing developments were intended for when they were built, in 1967, and I suppose this purpose was achieved, to an extent. The buildings attracted other white, middle-class families, along with Puerto Rican and black professionals and their children, to those condemned tenements, vacant lots, bodegas and garages. We lived, I felt, precariously, like isolated cliff-dwellers above a barbaric plain.

In truth, Avenue C was not only a lair for drug dealers and addicts, petty criminals, teenage gangs and derelicts; it was also home for honest, struggling black and Puerto Rican families who ran small shops and businesses: along our block was a corner bodega, a hair salon, a candy-and-newspaper stand, and a bar. At the bodega, the two Puerto Rican proprietors sat at a little counter behind a bulletproof, Plexiglas stronghold. To pay for your groceries, you slid a bill or coins under a thin slot in the fortification. These middle-aged men were trying to scratch-out a living under conditions that must have seemed as deadly and as eternal as a medieval siege. If it had been possible, they probably would have dug a moat.

The Puerto Ricans and blacks had begun moving into the tenements in the fifties, as the old Jews began to die off or flee with their children to the suburbs. For a white, Jewish, middle-class family to move *into* the Lower East Side just then was absurd. The Latino culture that enclosed us was utterly alien: we didn't understand the language of the people we lived among—the shop signs were Spanish; the stray

Top: Avenue C, in Alphabet City, in the 1980s; bottom: Avenue C in 1976.

pages of the *El Diario* newspaper in the gutters were in Spanish; the conversations along the streets—the men who drank beer on stoops wearing porkpie hats and flashing gold teeth, the women scolding their toddlers—were in Spanish. The kids who played on the stripped cars and in the water-gushers of the open fire-hydrants in the summer shouted at each other in Spanish. The graffiti curses spray-painted on the tenements were in Spanish. Frenetic, tinny Latino music blasted endlessly from transistor radios, and the horns of the flashy pimp cars cruising by tooted "La Cucaracha." Bodega windows displayed dusty yellow packages of Bustelo coffee and cans of Goya beans.

All of this—the Latino culture and Spanish language, the desolation, the endemic carnage, the drugs and violence, along with our location at the very edge of the island, by the East River—coalesced to sever the neighborhood from its surroundings, from the city itself. No subway line ventured so far east; our block was near the terminus for two bus routes. Even the air smelled different here—a mixture of rot from the river, dust from the rubble of ruined buildings, and urine and beer from the gutters. On Avenue C, in an alien, savage region that clung, unwanted, to the periphery of the city, our family was trapped deep within a sort of double solitary confinement: a cultural isolation within a geographic isolation.

Our neighborhood fell within the old designation of New York's Lower East Side: the thousands of 19th century tenements that sprawled from Canal Street north to Fourteenth Street. Our immediate vicinity, north of Houston Street, has often been included as part of the East Village (a name that emerged in the late fifties), but when we arrived, the bohemian culture hadn't yet reached us. The eastern boundary of the East Village was still Tompkins Square Park, a large, leafy square with bench-lined paths, a decaying, graffiti-covered band-shell, and basketball courts, lodged between Avenues A and B. In the sixties, the park drew Latinos, blacks, elderly East European immigrants, and hippies. In the seventies, the park became a haven for drug dealers, addicts, gangs. The paths were strewn with trash and hypodermic needles, the benches strewn with the homeless.

For me, the western edge of Tompkins Square Park—Avenue A—marked the border where, if you could reach it, civilization began. It was also, when I returned home by bus from elementary school in the Village each day, the line where civilization ended.

On that bus each afternoon, rolling eastward, the passengers would gradually exit, until we reached the park, and I would be alone among the rows of empty seats as the driver bore just the two of us through the increasingly decrepit tenements, the smashed pavements, the stripped cars.

And each day, as we passed the edge of the park, my stomach would start to churn, my heart would start to hammer, and I would peer, from low in my seat, through the dirty windows, desperately hoping that the bus would reach my stop before I was seen. My prayers on that empty bus each day were almost tearful entreaties for divine protection through that Valley of the Shadow of Death. And my fears were not the wild imaginings of a young boy: there *were* terrors outside. If the gangs spotted me, they would run beside the bus with their sticks or chains, grinning up at me, then wait for me to step off, as I had to, even as I knew what would come. Then they would rob me while the bus driver, who saw it all, would snap closed the doors at my back, and drive on.

The dangers were not only teenage gangs, but also adults. One winter twilight as I sat alone on the bus, which the driver had idling at the traffic light a block from our building, the door was suddenly struck by a force that rocked the vehicle like an explosion. Then, a second strike, a second thunderous crash. Outside, a man was shouting with insane fury. I saw through the glass doors a tall, gaunt man—a pimp in a long fur coat, his face half-hidden beneath a broad, feathered hat—was demanding the driver let him on, and had kicked at the doors with his boot. The bus driver's frightened stare darted from the pimp to the red traffic-light, which seemed never would change to green. I silently implored the driver: *please don't let him on this bus, don't let him on,* while the pimp raged through the glass, pummeling the door with his fists. Then, with a final kick, he struck with such force that the glass shattered and collapsed, and the driver, in panic, gunned the bus away through the red light, blasting the horn, scattering traffic.

The driver, a mountain of a Latino man, had been as frightened as I was. Where could a boy of eight turn for protection in that wilderness?

◇

I didn't fully realize we were living on Avenue C until a couple of years after we arrived. My first memory is of walking home from the bodega holding, in one hand, a paper bag with a quart of milk and, in the other hand, a few coins in change from the dollar my mother had given me to buy it. As I neared our doorway—a modern, glass-enclosed vestibule—three Puerto Rican boys holding sticks appeared around me, blocked my way.

They demanded something, but their words made no sense.

"What's in th' bag?" one said in English.

Another of the boys prodded the bag with the end of his stick. I moved to push past them. Instantly, my hair was seized from behind, I was grabbed from all sides.

"Give us th' bag!"

"Whachyou got in ya hand? Money?"

Sticks crashed on my neck, my head, my back, a furious rain. Fingers tore at my eyes.

"Give ovah the bag, maricon!"

"Yo! White boy! Let go of th' bag!"

A final blow on the back of my head. I went down. The bag was wrenched away.

When I sat up, the boys were running around a corner, holding their sticks like spears.

I sat on the pavement looking down Avenue C—this broad street of tenements that I did not know, that I was seeing for the first time.

I ran to our building and rode the elevator to our apartment.

"Some people don't have all the things we do," my mother explained. "But you shouldn't have fought them. If it happens again, just give them what they want. They could have really hurt you."

Such sensible words from my mother, who acted so insensibly! Well, there you were: a quick but effective introductory lesson in Evil and Poverty. Until that day, I had no fear, I had no awareness of where I was. After that day, I knew *exactly* where I was, and as the muggings continued, my days became a continual terror.

◇

It is difficult for me to convey the intensity of that terror—the deep sense of being trapped in the center of a vast, seemingly endless maze swarming with perils. The only person I know who can fully understand it is my brother, who is two years younger.

The terror was not only acute, but chronic; it churned my insides every day, from the moment those three boys attacked me with sticks nearly until I left for college, at age eighteen.

The panic intensified each year, with each mugging, before diminishing during the final few years I lived there. Shortly before I left Avenue C, I tallied up the number of times I was mugged and reached more than a dozen. I can no longer remember all, or even most, of the incidents. What remain are a few particularly nightmarish moments: I'm with a friend on a basketball court near an abandoned factory, while three young men hold knives to our necks and cars whiz by a few yards away on the FDR Drive; I'm in a tenement hallway, pinned at knifepoint to a wall, watching a neighbor's son violently struggling, until his captor waves a blade in his face and shakes his head warningly, "no"; I'm racing home, pursued by a half-dozen kids with sticks, am caught just outside our glass lobby—I swing at them until I'm beaten down and lose consciousness...

Usually, though, I wasn't badly hurt. They would order you to empty your pockets, then might strike a parting shot or two, shove you, kick you, humiliate you: look you in the eyes while they spat on your face, cursed you (and always your mother), cursed your whiteness, in both Spanish and English, for good measure. *"What'd ya say t'me?"* one of the kids would demand as a pretext for smashing a fist into your face, slamming you back against a wall. *"What'd ya call my mutha? You call my mutha a whore? Maricon! White muthafucka!"*

To sharpen your humiliation, they often put forward the smallest kid, some kid smaller than you, who battered you, spit at you, cursed you, grabbed your money, while the older kids—often nearly grown young men—taunted you to fight back: *"Hijo de puta! Hit 'im back! Why don' ya hit 'im!"*

"Dame los chavos carajo!"

"Hijo de puta!"

But it wasn't the pain of the blows or the humiliation or the racist hatred that caused the true terror. It was the sensation of being on your way to somewhere—the bodega, or the bus-stop, or a friend's apartment—and suddenly spotting those kids—perhaps just two, or perhaps a throng of more than a dozen that seemed to fill the entire street. You'd see them striding at you, or tailing you, in their worn sneakers and cheap coats, their stares fixed on you, and you would know, at the instant your eyes met theirs, just what was going to happen, inevitably. And then you'd be abruptly ringed by those deadened stares from those dirty faces, while standing in some broken, deserted street, or forgotten alley, or vacant playground, immeasurably distant from any aid or sanctuary. In those stares you saw that your life, and their *own* lives, were worthless to them. These kids *knew* they were fated to wander those streets until they were taken away by prison or death, and some of the older kids had already been locked up. The stares surrounding you reflected all the desolation of those streets, those destroyed cars, broken windows, crumbling tenement walls. Encircled by these dead stares, with a knife or heavy chains or a baseball bat in your face, the insane panic that rose in your throat was that of facing imminent death. And that was the real fear: you never knew how they would leave you, and I believed, each time I left our building, for fifteen years, that I might be murdered, tortured, maimed.

While in retrospect, it was unlikely I would have been killed, this fear, on Avenue C, was not far-fetched. They threatened you with death: *"Give us what ya got or we cut you up, white boy."* Once, a black kid, no more than seven or eight years old, standing in a gang that had surrounded me, slyly smiled and revealed to me a pistol, pulling it from his coat.

The evidence of violence and cruelty was everywhere. At night, guns of various calibers boomed and cracked through the streets below. In the day, we found bullet casings in the gutters. Dogs were tortured, squealing and shrieking in the night. I once discovered, as I cut through a weedy lot, the corpse of a pup, its legs bound with electrical cords, its fur charred, its eyes boiling with maggots. In the gutters lay rows of stripped cars—windows shattered, tires gone. Often cars, like dogs and tenements, were set afire, and their charred remains sat for months. When the nearby factory was demolished, the newspaper reported that a woman's skeleton had been discovered chained to a pipe. In the lobby of our apartment building, my brother and I came home one afternoon and found the glass walls spattered and dripping with blood, the floor covered in bloody pools. So when kids with dead eyes threatened to kill you and waved a knife in your face, it was not a joke.

I never carried a weapon, but my brother carried a number of them from age fourteen to eighteen—a chain, a knife, Mace canisters. Like me, he was mugged, beaten, nearly stabbed. (He wrote me: "I remember getting sadistically tortured in public by three kids—two brothers and a sister, who took turns beating me up.") He attended the local high school for a year, and one day came home and said that a corpse that had been sawed in half had been discovered in the garbage outside the school.

Where were the police, our neighbors, our parents? In my memory, adults or police never aided us. I remember, once, my brother and I ducked into a toy store owned by an elderly couple on Fourteenth Street, to evade a few kids who were tailing us. From the street, right outside the shop's glass door, the boys grinned at us, taunted us, mockingly urged us outside. We pleaded with the elderly couple to phone for the police or our parents, and while they clearly saw the kids outside their door, they merely shrugged, with that closed-off, shopkeeper air, and said we could not stay there, we had to leave. And of course, the moment we stepped outside, we were attacked and robbed.

As for our parents, my brother and I eventually realized that our mother and step-father could not grasp the depth of our sufferings. After all, our housing development was modern and pleasant, we seldom came home with more than a few welts and bruises, and violent crime was mostly confined to youth gangs, the elderly, and junkies; adults such as my parents, who spent little time on the streets (they drove through it in our old Pontiac), were generally left alone. Our step-father, a doctor, seemed to brush aside our complaints, and our mother replied in an exasperatingly distant way to our demands for explanation. As the years passed, three younger step-siblings arrived, and they too, came to hate and fear our neighborhood, and raised cries to leave.

On weekends, when my brother and I visited our father and step-mother, we appealed to them, asked why we were trapped in that slum, and though they urged our mother and step-father to get out, relations between the households were strained at best, and their urgings were futile.

◇

To say I was mugged a dozen times over the course of as many years is misleading, because it was the countless occasions that I avoided being attacked, that I spotted the danger and skirted it, which contributed to the sense of traversing a battleground and sharpened the sickening panic when I left the apartment for the bodega or got off the bus from school.

Each day, those fifteen years, when my brother and I walked through the neighborhood, we scanned every street before entering, scanned every face for signals of danger. The scan had to be instantaneous to avoid confrontation or engagement, and your own expression had to remain unreadable, a blank iron-mask for the panic that roiled your guts and made your hands tremble in your pockets. You learned to discern danger instantly by the eyes—those peculiarly malevolent, deadened gazes that became so familiar you could recognize them in a glance of less than a second. But often, even by the time you read their gaze, it was too late: they had also read yours.

When you walked, the stride was remarkably subtle in its unconscious calculation: purposeful but relaxed, confident but not a swagger, eyes locked ahead firmly at some distant point, never seeming to be uncertain of where one was headed. It all was meant to send an extremely specific message—that you knew your way around and weren't frightened, but you also weren't looking for trouble.

Our clothes were dull, non-descript, meant to avoid notice and any suggestion we had money. We camouflaged with grays and browns, the same colors as our slum, animals camouflaging against predators. The money we did carry was hidden in a shoe or our gloves, with a small amount carefully reserved for our pockets, to mollify attackers.

My brother and I eluded danger by crossing streets, backtracking, looping around blocks, hiding in bodegas and doorways. As we walked, we would arrange, with a murmured word or two, a place to meet—a certain bus stop or a certain corner—if we had to run different ways or were separated. A few blocks later, we would arrange a new place. I don't recall that we ever had to split up and meet at one of our arranged places, but in the back of my mind I always thought that if we ever did become separated and my brother didn't show up at our designated place, it meant they'd taken him, done something unimaginable. And there was a comfort in knowing that if I was captured someone would know to search for me.

We confined ourselves to a few familiar routes: most of the surrounding streets we *never* would venture through, especially after dark, when the neighborhood became even more nightmarish. From our tower, we looked down at those dark tenements with their windows glowing dully, heard in our beds the gunshots, the bird-whistles of the drug-dealer "lookouts," the drunken arguments on the corner outside Marvin's bar. We watched the prostitutes trolling the empty avenue and the fights with broken bottles and knives. Then, somewhere after midnight, quiet settled on the neighborhood. Avenue C stretched empty under the streetlights, except perhaps for some wandering shadows. An occasional car or delivery truck rumbled by on the old Belgian paving stones that had resurfaced through the tar. Cockfights were held, and each dawn, the crowing of a rooster or two pierced the silence of our sleeping ghetto.

Some nights, during the quiet hours, arsonists would torch a tenement, and the flames would shoot up into darkness while the occupants streamed down fire escapes. Fire trucks would arrive with wailing sirens, and families, standing in the street in nightgowns, underwear, and blankets, would be trucked off to shelters.

During the months afterward, the charred building would stand beside all the others that had also been burned for insurance, their rows of windows gaping blackly, or covered with cinder blocks, bricks, or sheets of tin, the doors painted with large, mysterious, vaguely biblical, yellow X's. The labyrinth of scorched ruins resembled an opera set for some war-ruined, 19th century European city.

The condemned buildings would stand for years, becoming defaced by graffiti, infested by junkies and derelicts. Wreckers might eventually arrive and knock down one of the buildings, leaving perhaps a ruinous, free-standing wall or two, surrounded by yet another vacant lot of rubble, which would soon become home for cast-off shoes, refrigerators, old tires, entire wrecked cars, newspaper pages, beer bottles, syringes, and stolen purses and wallets that had been picked clean and discarded. Over years, tall trees would grow among the weeds. Kids would play in the trash, and gangs would hang around in these wastelands, and size you up as you walked by. In these lots, where no police ever seemed to appear, life was debased nearly to the incarnation of Hobbes's nightmare-vision of primeval man in the state of nature, to the anarchy before the emergence of civilization:

> ...during the time men live without a common Power to keep them all in awe, they are in that condition which is called Warre; and such a warre, as is of every man, against every man....

When I first read that passage in *Leviathan*, in a study hall in college, the images of those vacant lots sprang vividly to my mind.

The worst aspect of life during such times, Hobbes notes, is the "continual fear, and danger of violent death…" And that certainly was true for me.

From the view of those kids in the vacant lots, however, Hobbes' other corollary was the truth:

To this warre of every man against every man, this also is consequent; that nothing can be Unjust.

Almost as if to illustrate this, my brother wrote me:

At age 14, I was in a street that was deserted and a kid told me it was a "stick up" and took my coat and wallet. He was actually not such a bad kid and he made it clear that it was simply an issue of someone with too little taking a little from someone who had more.

Violence and hatred are begotten in their victims. My pent-up rage burst out at school, where I continually got into fights, swinging wildly until some poor, dazed kid was lying bloody beneath me and I was pulled away. I knew school was a safe arena: here, the kids were not carrying weapons and adults would intervene.

Occasionally, though, even on Avenue C, I did fight back, if the odds looked reasonable: more than once, I simply shoved aside kids who demanded my money.

There were, thankfully, reprieves. On weekends, when we visited our father and step-mother, we savored the leafy lanes of townhouses, the cafes along Bleecker Street, the cozy, subterranean restaurants. But on Sunday evenings, the bus, like Charon's ferry, would always bear us back to our own neighborhood.

I spent as much time as I could away from the neighborhood with my friend Jack, who lived on St. Mark's Place. Or I went with school-mates to their apartments in the Village or played baseball after school in Washington Square Park.

The greatest respite came each August, when my mother and step-father took us on vacation. We traveled the country by car and visited my mother's relatives in the suburbs of Cleveland.

There were also the long summer days, especially in later years, when our street took on an almost homey feel. Ragged garments flut-tered on laundry lines strung across the tenement airshafts; the "Mister Softee" ice-cream truck with its familiar musical bells rumbled by on the paving stones; a Puerto Rican man selling "snow-cones" sat on a folding chair at a corner beside his cart, which held a block of ice and his row of colored bottles holding their sugary flavors; men and women smoked on the stoops listening to transistor radios while half-naked children played in the opened fire-hydrants, and shirtless men tinkered with their cars. On days like these, the danger abated, like a quiet day in No-Man's Land, and you felt almost free to walk around. But the respite always ended, eventually, with that blow to the face and that ring of deadened eyes.

◇

During the late seventies and early eighties, the muggings became less frequent and then stopped. In part, I was nearly a man, and the teenage gangs left me alone, and, too, as gentrification finally began to take effect, crime in our neighborhood slowly declined. We noticed that new cafes, restaurants, shops, clubs, bars, were appearing further and further eastward.

In high school, I adopted the styles of clothes worn by my art-student and musician friends—I bought an old military overcoat in a thrift shop and plucked a pair of black Beatle boots from a St. Mark's Place boutique. I wore everything black. But while the menace of our streets had somewhat abated, I wore these clothes with anxiety for the quick attention they always drew on our block. Sometimes, going out at night, I carried my coat under my arm until I had left our neighborhood behind.

The last time I was attacked came just a few weeks before I left for college. I was walking home very late at night, after leaving some friends. As I passed a drug-sentry standing on a stoop, I saw a man staggering toward me under the streetlights. From habit, I braced myself as we came beside each other—and he did abruptly pitch toward me, with sudden violence. He grabbed me, held me almost in an embrace, and began pounding me with his fists even as he tried to hold me, groaning. I thrust him off angrily and he fell to the pavement. He lay cringing, covering his face with his hands against the expected blows. And in my anger, I wanted to kick him, to beat him, to cause him pain. But seeing him lying helplessly, I instead quickly walked away. And as I began to walk, I heard him cry after me in a ludicrous, unrepentant threat, *"Yeah, y'bettah run! Y'bettah run, muthafucka!"* And I heard behind me the echoing laughter of the sentry on the stoop.

◇

The significant gentrification that my mother had for so many years predicted arrived too late for us.

In January, 1984—fifteen years after we arrived on Avenue C and just four months after I had left for college—the NYPD finally *did* move to gentrify Hell itself, with "Operation Pressure Point," a concerted campaign to eliminate the street sales of heroin and other drugs, which brought hundreds of police and undercover detectives to the area. Drug-sniffing dogs appeared and helicopters hovered over the roofs. The Law attacked the very center of the drug market: the streets a few blocks south of our apartment building. The police began sealing off the vacant tenements used for drug deals or as "shooting galleries" and erecting fences around the vacant lots.

The impetus for the campaign was reported as coming from the appointments of a new Police Commissioner, Benjamin Ward, and a new federal prosecutor, Rudolph W. Giuliani. "Both men wanted to make an impression and neither was adverse to positive publicity," *The New York Times* explained in an article about the operation that was published in February, 1984, one month after it was launched. The article described how entrenched the drug economy had become:

For the last decade, in scores of abandoned tenements on Manhattan's Lower East Side, drug dealers have flourished openly, serving buyers from throughout the region. The marketing system in what police described as the retail drug capital of America was so well organized that dealers employed local children as lookouts for $100 a day and used pregnant women to move drugs from one location to another. Drugs were so much a part of the community that addicts injected themselves openly in vacant lots and dealers used buckets to transfer drugs from their window to a buyer on the street below.

Last week, the streets of the Lower East Side were deserted, particularly the area known as Alphabetville, between Avenue A and Avenue D, from Delancey to 14th Streets. No longer were teen-agers steering out-of-state drivers to dealers' dens in abandoned buildings owned by the city. Gone were the queues of addicts buying drugs on the street.

...Operation Pressure Point, as it is called, ended its first
month with officers having made 1,780 drug-related arrests,
607 of which were felonies. Robberies in the area dropped by
48 percent.

By January, 1986, the *Times* was reporting:

In two years, the operation's officers have made 17,000
arrests on the Lower East Side—more than 5,200 of them
for felonies—and have seized 160,000 packages of heroin,
32,000 tins of cocaine, 16,000 bags of marijuana, 10,000
hypodermic instruments and more than $800,000 in cash.

But it was a long, tough battle. Meanwhile, a movement within the neighborhood had been intensifying since the seventies to reclaim the streets. Squatters, punks, skinheads, artists, musicians, and political activists began to move into the vacant tenements, and each year, new cafes, clubs, and galleries appeared. Real estate developers returned to the area, began to renovate the tenements. The gentrification—the rising rents, the eviction of squatters—led to protests and battles over the future of the neighborhood, culminating in a riot at Tompkins Square Park in August, 1988. But I was long gone by then.

The gentrification also came too late for my brother, who left the city the same year I did, to start a new life in the West. My mother, then in her forties, was diagnosed that year with Multiple Sclerosis, a disease that had already been deleting her memory and would soon confine her to a bed in a nursing home. Like us, she did not enjoy the gentrification she had so long predicted. Shortly before she entered the nursing home, when she was feeble and forgetful, she, too, was finally victimized—robbed of the coat she was wearing as she walked her dog outside our building.

◇

While I left Avenue C in 1983, the effects haunted me for nearly twenty years.

When I arrived at college—a tiny campus tucked away among Wisconsin farms—I was utterly disoriented. On the campus lawns and in the classrooms, I mingled with students who played golf, wore bright clothes, spoke loudly with sublime confidence that their voices would not attract—as I unconsciously feared—a knife-wielding gang into the quad. I despised my classmates as naïve and "soft"—they wouldn't last an hour on Avenue C. And yet, I also envied them, because I still could not speak loudly, wear bright clothes, walk those bucolic lanes without my intricate, self-defensive stride. In my mind, I was still on Avenue C, had brought it, intact, to Wisconsin.

I sometimes bolted awake in my dorm room from nightmares that were always the same: I was running through a bleak region of ruined towers, destroyed playgrounds, empty lots, pursued by kids, teenagers, young men, raging, swinging chains, firing guns. I run through streets, across tenement roofs, along hallways of abandoned buildings, and everywhere are strewn corpses—naked, bloody, dismembered corpses of entire families, casualties of endless gang wars. I'm frantically searching for our apartment building or an escape from the ghetto, but the wreckage, the corpses, stretch forever. Sometimes, it's daylight—the sky hangs gray, as oppressive as the concrete devastation—or it is night, and then I'm down among those fire-blasted hulks toward Houston Street, the center of the heroin market, those streets I had seen so many years from my high window and where I would never venture. There, I'm running lost among ruined walls that loom darker than the night itself, rows of windows gaping blackly, while gunshots crack and echo. I hide in silent hallways, in moonlit rooms strewn with the dead, and then I'm again outside, running, running…

And then I would wake—and brush it from my mind as only a dream. I did not reflect on the nightmares until years later, when I woke one night so shaken that I finally realized I had been having such dreams for more than a decade. They persisted until I was in my thirties, coming every several months. Other after-effects—the inability to wear certain clothes or speak without inhibition or walk in a relaxed way—also endured until I was in my thirties. I could not enter any street that appeared even remotely threatening without severe anxiety and a habitual scanning of everything around me. I could not pass a group of blacks or Latinos without a jittery stomach, a clenching of the fists and a preparation to run or fight. When I met my wife, at age twenty-four, I could not hold her hand on the street—even the most residential streets—without fear of appearing "soft," a target for gangs that roamed only in my mind.

When I saw the 1930 film *All Quiet on the Western Front*, depicting trench warfare in the First World War, I instantly recognized the shivering fear of the soldiers huddled in the trenches before leaping into No-Man's Land. It brought back the panic I had running home across the street from the bus stop or dashing to the bodega for groceries. In fact, I probably had a textbook case of the illness suffered by war veterans termed "post-traumatic stress disorder":

> post-traumatic stress disorder *n. An anxiety disorder arising as a delayed and protracted response after experiencing or witnessing a traumatic event involving actual or threatened death or serious injury to self or others. It is characterized by intense fear, helplessness, or horror lasting more than four weeks, the traumatic event being persistently re-experienced in the form of distressing recollections, recurrent dreams, sensations of reliving the experience, hallucinations, or flashbacks, intense distress and physiological*

reactions in response to anything reminiscent of the trau-
matic event...
    —A Dictionary of Psychology, Oxford University Press, 2006.

Still, the survival skills, the habitual, animal-like awareness that
my brother and I developed on Avenue C came to my aid in later years,
when working in foreign cities as a journalist. I often ended up walking
through poor neighborhoods late at night, and several times I shook off
pursuers—I was again a target, now, a rich American. But I spotted
them far faster than they knew, and even acquired the dangerous
vanity of pride in my street smarts. One evening, a decade after I left
Avenue C, I saw two young Russian toughs in leather jackets walking
toward me on an empty street in Moscow, and I saw in their pale faces
that predatory stare so clearly distinguishable from any other expression. I backtracked and ducked into a pharmacy before they turned
the corner, then watched them pass outside the window and saw their
puzzled faces as they searched the crowds. I knew more tactics of
evasion than they could ever guess. And I couldn't help but send them
off with a silent, scornful dismissal: *Go find another American to rob,*
you Russian bastards—I'm from Avenue C.

◇

For many years, I avoided Avenue C. I remained bitter at my mother
and step-father for setting up house on that Lake of Fire and remaining
while their children suffered. When we cried, "Why can't we leave?"
my mother's prediction of the coming gentrification was always so
weirdly calm and enigmatic that I sometimes searched for a Purpose
to this bleak tale, some meaning to my mother's oracular blindness.
Why that mysterious inertia? Why that exit, after fifteen years, at
exactly the instant when the police came marching in?

I occasionally read about the neighborhood, which in the eighties began being called "Alphabet City" or "Loisaida." I read about the continuing gentrification and the attendant battles among police and squatters and protesters. I became aware that my old neighborhood had become world-famous not only as a crime zone but also as a mecca for youth culture: its streets served as a locale for TV cop-shows and was also the subject of rock songs, even of the Broadway rock musical, "Rent," about struggling artists and bohemians, which was set only one block from our apartment, in the late eighties.

Magazines and newspapers began describing the eighties in Alphabet City as ancient history, which, given the vast changes, I suppose it was. In an article in the *Times* about the improvement of the neighborhood that appeared in February, 2008—almost exactly twenty-two years after its description of the then-two-year-old Operation Pressure Point—the paper reported:

> *Few parts of New York City have undergone a more rapid and drastic physical transformation over the past 20 or 30 years than the area below East 14th Street known broadly as the Lower East Side. In the 1970s and '80s the neighborhood was a gritty and often dangerous district where the population was dwindling and businesses were gradually being shuttered.*
>
> *Although the area is now bustling, filled with pricey apartments and a variety of restaurants and bars, 20 years ago entire blocks east of Avenue A consisted of little more than rubble-strewn lots.*
>
> *… The empty lots are no longer empty, and the abandoned buildings have been razed or rehabilitated.*

◇

Last August, I happened to be with my son near Avenue C, and on an impulse, I took him to see our old apartment building.

As we walked along the avenue that afternoon, I discovered that the neighborhood had improved almost beyond recognition. We passed new shops, groceries, restaurants, a modern dental-care center. The vacant lots where gangs and junkies once roamed were now community gardens, or the sites of new apartment buildings. Nearly all the tenements had been renovated; the spindly trees that lined the streets of my youth were now tall and broad. The fear and savagery that had once clutched this avenue had vanished. People were calmly shopping for fruit at a grocery; a deliveryman was wheeling a stack of boxes into a new supermarket without any sign of alarm; a young white man wearing preppy shorts and a polo shirt was walking a retriever on a leash while chatting on a mobile phone.

After I pointed out our old tower to my son—still exactly the same as I remembered it—we walked south, past the familiar blocks and then further, toward Houston Street, along those streets that I once would never have walked, that had troubled my sleep for so long—those ruins I saw from our apartment, their dark windows, their walls echoing with gunshots and the shrieks of tortured dogs. And now, walking those same streets, the sky a flawless summer blue, the people going about their business in the daylight, the scene was bewildering—as though the sun were a flashlight shining into a dark cave I had so long feared and now discovered was just an empty hole, after all.

We turned off Avenue C and onto Second Street, the old dark center of the drug market itself. As I strolled with my son along this pleasant street, I suddenly realized I was holding his hand without fear. And I knew then that I could truly bid farewell to Avenue C: I knew that, at last, I had left it behind.

3. The Forest in Grand Central Station

3 The Forest in Grand Central Station

L<small>AST FALL, MY FIVE-YEAR-OLD DAUGHTER AND</small> I <small>WERE SEPARATED BRIEFLY AT A</small> mall, in one of those enormous bookstores with a wilderness of aisles stretching across acres of carpeting.

"I want to get you a map, Daddy," she said suddenly and ran off. I was preoccupied reading the dust-jacket of a book. "Okay," I mumbled.

About ten minutes later, I went to where the maps were displayed, to get her. She wasn't there. Concern sharpened to worry as I searched the aisles. I was about to go have a look outside, when I heard a little girl's plaintive cries rising from among the books: "Daddy? Daddy, where *are* you?"

My heart leapt and I hurried over and saw her: her brown eyes, wide and brimming with fear, met mine and lit up with joy, and she ran to me, shouting, "Daddy!" and embraced me. And I, too, was relieved.

"Where did you go?" She asked, with consternation.

"I went looking for you," I replied.

She held out a map. "I got this for you." It was a map of Massachusetts.

As we drove back to our weekend house, in northern Connecticut, past the car dealerships and gas stations and strip malls, my daughter sat buckled-up in the back seat, quiet, thoughtful, clearly unnerved. And I was visited by a memory from my own childhood, when I had gotten terribly lost from my parents.

◇

In August, 1973, my mother and step-father rented a cottage in central Massachusetts from a family named Hansen for a couple of weeks' vacation.

I never met the family, and I don't recall how my parents knew the Hansens, but the vacation was arranged, and we arrived at their dirt yard one afternoon in our navy-blue, second-hand, 1966 Bonneville Pontiac.

My younger brother and I spent most of those weeks barefoot and outdoors like a couple of Huck Finns, catching snakes and insects, climbing the tree in front of the house, feuding with two brothers who lived nearby, and riding our bikes up and down the road. We got sunburnt, I got bitten on the hand by a snake just after my step-father snapped a photo of me holding it, and my brother tumbled from his bike and got badly bruised. We had a marvelous time.

The house was one of four at a crossroads. The area was working-class, more rural than suburban. A Manhattan kid, I hadn't spent much time in such surroundings. Previous summers we had driven around the West, visited my mother's family in the outskirts of Cleveland, and spent a week at a farm in Nova Scotia, but that was about the extent of my experience beyond New York. We lived in a new housing development on the Lower East Side, and while our building was modern and clean, the surrounding streets and tenements were plagued by drugs and crime, and so our weeks in Massachusetts were, for me, a respite from our neighborhood.

One morning, about a week after we arrived, my parents got in the car to drive the couple of miles to the grocery store—really just a shack in a dirt patch on a back road. I said I would follow on my bike. I hadn't made the ride before, and my parents looked doubtful but acquiesced.

"Stay close," my mother said.

My step-father eased the Bonneville slowly along the road, and, at first, I did stay close. In the car's rear window, my brother waved at me, stuck out his tongue, made clownish faces (those were the days before the law required riders to wear seatbelts). But the car began pulling away, despite my manic pedaling; my brother's silly expressions and waving hands became smaller and smaller. Then, the immense, dark, low-slung car slipped around a bend in the woods. I chased still faster, but when I flew around the curve, the country road lay empty before me, split off in a fork. Without slowing, I followed the way that veered off to the left. Almost immediately, I sensed that this was the wrong direction, but I rode on, figuring that if I didn't find the store ahead, I would turn back.

The road broadened to a small highway, led up a long hill that made for hard pedaling in the hot August morning. I worked along the road's shoulder as cars sped past. At the top of the hill, I halted. It seemed I had gone further than I should have, but I decided to ride a little further.

A little further became quite a bit further, but I did not turn back. I reasoned that I had already come so far, it would be best if I kept on until I found a gas station where I could ask directions for a shorter way back to our house. I did not factor into this plan that I didn't know our address or even the name of our road, knew only the name of the family that had rented us the place.

I followed the highway through a few intersections and it narrowed again to a back road and began to wind into the woods. Eventually, the blacktop gave way to dirt, and after a while there were no more houses, no more passing cars. The forest closed in, cast a cool, layered, green dimness that blocked out the sky. But I rode on, long after I knew I should have turned back. I was certain my parents were searching for me. They would probably appear behind me soon in the big Bonneville, my step-father blasting the horn and smiling at my foolishness. Some-times I glanced back, but the Bonneville did not appear, and as the afternoon grew later, the dirt road wound still narrower, became treacherous with ruts, roots, stones and potholes, little more than a dim trail through the trees, and my fear, which had been intensifying all day, became panic—the child's primal dread of getting lost in the forest. I had started out on my bike on a sunny morning and taken a wrong turn into a terrifying fairy tale.

◇

The forest, in myth and legend, presents a trial through which the hero intentionally journeys, from Gilgamesh to Lancelot, and onward. But for children in literature, the forest is a menacing region into which they stumble or are led and for which they are unprepared.

Hansel and Gretel, Little Red Riding Hood and other fairy tales represent the forest as we once consciously perceived it and as chil-dren still do—a vast, shadowy, magic place, a lair for ogres, witches, fairies, and dragons. In the fairy tale forest, as in dreams, appearances deceive: birds and bears suddenly speak to humans as equals; kindly farmers morph into hideous trolls; the resting dead leap back to life. For children in fairy tales, to enter the forest alone is always the beginning of woe, and that August day in 1973, at age nine, as I rode deeper and deeper into the darkening woods, I was, in my mind, no longer riding a back road in Massachusetts, I was riding through the pages of one of my fairy tale books, was trapped in a Gustave Doré illustration. And my own story would require few changes to turn it into the start of a typical Grimm's narrative: my parents' drive for groceries at the shack would become a ride in a cart to buy an enchanted goose or magic beans, while on the way, the boy, seeking a little fun, decides to follow on his pony but falls behind and gets further and further lost in the woods.

My distress was exactly that of Hansel and Gretel after the siblings are abandoned by their parents—the fear that a way home might not ever be found in the enormity of the forest:

> ...*they walked the whole night long and the next day, but they still did not come out of the wood; and they got so hungry, for they had nothing to eat but the berries which they found upon the bushes. Soon they got so tired that they could not drag themselves along, so they lay down under a tree and went to sleep.*
>
> *It was now the third morning since they had left their father's house, and they still walked on; but they only got deeper and deeper into the wood, and Hansel saw that if help did not come very soon, they would die of hunger.*

This, precisely, was the source of my anxiety—that I would die of hunger and weariness. Yet, as strange as the woods appeared, there was something in the quality of this fear that was familiar, although I only understood why years later: it was the same fear I lived with each day in our neighborhood on the Lower East Side—the panic of a boy journeying alone, beyond aid, encircled by peril.

The slum of tenements that surrounded our housing development was as riddled with macabre decay, was as nightmarish as any setting of a tale by the Grimm brothers. Instead of trees and caves, ours was a brick-and-concrete wilderness where gangs crouching in alleys were the equivalent of ogres and trolls concealed under bridges, and bands of giants roamed with knives, chains, and sticks. For a boy, everything appeared immense and even more frightening. Expanses of trash and rubble, where buildings had once stood, stretched like blighted wastelands; wrecked cars lined the gutters like slain beasts, some in flames. Avenue C *was* a ghastly fairy tale

A fairy-tale city: the Lower East Side in the 1980s.

place, and I was forced to negotiate its streets alone each day, at an age when I was, like most children, still afraid of the dark in my own bedroom.

In fairy tales, large towns and cities appear less often than the forest, but they, too, are presented as a warren of traps, fatal temptations, magic. The story *Pinocchio* places its initial danger at the town square itself, where the boy-puppet sells his school book to pay for admission to a show and ends up imprisoned by a villainous puppet-master. In *The Pied Piper*, a seemingly kindly stranger enchants with music all the children of a German town and leads them through the central streets in broad daylight to their deaths in a cave. Yet the menace particularly associated with urban life, to the point of cliché—the depraved stranger that lures children with candy—appears most famously not in a fairy tale city but in a forest: in *Hansel and Gretel*, a witch disguised as a kindly old woman offers sweets to the children, then tries to roast them in an oven. Here, forest and city have become almost interchangeable in their hazards; each is a symbol for the other.

The underlying similarity of town and forest as portrayed in fairy tales was made evident far back: Charles Perrault's moral in the 1729 version of *Little Red Riding Hood* warns children, particularly girls, that the dangers of their world are akin to those of the magical forest. Strangers, like the apparently benevolent wolf that Red Riding Hood meets along the path to her grandmother's house, are often evil beneath deceptive appearances:

Moral
Little girls, this seems to say,
Never stop upon your way.
Never trust a stranger-friend;
No one knows how it will end.
As you're pretty, so be wise;
Wolves may lurk in every guise.
Handsome they may be, and kind,
Gay, or charming never mind!
Now, as then, 'tis simple truth—
Sweetest tongue has sharpest tooth!

As a parent in New York City, I find this is still sound advice almost 300 years later.

At root, the child's angst at being lost is always the apprehension of being exposed to *some* kind of potential harm—adults, other children, the elements, or fairy tale creatures like Perrault's wolf. The trauma of being lost can be profound and memorable, even when the experience is not a long bike journey down a shadowed trail, or years navigating a crime-infested slum. Panic can strike a child anywhere, and a misadventure of only a few minutes can transform the densest urban places into dark forest. A friend who is in his forties recently reminisced:

> When I was six or seven my step-father took me to the
> Museum of Natural History in New York, and when we
> were at Grand Central Station I followed his tweed coat
> into a huge (to me) room filled with similarly clad men
> reading newspapers and smoking. I looked up and discov-
> ered that the particular tweed coat I'd been following
> did not belong to my step-father. I remember crying and
> looking everywhere until finally a man in a railroad-
> employee uniform came up and comforted me and then
> helped me find my step-father, who was wandering around
> looking for me.

For my friend, Grand Central Station melted into a forest for a few minutes—minutes that became ineradicable from memory.

Still, my fear that day in the woods differed from my fear on Avenue C in one aspect, because it comprised a new sensation for a city boy—an apprehension of the vastness, the unreal stillness, the indifference, of the *natural* world. On Avenue C, the threat was of being attacked; the forest passively, silently yet frighteningly, received you as you wandered deeper and deeper within.

❖

As I rode, the trail became even more deeply rutted, strewn with rocks and branches. The woods were hushed but for my labored breathing as I pedaled, the whirr of the spinning rubber tires, and the metallic jangle of my bike as it jounced ahead. My legs and backside were sore and I was covered with dust. At one point, the image of my brother making silly faces and waving at me through the car's rear window surfaced like a memory of long ago.

The trail dwindled into hardly more than a footpath. I knew that I was nearing its end, yet I kept pedaling, as senselessly as though I were under a witch's enchantment.

At last, the trail did end: the path swerved left, and I stopped before a clearing and a blast of red sky. The grass led to a tall wall of corn that blocked out the setting sun. About twenty yards away, at the edge of the cornfield, were parked a half-dozen motorcycles and a white pickup truck.

It was a motorcycle gang—men and women, decked out in leather, were sitting on the machines or in the grass, drinking from beer bottles, blowing clouds of cigarette smoke, their rough laughter and taunts carrying across the clearing. The men with their wild beards and massive, tattooed arms, the women with their fierce voices and leather boots, struck me with the same freezing fright as if I had stumbled into a lair of ogres.

I quietly walked my bike backward and remained uncertainly in the cool dimness of the leaves.

There was nothing to do but start the long ride back home. I began once more to pedal the bike, but by now, the soreness of my legs and my backside was excruciating. Moreover, the way back was uphill. Exhausted, in pain, unable to pedal any further, I got off the bike and began to walk with it. But the prospect of retracing all those miles, all those hours, appeared impossible, and I knew I would not reach even the paved road by nightfall.

An engine's roar jolted me around, as one of the bikers from the cornfield flashed by, a black, ferocious blur. Another rider flashed past and then several more, in a thunderous black procession. My arm shot up, as though by its own impetus, above my head and waved for them to stop. The last motorcycle passed, and I felt tears welling in my eyes, but then I saw the cycle slow and halt. The rider turned. His face was nearly concealed by a black helmet, black visor and a black mustache. Sitting on his black, snorting motorcycle, he called out to me, asked what was the matter. I explained. He thought a moment, then dismounted. He said he would bring me to the sheriff. I watched as he buried my bike in leaves beside the trail and built a little tower of rocks by which I might find it. I got on the motorcycle behind him and we shot away uphill along the trail, which quickly widened, then became paved and lined with homes, and we flew along the roads, covering in a short time, with the surge of an engine, the miles that had taken me so many hours to pedal.

We arrived at the sheriff's house, and the sheriff's wife, a middle-aged woman in a housedress, opened the door. The biker spoke with her briefly, then roared off—as in fairy tales, where appearances deceive, the ogre in the woods was revealed as the tale's benevolent huntsman.

The sheriff's wife sat me on a sofa in a living room, phoned her husband, then brought a plate of cookies and a glass of milk.

When the sheriff stepped through the front door, tall, lean, gray-haired, in uniform, he spoke with his wife, then knelt by me and asked questions, made a few phone calls. He took me out to the patrol car, and, once inside, he said that he thought he knew where the Hansen's place was and that a call had been received at the station some hours before about a boy missing on a bike. And he drove me back toward our house.

I sat in the back seat, and my fear of the forest was replaced by fear of my parents, who would be furious at me for my adventure, for losing the bike, and would certainly punish me. But when we rolled onto the dirt yard and the sheriff hit the car horn, my parents dashed through the cottage's front door toward us and I saw framed in the back seat window their wild, tearful faces in the twilight.

◇

Over the years since that day, I had come to understand the fairy tale aspect of my ride through the forest, but when that day returned to me last fall, as I was driving home from the mall with my daughter, I perceived for the first time how my parents must have lived those hours. Now, I saw myself as they had—a dirty, tired, frightened boy who had been lost all day and had been brought home at nightfall in a sheriff's car. I understood their tearful joy at seeing me in the back seat. (The sheriff was the kindly huntsman of *their* tale.) And I understood why, when I had said, first thing, "I'm sorry I left the bike behind," they brushed aside my words with embraces.

My parents had been enduring their own primal fairy tale horrors those hours I was missing. I could imagine what worries must have stabbed them when I had vanished on my bike from the Bonneville's rear-view mirror and during the long hours while (as I later learned) they had searched for me along the back roads and waited for word from the police. A lost child sets loose in a parent's imagination the converse fears felt by children in fairy tales—fears that one's offspring could become, like Hansel and Gretel or Red Riding Hood, victims of some unimaginable evil. And headlines regularly confirm our deepest dread, with gruesome, tragic reports that remind us the world is filled with monsters as terrible as those in fairy tales. (Only a few weeks before we arrived at the Hansen's house that summer, the newspapers reported that a seven-year-old girl, Janice Pockett, who had been riding her bike on a dirt road less than fifty miles away, had been abducted after asking her parents' permission to ride off alone to recapture a butterfly she'd found on a rock. She has never been found.)

Fairy tales do truthfully reflect, as dreams do, the basic and perennial anxieties and yearnings of not only children, but parents.

It is the parents' fierce, elemental urge to protect their children that prompts those trite-sounding admonitions to "be careful" and "stay close to home," which children find so superfluous and irritating. But those words must be spoken, are a compulsion for parents. Now, when I read my daughter her fairy tales of forest cottages and witches and woodcutters, I know that the fears they raise in us, as parent and child, are different, yet correspond, like a matched pair. And always some part of me shudders at the deceptively quaint words "Once Upon a Time…"

◇

The next morning, when we drove the Bonneville along the roads to retrieve my bike, my parents asked me to guide them. They were astonished at how far I had ridden, as was I. My backside and legs were still sore, my body sagged with exhaustion. They repeatedly asked me why hadn't turned back, but I had no real answer.

We rode far along the dirt road, the big car's axels scraping rocks and roots, the seats pitching as though we were on a turbulent sea. Finally, we could drive no further, parked on the side of the trail, and walked.

I found the place where the bike should have been, the little tower of stones, but the bike was gone. It seemed unlikely that the man who had come to my aid had returned and snatched the bike. Puzzled, we returned to the car and drove back to the house.

I remembered all this while I drove with my daughter toward our weekend place that afternoon years later, and I wondered if she would recall into adulthood her moments lost in the bookstore, as my friend remembered his brief time lost in Grand Central Station, and how she had embraced her father when he found her and then angrily demanded where he had been.

It was then that my daughter, in the back seat, asked me if she could ride her bike when we got home.

Startled, I replied, "Yes, of course you can." Yet I couldn't help but add: "But don't ride too far away."

4. Crossing into Poland

4 Crossing into Poland

We cannot escape our origins, however hard we try, those origins which
contain the key——could we but find it——to all that we later become.

—James Baldwin

ONE DAY, WHEN I WAS IN THE SIXTH GRADE, I DOVE INTO A FISTFIGHT WITH A
black kid in the school cafeteria—I struck first, swung at his face
until his nose spewed blood as he lay pinned beneath me on the worn,
sea-green tiles. His glasses flew off and he tried to protect his face
with his bloody hands while a crowd of kids circled us and chanted
in savage glee, as they always did for such battles, "*A fight! A fight!*
A nigger and a white!" and the teachers raced over and struggled to
separate us.

Fights were common at our school, and I was also quick to fight.
But this scrap was significant because that afternoon, in that basement cafeteria, I confronted, for the first time, anti-Semitism.

The boy I had fought had been sitting with a couple of his friends
at the next table, and they had begun throwing balled-up napkins, bits
of food, then metal silverware—laughing and shouting with increasing
hilarity, while we tried to ignore their volleys. A couple of the boys I
sat with brought their trays to other tables. Finally, the kid beside me,
a pale little boy with angelic yellow curls, after being struck in the
face by a cardboard milk carton, protested, in a voice both angry and
frightened. That's when this kid approached and loomed over him,
shoved him roughly. "*Yo, white boy, you got something t'say?*" Shove.

"*What you say t'me?*" All of us sat staring at our plates, as though nothing was happening.

He was a tall, skinny kid, maybe a year or two older than we were, and suddenly his long, narrow face bore down on mine, his eyes enormous and menacing behind thick glasses. "*Yo, muthafucka, you got something to say? You wanna mess with me?*" Shove. "*I'll fuck your white ass up.*" Shove. "*You a fuckin Jew boy?*"

I don't know what prompted this question unless, I suppose, I "looked Jewish." But I met his demand with defiant silence, so he repeated it, louder—"*Yo muthafucka! You a fuckin Jew boy?*" Shove—and then again—shove. Finally, I gave him the answer he wanted, and after the next shove, I lay into him.

His demand had disturbed me, not so much for its senseless threat and its profanity—I was already as accustomed to these as I would ever be—but because I had never faced a question about my Jewish identity. I was awakened to the startling fact that my religion, which I had seldom given a thought to, *mattered* to others and was somehow, mysteriously contemptible. But I also intuited that this kid had been driven, not primarily by religious hatred, but by the racism and class animosities that, in the 1970s, roiled our public school—as they roiled all of New York City those years.

After that fight, I would deny my Jewish identity, although I knew the tactic had limited efficacy: If some kid wanted to fight, he'd find an excuse to take a swing—and during subsequent years at that school, there would be many more battles. And I knew, too, that verbal evasions would be irrelevant in my own neighborhood, on the Lower East Side, where the racism was far more brutal, devoid of any religious overlay, and the gangs didn't bother with such interrogations when they beat you and snatched your money.

◈

The Lower East Side of my grandfather's day—he was born in a tenement on Madison Street, in 1907—had also seethed with crime and
bigotry. But by the time we arrived, in the winter of 1968, our neighborhood had descended into a sort of primeval human darkness. If
the police of the Ninth Precinct did venture out, they walked in pairs;
bricks were flung at them from tenement roofs along with wild taunts,
while a cacophony of bird whistles went up along the streets, as in a
jungle, to warn the drug buyers and dealers.

When my mother brought my brother and me to Avenue C, after
she and my father separated, our little remnant of a family was in the
incongruous position of middle-class, assimilated Jews moving *into* a
Puerto Rican and black ghetto besieged by drug-and-poverty-related
crime. We arrived, ironically, just as the last survivors of the Jewish
community, which stretched back to the 19th century, were vanishing.
All that remained of that past in our vicinity were a kosher butcher
and a men's clothing store, both of which had soon closed. Their shop
fronts remained gated, rusting, and graffiti-covered for decades.

While we waited, year after year, for the neighborhood to improve,
as our mother promised it would, my brother and I were utterly lost.
We were four generations from our Jewish immigrant ancestors—we
certainly didn't belong in the dying Jewish Lower East Side. But we
also didn't fit among the impoverished blacks and Latinos who had
taken over those tenements. We should have been in one of Manhattan's middle-class neighborhoods—perhaps in the Village, where my
father and step-mother lived. And over the years, our isolation in that
slum would make all the difference—would make our heritage, which
was, in many ways, so distant and irrelevant, acquire in our minds a
life-and-death significance that it would not have, if we had grown up
outside that ghetto.

In our neighborhood, we quickly learned, we were targets
because of our white skin, which, in those streets, shone like the

coins those gangs suspected we carried in our pockets. And when those gangs, with their sticks or chains or knives, slammed you against a wall and spat in your face, they invariably threw that same word—*white*—that was thrown at us in school, and with the same hatred and contempt—*"Empty ya pockets or we'll cut your fuckin white ass up"*—and the hatred lodged in memory, a seeping poison, years after the welts and bruises and blood had gone. That word, *white*, flung like a curse, held all the fury of those boys, held innumerable shades of meanings. It told us that while we may have lorded it over the rest of the world, here, now, in *this* alley, in *their* Lower East Side, *they* would now lord it over *us*, and we would learn just how weak we were without the apparatus of our middle-class protections. That word *white* was hurled vindictively, as though we had finally been ensnared, like elusive, delicate, but evil animals, after straying from our haven, and now they would exact a steep price for all that we, as whites, had done—*"Yo, white muthafucka, why don't you start somethin?"* Shove. *"I'll kill your fuckin white ass--"* Blows, chanting—*"Yeah man, fuck him up!"* *"Fuck his white ass up!"* Laughter, shouts. *"Yeah! Kill that muthafucka!"* Then there was nothing to do but endure the pain, endure the terror that the blows might go on until it didn't matter anymore.

The muggings, the racism, our fear on those streets, the knowledge that we were part of a tiny white minority within a minority slum, all led my brother and me, absurdly and yet also logically, on a path similar to the downward assimilation that so many of those young blacks and Latinos were following into the surrounding culture of drugs and crime. During the years after our arrival, we sought, by mimicking the clothes, gait, and speech of those kids, to conceal all that made us different. We could not hide the whiteness of our skin, but we could suppress, or try to, everything else: our education, our literate home, our middle-class manners—all that made us *civilized*.

And yet, we didn't want, quite, to assimilate into that ghetto. Our hatred of our attackers and of the squalor was too great a barrier, and the difference in culture and economic status was too vast to bridge. We wanted simply to get by, to blend-in, to escape notice, and to *get out*, someday, in one piece. When we went outside, we assumed those street kids' appearance, and when we returned home, discarded it. But this quick trick of denial and recovery of our true selves, which we learned so young, became increasingly untenable. During those many years, our adaptations did not, probably could not, remain superficial. We unconsciously began to adopt not only those kids' appearance but also, more significantly, their desolate view of the world as a field of perpetual battle that required, for survival, ruthless *hardness*. And this view was, in fact, tragically accurate for those boys and young men: their world *was* brutal and deadly, and many of them would end up casualties—junkies, convicts, derelicts, corpses. And their view of the world was, now that we lived among them on those same streets, true for us. This hardness we adopted was nothing like the old virtue of courage, there was nothing virtuous about it—it was merely an acquired capacity to withstand and dispense brutality, and carried with it the corollary of contempt for those too frail to fend for themselves. And, as the endless blows and racist curses over the years drove into my brother and me that we, as whites, were pathetic and privileged, we began, in our minds, to sever ourselves from our heritage, and to bury it so thoroughly from both those gangs and ourselves that no one would ever know of it, and perhaps even we could forget.

While many American children of Jewish immigrants had sought, in earlier decades, to obscure their heritage, in order to assimilate into middle-class America, my brother and I had been born into that coveted stratum. But our peculiar descent into a violent black and Latino slum caused us to become ashamed of precisely that identity which those earlier generations of American Jews so desperately sought to acquire. And we were not only rejecting our Jewish identity, we were rejecting, trying to eradicate, our race and our class—*everything* about ourselves.

Our response was, in certain aspects, similar to the psychological survival tactic known in the social sciences as "identification with the aggressor." The concept, introduced in the 1930s, describes a tendency observed among victims of prolonged exposure to violence or the threat of harm—abused children, hostages, even Jews in German concentration camps—to unconsciously identify with their tormentors, to adopt their outlook, or at least to mentally disassociate themselves from the aggressor's victims, in order to ease the anxiety of vulnerability experienced before a threat. While our impotent rage at our attackers and the chasm between our cultures prevented my brother and me from fully identifying with those Latinos and blacks, we did seek, through imitation and our mental rearrangements, to ally ourselves with them by cutting loose from all we were, by positioning the white middle-class, the Jews, as the *other*. The Jews, in particular, received our contempt, not only for the stain of the Holocaust but also because so much of the world—as evinced by the anti-Semitic attackers at school—still openly considered the Jews vile, deserving of extermination.

Our shame intensified, as a result of the years of attacks at school and in our neighborhood, to a degree unusual for a couple of assimilated, fourth-generation, American Jewish children. Our shame, our hatred, was as potent as that described by the Jewish writer Jakov Lind, when recalling his adolescence in Nazi-occupied Holland: "I hated the Jews because I hated the sight of death. Each of them was to be destroyed. I did not wish to belong to this kind of people."

Had we belonged, even tenuously, to a Jewish community, we might have had enough support to shrug off those anti-Semitic and racist attacks and accept our identity. But our deep cultural isolation during those years left us few resources to defend our heritage to ourselves. Our sense of identity became increasingly fragile and ambiguous each year we lived on the Lower East Side. Were we really Jewish? By birth, but little else. Our skin told us, unmistakably, that we were white, but were we really the hated middle class? Or were we slum kids? Our parents were college-educated, intellectuals, writers, were knowledgeable about the arts, widely travelled. We visited our father and step-mother at their pleasant Village apartment on weekends. Yet we were living in one of the country's most violent ghettos, in an over-whelmingly Latino and black culture. Among my white classmates, I felt isolated by my experience, felt harder, tougher, possessed of a bitter knowledge they couldn't know. I was, in some ways, as distant from them as I was from the Latinos and blacks in our neighborhood.

The nickels and dimes those gangs stole from us over the years amounted to little, probably wouldn't cover the cost, today, of even a taxi across town—the real theft was of our early, natural, unam-biguous attachment to our family and heritage. On Avenue C, we were wandering lost between two cultures, hating and fearing the Puerto Rican and black ghetto, while bitterly despising ourselves, our family, our religion.

◇

My family, on both sides, as I knew all too well, were among the hundreds of thousands of Jews who fled, during the decades around 1900, the persecution, restrictive laws, ghettos and muddy villages of Belarus, Lithuania, Poland, Rumania, Russia, Ukraine. They were shopkeepers, butchers, factory workers, soldiers, though there were also anti-Czarist revolutionaries, artists, writers, musicians, several of whom were famous in their day. By the late sixties and early seventies, however, nearly all of the first-generation immigrants of our family had died or were elderly and scattered: to Cleveland, Philadelphia, Pittsburgh. Their children had Americanized their names, risen into the middle class. Religious observance had faded. I had never so much as glimpsed the inside of a temple, nor read a page of even a children's Bible. I was completely ignorant about Jewish and Christian history and beliefs, had no knowledge whatsoever about Jewish holidays or when they appeared on the calendar—I didn't know the Jews *had* a separate calendar, for that matter. And yet, in my youngest years, I watched my mother lighting Hanukkah candles and reciting the impenetrable Hebrew litany with a kerchief around her head in our dingy kitchen in our housing development, and my father held a Seder a few times in his apartment. But these memories are as anomalous as our position in our ghetto, since our parents had not been observant.

Still, like those baffling Hanukkahs and Seders of my earliest childhood, two other Old World vestiges—two family tales—somehow had survived. Our father's mother, Bertha—a short woman with round glasses, jet-black hair set in a bun, and a voice raspy from Kent cigarettes, who shuffled endlessly within her pleasant, carpeted home in Philadelphia—told my brother and me of her earliest memory: a pogrom. Her family had hid in their basement while the Cossacks' boots pounded above, and her mother clamped a hand over her mouth and nose to keep her silent, and she panicked because she could not breathe. Her family left for America after her father was severely beaten in an anti-Semitic attack.

On our mother's side, we heard the reason why our elderly aunt Ray was crazy. We saw Ray during our summer visits to my mother's family in a Cleveland suburb. Ray had dementia and was cared for by our relatives. We were told that as a young girl, in Rumania, she had suffered grievous harm at a village market. No one knew just what had happened—the story was that a soldier, impatient to clear the way for a military parade, struck her on the head with a rifle-butt, cursing her as a Jew. She returned home that snowy afternoon in a state of shock, mumbled about Christians, and collapsed. The next day, she had no memory of the incident, but "she was never the same again," we were told. "Poor Ray, she wasn't quite right afterward." Our aunt, who was missing half her teeth, had a wizened face and lank gray hair, used to shriek maniacally in another language—Yiddish? Rumanian?—at my brother and me when we played on the lawn those summers, waved at us urgently to get in the house. We laughed at her, yelled nonsense back at her, mimicked her to her face, then ran into the backyard woods.

Those tales of long ago, of vanished villages, of distant countries, were no doubt meant to enlighten us Avenue C boys, to remind us of our heritage, but they drew from us only contempt, resentment, an urge to bolt. When my grandmother told us of hiding from Cossacks in that basement, my brother and I exchanged derisive glances. Our disgust could not have escaped her, and I have since thought how dismaying it must have been for her to see her family rejected, despised, in the insolent faces of her American grandchildren. But while we were ignorant of our religion and our Bible, we had picked up from books, newspapers, and documentary films on television just enough historical facts to conclude that Jews had wandered through the centuries as the world's wretched victims. We had seen the ubiquitous, gray images of the *shtetls* of Eastern Europe, the burning Warsaw ghetto, the Jews during World War II wearing the Star of David on their coats, the shop windows smashed and synagogues destroyed in Germany after *Kristallnacht*, the hills of the naked corpses in concentration camps. Jewish history was a series of calamities and humiliations. We did not register, or perhaps did not know of, the military triumphs, such as the Israeli wars of 1967 and 1973, nor triumphs of the spirit, such as the Warsaw ghetto uprising or the ancient Jews' defiant mass suicide during the Romans' siege of Masada.

My father, though not observant, supported Israel, was proud and knowledgeable about Jewish history. When I was thirteen, he gave me for my birthday a paperback of Isaac Babel's collected stories. He knew of my interest in literature and may have simply thought that he was providing a book I would enjoy. He may or may not also have been trying to coax some interest in my background, but if so, he didn't realize how deep and bitter my estrangement already ran. I read Babel's stories of his experience in the Red Army, of his Odessa boyhood, with revulsion for their Jewish themes, mingled with grudging admiration for the poetic, terse prose. I read the story "Crossing into Poland" (as it was titled in that edition), in which the narrator describes staying the night in a hovel where the father of a Jewish family had been murdered by Poles, his throat "torn out and his face cleft in two." In another story, "My First Goose," Babel wrote of his—to my mind—pathetic pride in killing a goose waddling about an old woman's yard, an act that brings him acceptance among his Cossack comrades. And I read "The Story of My Dovecote," of the 1905 pogrom in Odessa, during which the narrator, then a nine-year-old boy, suffers humiliation and injury at a marketplace and sees his grandfather murdered.

Later, I discovered that Babel was writing of his efforts to resolve many of the same obstinate dilemmas presented by his inheritance that I was struggling to work out—the Jews' seemingly irrelevant insistence on book-learning in a brutal world; the bewilderment of being torn between an alien, hostile culture and a tradition that can't quite be embraced; the maddening inability, for a gentle, bookish Jew, amid desolation and cruelty, to inflict pain. But at thirteen, I perceived these stories as merely describing still more Jewish sorrows and degradations. Those Old World Jews had cowered before those Poles, those Russians, those Germans, but *I* would have battled back proudly, would have mastered my fate. I overlooked that I did not battle my attackers, proudly or otherwise, on Avenue C—or rather,

I *did* know this, somewhere far down. And so I also knew that, by those street kids' remorseless standards, I *was* weak, because while I could endure the violence of that ghetto, I could not, just as Babel could not, inflict pain with pleasure or indifference. This murky self-knowledge sharpened my sense of helplessness, terror, self-hatred. At school, when some kid threw at me the word "Jew," he exposed my darkest shame, showed me that I could not escape my identity, and I would resolve all the more that I *would* escape, and I'd unleash my pent rage with my fists—but only at school, where it was relatively safe to fight.

At home, I loathed those old snapshots in our album, the bespectacled Jewish men standing stiffly in suits, the dark-haired Jewesses in elaborate dresses. I loathed my parents' bookishness, which indicated privilege, vulnerability, our Jewishness. But I was also profoundly, if unconsciously, conflicted, because I was certain I wanted to be a painter, later a writer, and in either case, a bohemian intellectual, like my parents. Looking back, I believe some portion of this ambition was driven by a lack of any other available path: I had rejected my entire white, middle-class background, and so, bohemia—classless, secular, rebellious—was the only path into adulthood that remained. That path also provided the comfort of fitting with the adolescent culture of rebellion that was common at Music & Art High School, which I entered at thirteen. At Music & Art, I had left the racism, anti-Semitism and class hostilities of intermediate school, although I still faced each day the violence and hatreds that gripped our neighborhood.

Until adolescence, I stifled my fury at my attackers and at my parents for seemingly abandoning us to Avenue C. But in high school, I exploded. I initiated venomous arguments with my parents and my brother, launched into innumerable fistfights, ruined friendships. When I walked outside our neighborhood or rode the subway, I had to clamp down tightly on my churning contempt for the white, middle-class adults surging around me, with their polite manners and suits, and toward the orthodox Jews, who appeared pitiably comic and also infuriatingly obvious to me, after having covered-up my identity so thoroughly, for so long: the kids with skullcaps, the pale Hasidim with their broad-brimmed, velvet hats, their side-locks and beards, their Yiddish chatter. I wondered how on earth they could display their religion, their conspicuous, absurd costumes, with such ease, without fear—on Avenue C, they'd all be destroyed before they'd walked a block. The only difference between my hatred and that of the street kids in my neighborhood or at my intermediate school was that I didn't *act* on my urges to physically attack these affluent whites, these repellent Jews.

Yet, in the end, even though I was growing up in Manhattan in the late 20th century, was several generations and an ocean removed from a world that had been incinerated by World War II, I could not quite, in my mind, completely separate myself from my Jewish identity, which was so stubbornly entwined with those doomed Jews in the newsreels, with my family's Old World stories of persecution, with those bloody, grotesque tales by Babel. And the precise point where we had settled on Avenue C, by an unnerving coincidence, helped make it impossible for me to forget any of this: I was reminded of all of it each time I looked out our windows.

◇

Our windows, high above the tenements, faced both south and west, framed not only Madison Street, where my mother's father had been born of immigrant parents, but also the Empire State Building—which he had, at age twenty-three, helped build.

The fact that my grandfather had been on the construction crew of this most American of all buildings made our family Americans,

The author's grandfather.

in my mind, in the same way as if he had been a cowboy or a Revolutionary War soldier. The fact was, to me, as extraordinary and as questionable as a Homeric myth. I sometimes asked my parents if it was really true, and my mother would smile and say, yes, that's what her father had said when she was a girl in Cleveland— her smile had some pride in it, I thought. My father told me how my grandfather walked with him one day in the 1950s through the great building's lobby and pointed out areas of the stone walls that were his work.

My grandfather, a tall, rugged man with red hair and a genial, craggy face, who changed his name from Reuben to the more American Roy, endured a tough early life. He was the youngest of six surviving children of twelve. His father, after arriving from Vilnius, worked as a plasterer on the Lower East Side. When Roy was a teenager, he

The house the author's grandfather built in Ohio.

escaped Madison Street and became an itinerant laborer. When he worked on the Empire State Building, he was still an unskilled hand, one of 3,400 laborers and craftsmen who, in early 1930, swarmed into Fifth Avenue at Thirty-Fourth Street, site of the old Waldorf-Astoria Hotel, to construct the world's tallest tower.

In his later years, Roy told my father he could not eat doughnuts because he too well remembered, during the Depression, standing in the cold, looking for a job, with only doughnuts to eat. He became an apprentice bricklayer, then a bricklayer himself and eventually owned a successful home-construction company in Ohio. By the time he died, of lung cancer, in 1965 (one year after I was born; there is one snapshot of him holding me as an infant) he had raised a family in a pleasant house which he had built himself, in suburban Cleveland. His daughter—my mother—was educated at one of the country's most prestigious colleges. There, she met my father, and during the sixties, when he held a coveted position as an editor at a mass-circulation magazine, they lived well in the Gramercy Park neighborhood of Manhattan.

It was a perfect immigrant-family success story. But then, my mother, after she and my father separated, suddenly swerved off course, took a U-turn, and brought my brother and me right back into the very same ghetto where our family had started—less than a mile from the street where my grandfather was born. Her decision was particularly galling because my grandfather had escaped, not to Brooklyn across the river, nor to Manhattan's Upper West Side, a subway-ride away, but all the way to Ohio. My mother led our family along the American Dream in reverse: from a Midwest, suburban home to the immigrant slums of the Lower East Side.

While our windows neatly framed my grandfather's journey from a tenement to the scaffolds of America's triumphant symbol of its ascent, I did not, gazing out those windows all those years, meditate on the glories of the Melting Pot and the Land of Opportunity. I only felt, year after year, fury at my mother for bringing us to Avenue C.

◇

Eventually, like my grandfather, I, too, fled the Lower East Side for the Midwest, where I attended college. But I went with misgiving, a sense that I was betraying my identity as an Artist, which I had clung to for so many years. I also brought, along with my duffle bag, all my identity concealments.

During my first year at college, I continued to disavow my religion. I denied it to the parents of a friend when I visited his upper-class home in Massachusetts; I even denied that I was Jewish when a kind, middle-aged woman in a bookshop in our college town asked me, during a discussion, if I was "a Hebrew" in her over-polite way. Still, the question of my religion was seldom directly put to me by other students and when it was, the motive clearly was not malice, but curiosity, based on the widespread assumption among white, middle-class American teenagers that probings of another person's heritage could cause no apprehensions.

Often, questions about my family were not directly, or solely, concerned with my religion, but were more general inquiries regarding where my family "was from," usually prompted by my appearance. I had a lot of curly thick hair—was I Italian? Jewish? Russian? I would instantly become anxious, would reply with layers of well-practiced evasions: my family was from New York, or from Cleveland, or Philadelphia, and I would feign ignorance of what they were really after, and try to end or change the conversation. When the questions persisted, I would offer that my family was from "Russia" but would not mention or admit that they were Jews. On occasion, I did receive a direct question about my religion from other Jewish students, and then I denied my identity with particular vehemence.

But at college, the process of self-acceptance began. Gradually, I cast off my slum gait and my street clothes. The fistfights stopped. I could begin, at last, to relinquish the illusion of my hardness. I would never feel entirely comfortable with my religion, would never be observant, would always feel like "a Jew among Gentiles and a Gentile among Jews," as one of Philip Roth's fictional characters famously describes himself. But I began to understand that, like those Old World Jews, I too, in my own way, in the New World, had been tossed by forces beyond my control.

◇

During my second year at college, when the winter holiday arrived, I returned home for a visit.

On a Saturday night, I arranged to meet with a few high school friends in the East Village. We met at a bar housed in a tenement, a few steps below the sidewalk. It was a Polish working-class dive with a few battered booths, a pool table, an antique jukebox that played polkas. In recent years, the place had also become a rendezvous for musicians, artists, and students, who had been moving into the neighborhood.

It was near Christmas, a snowy night, and the place was festive, strung with colored-lights, hot, smoky, noisy. There were about six in our group, all young men, and we were standing by the counter. It became late, and we were getting a little boisterous. It was then we heard an insistent, agitated voice rise above the clamor. We turned and saw that a gray-haired man sitting halfway down the counter was pointing at us, had apparently been demanding something of us. He said to the young bartender: "What is he doing here?" And I saw, with surprise, he was indicating *me*. The bartender, glancing vaguely my way with an expression of discomfort, spoke softly, in Polish, to the man, but he would not be placated. The man stared directly at me and asked, outraged: "What are you doing in here—in *this* bar?"

I was too dumbfounded to reply. The Pole turned back to the bartender, and now, also, to a few Polish working-men sitting along the bar. "Who let him in here?" He cried. "Who let in *this*—*this*—" He stopped; his lips trembled before the word. He could not quite utter the word, but my friends heard it, and those onlookers heard it, and the bartender heard it, and as I stood there, the sole focus of a surrounding sea of turned faces, with the old Pole fiercely pointing his finger at me, his lips trembling vengefully before that one syllable that the world had made for him unspeakable, I finally heard it. I finally understood why that old Pole was enraged by my presence in that bar, in *his* bar, and I felt shock and disbelief seeping down and down that this scene was happening to me. I had never been slammed by 100-proof, Old World anti-Semitism, had never experienced true religious hatred from an *adult*, from another *white*. I searched wildly around to see if I was imagining this entire, unlikely incident and was rebuffed, like a blow, by a row of pointedly stony workmen's gazes.

The bartender tried again to soothe the man, placed a bottle of beer before him, but there could be no reasoning with him, as he continued to insist, in escalating indignation, on his question of my presence there, drawing more and more onlookers.

My friends began to rebuke the man, but I didn't stay. I pushed through the crowd to the door.

Outside, in the cold air, I buttoned my coat. I stepped up to the sidewalk, leaving behind the music, the confusion of voices. Ahead, the snow-driven street shone beneath the lights. As I started home that night, it seemed to lead on like a street returned from a vanished world.

5. Lost Lustre

5 Lost Lustre

Nothing can be of less importance to any present interest than the fortune of those who have been long lost in the grave...

—Samuel Johnson

I.

SEVERAL YEARS AGO, DRIVEN BY SOME COMBINATION OF NOSTALGIA, CURIOSITY, a wish to mend a few fences, and the claustrophobia of encroaching mortality that often accompanies the approach of middle-age, I began seeking out certain old friends, girlfriends and acquaintances, going back to childhood, high school, and college.

This endeavor, which in the days before the Internet would have been difficult, if not impossible, turned out to be surprisingly effortless through the use of search engines. I was able to track down almost everyone I sought in a matter of minutes by employing a little detective work and hunting for clues among memories.

I wound up having reunions by e-mail and telephone. Now in our forties, we shared memories and gossip about mutual friends and updated one another on our marriages, children, careers, and travels. This searching became addictive, a diversion to be indulged. But I avoided reaching out to one old friend—the closest companion of my youth.

My friend, Tim Jordan, and I had been almost inseparable during early adolescence, but we had drifted our separate ways during our teenage years, then had a falling out. I hadn't seen or spoken with Tim, or with any of our old crowd, for twenty-five years, except for one meeting with Tim back in 1990.

Anyone who was a regular of New York's downtown club scene during the end of the seventies and into the eighties probably either had met Tim, seen him sing with his band, or knew others who knew him. It seemed so many people knew Tim Jordan or heard of him—and he was certainly memorable: blond, strikingly handsome, cool, slender, with a wicked wit and a "leonine self possession," as his former girlfriend aptly remarked. He was lead singer and principal songwriter in his band, the Lustres—a sly wink of a name, at once quaintly retro, evoking groups like the Five Satins, the Elegants, the Moonglows, the Silhouettes—yet current in its vulgarity, a racy play on words typical of Tim's humor.

He was, when I knew him anyway, confident that he was on the brink of being "discovered" and cutting his band's first smash album. This did not appear to most of those who knew him as a grotesque fantasy. Most of our friends were also playing in bands around the clubs, chasing fame and fortune on their stages, and Tim, and his band-mates, certainly had everything going for them. And as teenagers, after all, anything is still possible. The Lustres played at CBGB, Tramps, Snafu, Armageddon, Trax and other nightspots of the day. In August, 1983, the band

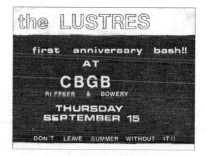

the LUSTRES

first anniversary bash!!

AT

CBGB

BLEEKER & BOWERY

THURSDAY
SEPTEMBER 15

DON'T LEAVE SUMMER WITHOUT IT!!

played Danceteria, at the time a premier New York club (only eight months before, Madonna was still performing for a $5 cover).

But Tim's drinking, excessive through our teenage years, became alcoholism, and the last time we had met, sixteen years earlier, in 1990, he was twenty-six and in very bad shape. At that point, I was entering law school and had only recently returned to New York from the Midwest, and hadn't seen Tim for about six years. I brought my wife along

to join us at a Midtown
diner, the Delphi, on a
Saturday night, for coffee.
I had wanted her to meet
Tim, since I had frequently
spoken of him. It was the
same urge that later led me
to take her to my old neighborhood on the Lower East

Side and other places of my past. We waited for him outside the diner
in the warm evening air. A few minutes after the agreed meeting time, I
recognized Tim walking toward us amid the crowds and the shop lights.
He walked with his familiar, slightly unsteady gait, verging on a swagger.
He wore the same smart look I remembered: black sport jacket, black
Levi's, and scuffed black boots. Always a heavy smoker, he held a lit
cigarette. He smiled and we shook hands. I introduced my wife.

"Nice to meet you," he said, and we went inside the diner and sat
in a booth by a window. Seated opposite him at the little table, I was
startled by the decay that had beset him. His blond hair was thin-
ning and lank. His face was sickly pale and his fingernails were dirty.
His teeth and his fingers were stained nicotine yellow and he'd given
himself a spotty shave that day. He had returned to wearing glasses—
round, and stylish as to be expected, but they looked as though they'd
been poorly repaired and sat slightly askew on his face. His clothes
were worn, rumpled. He looked like a man who had something very
wrong with him—as, of course, he did, as a severe alcoholic trying,
that evening, to keep up appearances.

"What are you having?" the waitress asked.

"Just coffee," he said and closed the menu. He turned to me and
flashed a dingy grin. "So, how've you been?" And I gazed at this man's
wasting face, which I had known since we were grade school boys.

◇

Over the years since that final meeting, I had occasionally wondered about Tim, but a fear, a foreboding, had prevented me from searching for him on the Internet as I had searched for others from my past.

One morning in September, 2006, at the Midtown law office where I worked, on an impulse, I typed in Tim Jordan's name on an Internet search engine and hunted around a few online directories. But I found no trace of him on the Internet. My suspicion that some tragedy had befallen him began edging reluctantly toward certainty. Still, perhaps he was in Europe playing gigs, or maybe he had gone back to the small town in Indiana where his mother's family was from, and where she brought him during summers as a kid (and which he had derisively called "the sticks").

Most of the decade I had known Tim well, from age ten through twenty or so, he had lived with his divorced mother in a well-kept, little apartment on the sixth floor of a tenement on the Upper East Side. That morning at my office, searching the Internet, I did find that his mother, Jayne, was still listed in the New York directory as residing at that address. I avoided contacting her for about a month. Then I mailed a brief note, asking about Tim.

About a week later, I received a dark gray envelope that was distinctive from the letters piled in my In Box. When I saw Jayne Jordan's name on the return address, I tore open the envelope, which contained her two-page, handwritten reply:

> *Dear Josh,*
> *I can't begin to say how happy I was to hear from an*
> *old friend of Tim's. Tomorrow, September 21, will be the*
> *14th anniversary of Tim's death. He was just twenty-eight*
> *and it still seems like yesterday. I am so sorry to tell you*

this, and I'm sorry that you did not know at that time.
Tim fought a long, hard battle with alcoholism, and
eventually lost.

As I read the letter, I felt as though I had been given a shot of anesthesia: the words on the page began swimming, and my body went numb and limp. Several old snapshots had tumbled out of the letter. A couple of photos of Tim, whose face I had not seen in sixteen years, filled me with sadness. But one photo in particular threw me back in time. There I suddenly was, smiling out at myself, two decades younger, age twenty or so, sitting beside an old friend I immediately recognized, named Vincent Metzo, both of us lean and young, a couple of guys grinning out at me from half a life-time ago; a crooked instant captured at the launching moment of our adulthood, before marriage, before children, before career. With an inner shudder of tenderness, I recognized the squalid surroundings framed in the snapshot—the soundproofed walls, the wall lamp: the studio in the cellar of an East Village tenement where Tim and the Lustres used to rehearse and where I and others used to drop by to listen, drink beer, joke around. Then we would go out—usually to a few Polish and Ukrainian dives around St. Mark's Place—and we would stroll over to nearby clubs, or to someone's SoHo or Tribeca loft or apartment for a party. I even recalled that particular night because, almost the instant I saw that photo, I remembered that Tim had snapped it himself.

It was the only photo that Tim had taken of me in the years I had known him. I even remembered the moment he pressed the shutter on the cheap camera, standing before us in that cellar, and after the camera's flash had blinded us, he had smiled, raised a half-mocking "A-OK" sign, and sauntered away and taken some more shots of his band-mates. I had been startled that he had taken that photo—it was very unlike him—too sentimental a gesture. And now, a generation later, that cheap camera, and Tim's uncharacteristic impulse, had salvaged 1/60th of a second of that long forgotten night from my youth, and presented it to me, in my middle-age, at the sleek law offices where I worked, twenty-seven stories above the pavement.

As I sat at my desk studying the photos of Tim and of old friends, re-reading Jayne Jordan's letter, I urgently had to get outside. Despite the pressing work and the gathering e-mails demanding replies on my computer, I rode the elevator down to the lobby, then joined the crowds on Sixth Avenue that overcast September day and took a dazed walk through Bryant Park.

Wandering the gravel paths, nearly empty at mid-morning, I felt the shock that continued to penetrate came not so much from the news of my friend's death, but that he had departed this world at age twenty-eight—fully fourteen years before; that he had already been dead all the years during which I had still been assuming, in the back of my mind, and sometimes consciously, that I might just run into him sometime in Manhattan; that I might spot Tim one day, perhaps waiting for a traffic light on a curb, or striding through the crowds with his long, cocky strides, wearing his black outfit, his tousled blond hair blowing away from his handsome face, the ever-present Marlboro in his hand, maybe carrying his vintage Gibson electric guitar in a case. And he would be still singing with some rock band in the downtown clubs, still writing songs, still waiting for fame to find him.

◈

But, of course, fame didn't find my friend. Death found him, instead, at age twenty-eight—gathered him away as he lay alone on his bed after an alcohol-related seizure, in his disordered tenement apartment, six stories above the traffic of First Avenue.

Tim Jordan, performing at
Danceteria, 1983.

I'm not sure whether fame ever would have found Tim, and if it had, whether he would have survived long enough to savor it. But I've more than once considered that to write of my friend is perhaps a bit what it might be like for a classmate of, say, Jim Morrison, to write of the rock singer's dark charisma, talent, and death, if Morrison had died before recording the Doors' first hit, "Light My Fire"; or for a friend of Tim's early idol, James Dean, to write of the actor if he had died in that car crash before his first film, *East of Eden*. In both cases, the writer would have to convey, to an audience who never saw these young men perform, their charisma, the singular impact on their friends of their extraordinary personalities. Tim seemed to have some unquantifiable piece of this sort of magnetism, this larger-than-life quality.

Like both Morrison and Dean, Tim Jordan was a deeply troubled young performer who passed away too soon. Tim had been given, it seemed, an enviable portion of everything: blond good-looks, a muscular physique, an unerring hipster style, lightning-quick wit, a facile talent as a song writer, singer, performer, musician, and visual artist. And he had, during adolescence, a confidence that most of us lacked; he was fearless about the use of drugs and alcohol and abandoning high school. Yet underneath it all, even before the alcohol began to ruin him, there was also a sense of some troubled core that would remain oblique and pained and unreachable. And this, too, contributed to that enigmatic quality.

In the days after I learned of his death, when I thought back on Tim as a performer, I kept remembering one night, about 1980, at CBGB, where, as Tim well knew, only a few years before, the Ramones, the Talking Heads, Patti Smith, and so many others had performed, and now it was his turn to climb that stage and launch his career, he no doubt thought. I remember hanging around with the band before the gig in the graffiti-covered, plywood-walled room backstage that was separated from the club by only a ratty curtain. We drank beers, smoked cigarettes and joked around, and they ran through their set list. When it was time to go on, Tim called out to his mates, like a war cry, as he strapped on his guitar: *"OK! Lustre Up! Lustre Up!"* Then, on stage, the band launched into the opening chords of their first song, and Tim belted his savage, clever lyrics into the microphone, his black Gibson hanging at his hip. He sang sometimes with his eyes closed and sometimes he turned and grinned broadly at his band-mates, clearly enjoying himself. Snarling out songs between swigs from a beer bottle, he exuded a youthful defiance that was clearly the real thing, not an act. I could feel the girls at the tables around me adoring him—a primal, feminine force.

Martin Blazy, the Lustres drummer, whom I contacted after I learned of Tim's death, wrote to me in an e-mail:

> When I was in the band, there was an aura around Tim that
> he was James Dean cool. Even the girls said it. He just had
> this wonderful presence. When we would play, Tim would turn
> around at times and give me the greatest smile—I knew it
> wasn't a stage smile. We knew we were a band to be reckoned
> with. We were a great live band. When you think of some of the

three part harmonies and double leads going on, the experimen-
tation was awesome. This band had so much potential. To this
day, the Lustres were one of the best bands I played with.

Tim's other surviving band-mates still share Martin Blazy's belief
in the unrealized potential of the Lustres and in Tim's talent as a
performer and a songwriter. Former guitarist JZ Barrell, who now
teaches audio at Parsons and runs a music studio, reminisced with me
about the band over drinks one night at a Midtown bistro after work:
"I think Tim had a good read on rock and roll," he said thoughtfully.
"And he had a really good ear for leads—an inventive and fluid style,
with a gift for melody. His phrasing was dead on, his pitch was really
good, and his lyrics were clever. He was passionate about his music
and he worked really hard."

So, what happened? What chain of events led to the dissolution
of Tim Jordan's band and finally to my friend's death, at age twenty-
eight? During the following months, I reached out to many of our old
friends to learn more about his final years. I discovered that I was the
last to know that he had passed away, having been cut off for twenty-
five years. Meanwhile, word had slowly spread.

◇

I had been avoiding this group of friends, in a sense, since I was twenty.
I had become troubled and sullen during high school, and my friendships became increasingly tenuous until, one night, when I was home
for the winter holidays from college with a group that included Tim, at
the Four Winds Tavern, on St. Mark's Place, I stormed away, I thought
forever, in a torrent of misplaced righteous indignation. So when I
began to contact this group, it was with some unease. Yet I found that
our meetings were surprisingly cordial; old conflicts were set aside

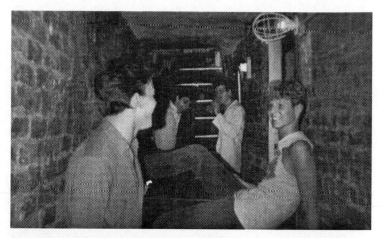

In the cellar passageway outside the Lustres' rehearsal studio in the East Village in the early eighties. Front: Tim Jordan, JZ Barrell; rear: James Noonan and the author (in white jacket).

or were by now too hazy to care about, and mostly the good times remained. After all, we were now parents, deep into our adult lives, and adolescence was very long ago. But for me, having just learned of Tim's death, and meeting our old crowd for the first time in decades, I felt like an urban Rip Van Winkle waking, not on a grassy knoll in upstate New York, but in a Bowery bar. We met in groups of various constellations over several months at the dives we used to go to that remained, from nostalgia. We cleared an evening on our calendars, hired babysitters; some brought along spouses, drove into the city from houses in New Jersey or Queens. Finding myself amid their faces at the same bar tables of thirty years earlier occasionally made me a bit lightheaded; time seemed to collapse and expand disorientingly while we reminisced about our years together in the New York of our teenage years.

We had been a large yet tight-knit group in high school, and many had stayed in contact, so these gatherings were less of a reunion for them than for me. Most of us were children of artists and professionals—musicians, painters, writers, performers, composers, literature professors, corporate lawyers—and had been sophisticated beyond our years. We were a precocious and ambitious group of New York adolescents, who saw a career in the arts as being as natural as the children of more conventional families consider a career in banking or accounting or taking over the family business. We came of age as neighbors on the Upper West Side, in the Village, in a nascent SoHo or Tribeca. Many, like Tim and me, had wound through Manhattan public schools together since childhood. Most of us had attended Music & Art High School, though some gone to Art & Design, Stuyvesant, Bronx Science or other schools for talented and bright children of the city.

During our four years of high school, we spent weekends together at the same parties, the same clubs, the same bars and diners. We slept at each other's apartments. We dated together. Most of the boys played in bands together. The ambitions, among the bands, had been enormous. And in one aspect, our friends were unlike teenagers anywhere else: they were growing up in the world's music capital and were playing, or were poised to play, at CBGB, Max's Kansas City and a dozen other leading clubs. There was an atmosphere of grand ambitions being achievable. ("We were already playing CBs," one old friend, now a high school music teacher in Westchester, remarked to me one evening. "How could we *not* have had high expectations?") In this milieu, Tim's own stratospheric aspirations were hardly out of place.

But thirty years later, I saw that, for many, those ambitions had, perhaps predictably, faded, had been replaced by concerns over mortgage payments and elderly parents' illnesses and children's schools. And while a few still played music together around the city, it was mostly just for fun. The torn T-shirts and biker jackets had been replaced by more conventional clothing. We were going gray, were no longer hollow-cheeked adolescents with thick hair. One woman whom I had last glimpsed standing in front of a bar with pink hair, puffing on a cigarette, was now a private school teacher in Connecticut, married to a banker with two sons. I certainly wouldn't have recognized her on the street. And yet, in certain respects, there was continuity: many had pursued careers in the arts—as music teachers, studio musicians, writers, graphic designers.

Tim had been closer than I had with this group, had remained with them after I had left for college, so I had expected that our friends would fill me in about what had happened to Tim during his last years. But I learned that he had become increasingly isolated after his band dissolved, had gradually lost touch with everyone.

When I asked about Tim, the responses were inevitably the same: expressions became somber, gazes turned inward, and I could see in their eyes how their minds were traveling back across the years as they studied their beers. No one had the complete story. Instead, I heard fragmentary facts, old rumors, dreadful anecdotes, all related with subdued sadness: *"The last I heard about Tim he'd been in detox—" "He was living in Brooklyn, in some dump, I think, with someone—" "I ran into him on the street in Midtown, and he had a delivery job of some kind—" "I remember seeing him at some club in the late eighties, and he looked dreadful—"*

But there were also old stories that still made us laugh, even if sadly (*"That was the night Tim was so drunk on stage he fell into the kettle drum and couldn't get out—"*).

I also found that everyone remarked on the same two things that I had also felt: how they had seen Tim's death coming years before they had learned of it, and how striking his personality was, how he had stuck vividly, if poignantly, in their minds, even these decades later.

Just about everyone had liked Tim: somehow, his ironic detachment, his arrogance, had not been a put off. We had tweaked him about it, were amused and skeptical, but he would laugh with us, a disarming laugh—seemingly relishing the humor while impervious to the taunt, just as he had during my verbal jousts with him back in grade school. While most of us boys were concealing our adolescent uncertainties behind bravado and poses, hiding inside our leather jackets ("like inside turtle shells," as JZ Barrell remarked), Tim radiated a splendid self-assurance. If we sensed, as some of us did, a troubled soul within, it remained vague, and if we felt that some of Tim's cool was a pose, the pose was so seamless and impenetrable that it was impressive, worthy of respect.

Christopher Sorrentino, now a writer in New York, articulated in an e-mail his perception during those years after high school that our friend had become entrapped in some terrible, irrevocable descent, and, also, that special, memorable quality of Tim's:

> *I thought a lot about Tim over the years, mostly because it often seemed that it might have been any of us who just spun out. Certainly Tim had enough talent, looks, brains; as much or more than a lot of us. By the time he died I guess I wasn't surprised that he hadn't been able to find his way back to a good place. That final act played itself out for a while. But I've often considered him; it's almost unexpected how much of a place he occupies in my memories.*

Sorrentino's conclusion—"it's almost unexpected how much of a place he occupies in my memories"—holds true for most of Tim's old friends today. Certainly it does for me. I'd known Tim had had many girlfriends, but several women surprised me at those evening gatherings by confiding that he had been their first love, that they had given him their virginity, or they had harbored a secret crush on him for years. Some of the men told me how much they had admired him.

Chris Standora, who played bass in a band that Tim had formed before the Lustres, recalled:

> *I remember Tim sitting at the Triumph diner, surrounded*
> *by band-mates and admirers, looking happy and satisfied,*
> *flinging out the sarcasm. He was rough with some people,*
> *although he was pretty merciful to me. I think I was a little*
> *in awe of Tim. Sure, the girls loved him, and he had his own*
> *style and adoring entourage—these attributes were enough*
> *to make any teenage boy feel a mix of envy and loathing—*
> *but when I look back, I mostly remember how other singers*
> *pretended their way through songs, trying to be cool and*
> *tortured (yet oh so fatally cute). None of Tim's performances,*
> *even at rehearsal, seemed to be a put on. That, I suppose,*
> *is talent.*

Contact sheet of a Lustres photo session.

We all knew Tim had talent. But I wondered, when I left our friends those evenings, just what was it about him that was so peculiarly haunting all these years later. What did he give to us—or, perhaps, take from us—as teenagers that he remained such a presence in our memories for three decades? To an extent, our sadness was for a lost friend, or boyfriend, whose memory also had become intertwined with nostalgia for our youth, who was frozen in our minds in our teenage years in New York in the eighties. But the haunting quality of Tim's memory derives, I suspect, from something even more than the grief that surrounds any young man's early death from alcoholism—derives, I believe, for many of us, from the ghostly image of a young man of promise who grinned at us inscrutably as he sauntered into the flames and ashes, while we, still so young ourselves, watched in helpless horror.

◇

Still, for me, there remains another image superimposed on that grinning, dying young man. It's the face of an Indiana boy with round, gold-rimmed specs who had recently been transplanted by his mother to New York. But the boy's smile, unlike the young man's, is open, has not yet become closed off. It's the face of my friend when we met in fifth grade at the Greenwich Village School, at age ten.

Tim Jordan, age ten.

At that age, Tim's straight, attractive features and his dark-yellow hair, the color of wet hay, gave him the incongruous appearance, in Manhattan, of a farm boy in an illustration by N.C. Wyeth in an old children's book—perhaps walking beside an idealized wheat field wearing a straw hat, or feeding horses. But the glasses he wore, his pale, indoor complexion, and his solitary air modified this farm-boy appearance, as though he'd usually be found, not in the fields, but holed up in the cool of a barn, reading. And it was this boy's face that had risen up to me when Tim and I had sat across from each other that night at the Delphi Diner.

I think Tim's appearance at ten was, in fact, expressive of the boy within. Even as an adult, despite his urban-hipster outfit, on a subway or in a dive bar, he still resembled a displaced farm boy, with his flash of blond hair and wholesome features. And he always would carry a deep sense of home toward the towns and farms of Indiana, where he returned with his mother each summer, despite his outward scorn of them when he reached adolescence. And he always would remain somewhat bookish and solitary, even amid the teenage parties and city night roaming. He carried used paperbacks in the pockets of his overcoat and read on the bus or subway—he once had with him a copy of Edgar Allen Poe's short stories and, another night, *On the Road*.

Yet his farm-boy appearance also concealed the most striking aspect of his personality: his cynical, urbanite's world-view, which had already begun to encroach on that Indiana kid by the time we met. I cannot know why Tim developed such a hard view of the world so young—perhaps his parents' separation, perhaps an innate predisposition, perhaps the city's relentless hardness rubbed off on him. But it appeared in him early, and over the years seemed to eclipse the sweet boyishness until, toward the end, I couldn't see it anymore.

I'm certain it was I who cottoned onto Tim, since he seldom reached out to anyone. At school, during recess, most of the boys would chase around in frenetic clusters; he was serenely content alone. He would sit in a quiet corner of the yard, engrossed in a comic book, and with his air of solitariness, he might have been in the barn he seemed to belong in. In class, I would find him bent over his notebook, sketching caricatures of teachers and classmates.

Eventually, Tim invited me to the apartment where he lived with his mother in a renovated walk-up on the Upper East Side. They had recently arrived from a loft in the downtown area of warehouses that would become Tribeca.

I discovered, in his tiny bedroom, the possessions representing his various interests. He had accumulated hundreds of comic books; he had a menagerie of reptiles. War and martial arts fascinated him: he collected model tanks, soldiers, and far-eastern weapons. He filmed elaborate, stop-action war and super-hero movies, which he showed me on a viewing-box, and he and his mother believed that film-making— acting or directing—would be the path he would follow.

Although Tim enjoyed drawing, would attend Music & Art High School, and could have had a successful career as a commercial artist, he never took it seriously. We differed in this, for I already had ambitions to be a painter. And there were, in fact, many differences in our lives—he lived uptown, while I lived with my mother and step-father in a housing development on the Lower East Side; he was an only child, while I had younger siblings; his family was nominally Protestant, mine was nominally Jewish. He was an Indiana boy, who knew fields and porches and main streets as I never would. But in certain ways, and perhaps the most crucial ones, our families were strikingly similar. Both of our parents had divorced, and Tim's mother, like my parents, had come to New York from elsewhere. But perhaps the single most important similarity was that our parents had been bohemians, had instilled in us a sense that Art was not only an acceptable, but even a realistic possibility as a profession, that pursuing one's own way in the arts was justified rebellion against convention. My parents were writers, his mother and father had met while studying art at Indiana University. When I befriended Tim, in 1975, his mother had recently taught art classes, and was a freelance mechanical artist.

With such families, it is hardly surprising that Tim and I developed, even by age ten, strong identities as Artists, along with dislike of the regimentation, authority, and class-work of school. I think, at bottom, it was this shared identity—and a subversive, custard-pie-in-the-face humor that partly grew from it—which bound us as friends.

Our friendship was also close because, by some ghost in the New York City Board of Education machinery, we were placed in the same public schools and classes for five years.

During those years, we passed from boyhood into adolescence together, sitting side by side in a seemingly endless series of squalid, chaotic classrooms, listening to tedious lectures.

Mostly, I recall laughing at classmates and teachers, and drawing caricatures of them by passing our notebooks under our desks, taking turns adding to the images. Often, we couldn't stifle our laughter or resist some cutting remark, and Tim would flash a broad, toothy grin, his green eyes crinkled and sparkling delightedly behind his round glasses. And then the teacher would scold us to be quiet, occasionally would even eject us to the hall or an empty classroom to "cool off." Our home-room teacher in intermediate school, a burly, sandy-haired young man named Mr. Durko, called us "the Bobbsey Twins," in reference to the children of the serial novels. (*"Hey, Bobbsey Twins! Keep it quiet in the back, or I'll separate you two!"*)

When we weren't ridiculing others, we turned our pens and wits against each other.

"Where did you find that ratty old book-bag, anyway?" Tim might scoff. "You look like a war refugee. What do you have in there—orphans?"

"How can you see anything through those thick glasses?" I would
retort, and we would veer off into a silly, boyish banter that had us both
in stitches, gasping for air. But Tim always seemed ahead of me in his
world-knowledge, his artistic talent, his adventurousness, his quick
repartee, and I kept trying to catch up. He made references to Sopwith
Camels and *panzers* and Fidel Castro and odd animals like orang-
utans. He relished foreign and old-fashioned words, many of which I
didn't know: *Lederhosen, behoove, lollygag, fiddlesticks*. He was only
three months older, but far ahead of me, was like the older brother I
didn't have. None of our classmates had the sort of electric mind that
Tim seemed to possess; they were dull in comparison. Through the
years, his ridicule stung deeply but in the end it had a salutary effect:
it woke me from of the haze of childhood, made me aware of how I
appeared to the world.

The deep bond of our friendship, before we drifted apart in late
adolescence, is difficult to fully describe, because ours was the special
comradeship of pre-adolescent and teenage pals. For adults, even
our closest and oldest friendships dwindle to merely a small piece of
the complex lives we accumulate. We find it hard to remember when
friendship—and especially our *best friend*—had filled so much of our
lives, had been the center of our world. With a best friend, we were
always on the same frequency, a frequency that no one else seemed to
quite share. Such intense friendship is the first exciting discovery that
beyond our families there are like-minded others; we are less alone
in the vast adult world that we are starting to discover. And Tim and
I did discover this world together as we entered our teenage years:
we embarked on explorations of Manhattan after school. We would
roam—in memory, always laughing at something or other—through
Central Park, Herald Square, the Upper West Side. Sometimes we
sparred, bare-fisted, on his tar roof and mimicked, to our hilarity,
the wooden, awkward poses of John L. Sullivan and Jim Jeffries, and

taunted each other with ridiculous put-downs as we threw harmless punches. *"Now, I'll whip you, laddie!"* Tim would say in a broad Irish accent, and laughing, off we'd go around the roof.

Last fall, I was reminded of the particular intimacy of our early comradeship when I was taking my ten-year-old son and his friend to the movies. I saw them walking before me, laughing and giggling over some bit of pre-adolescent silliness, their curly heads close together as they shared whatever it was that drew their laughter, oblivious to the serious adult world rushing past. It occurred to me that Tim and I had probably once appeared just like them. And I silently said to my son and his friend: *Boys, savor this time together—friendship will never again be quite so sweet.*

◇

Music & Art is a prestigious high school, requiring an examination for admittance. For many years, the school has been housed in a modern building at Lincoln Center, but in our day, it was at its original site: a neo-gothic, castle-like structure built in 1926, which still towers over St. Nicholas Park, in Harlem. The stone architecture and leafy surroundings lent the school an atmosphere of deep age, of magnificence, of importance. Students of every background journeyed from the most distant outposts of the city for the privilege of attending. They carried instruments in black cases and toted art portfolios, giving the place the rarefied air of a conservatory.

When Tim and I arrived, in the fall of 1978, we felt that we had entered not only a venerable institution but also an alien civilization comprised of a bewildering array of teenage cliques. They collected on the pavement amid the amorphous throng of students, each group with its own costumes, as distinctive as the feathers, paint, and masks worn by New Guinea tribes. There were still remnants of the Age of

Aquarius—the children of hippies: girls who wore sandals and long, cotton skirts, who smoked clove cigarettes in the park, and shaggy-haired boys who wore tie-dyed T-shirts and played Frisbee and listened to psychedelic music. But there were also the disco freaks, who were perpetually exchanging insults with the rockers. And there was the newer, smaller tribe of punks—skeletal and pale, with Mohawks and biker jackets, they wandered like flocks of long-legged, black birds. Then there were the even more recent arrivals, the New Wavers, with their more civilized look of narrow-lapelled, garish sport jackets, thin ties, and multicolored pants.

Toward the end of our freshman year, after getting our bearings, Tim and I found our place among the latter two groups, and met the friends we would spend so much time with in the coming years, the friends I would meet with again three decades later. But during our first months, we stuck close together, in a protective alliance. As at intermediate school, we were thrown into all the same classes. We sat at our desks together, ate in the cafeteria together, took the subway downtown after school together. We almost immediately resumed our banter, our caricatures, and mockery of teachers and classmates. And, as in intermediate school, we sometimes were ejected to the hall or an empty office to "cool off."

We particularly couldn't resist mimicking our art teacher, a genial, feminine, middle-aged Jamaican man named Mr. Bang. We mimicked him while he demonstrated drawing techniques to the class at an easel, until the students' laughter would alert him.

"*Out!*" Mr. Bang would shout with his ripe Jamaican accent, half-laughing himself. "*Get out you two—criminals!*" And we would be exiled, to the astonishment of our well-behaved classmates, to Mr. Bang's office down the hall. His huge, battered, roll-top desk sat by a window that faced a quiet courtyard, and Tim and I spent innumerable hours hanging around that desk during that fall and winter.

In our other classes, too, we pressed the limits of acceptable behavior. Our math teacher, Mr. McCann, was a tall, black-bearded man, a bit of a rustic, who wore corduroy shirts and had a colorful way of speaking. One afternoon he described something to the class as being "yea big," extending his arms. "*Yea big?*" Tim smirked at me and others near us, savoring the expression. "What the *hell* is that?" Then, in a mock-hillbilly accent: "Well, Mabel, my *dick* is about *yea big*—as the fucking crow flies!" and all of us burst into uncontrollable laughter. That was vintage Tim at that age—crude, rebellious, puerile, yet irresistibly funny to a bunch of teenage boys.

But his humor could be devastating, even to adults. After school one day, a classmate brought us to his apartment on upper Broadway. His mother, who had been married and divorced several times, was a pianist. Along one wall were long rows of portraits of the great composers. Tim glanced at the bewhiskered old men glaring out from the gold frames and off-handedly asked our friend's mother: "Who are all these guys? Your husbands?"

◊

Tim's adolescence seemed to launch abruptly, in a single day, that spring of our freshman year: he arrived at school one morning transformed from a school-boy into James Dean.

The metamorphoses was startling for its suddenness, weird for its thoroughness. He had gone home the previous afternoon wearing an ordinary brown coat with his hair parted on the side, and he appeared outside school the next day wearing jeans, a new, white T-shirt, a red windbreaker of the sort Dean wore as the troubled teenage protagonist in the 1955 film *Rebel Without a Cause*, and with his hair combed back, like Dean. He seemed to have aged about five years overnight. He had recently replaced his glasses with contact lenses, and had grown taller; suddenly, he wasn't a boy. He was a stranger. That morning, he opened a pack Chesterfield cigarettes—Dean's brand—and began puffing on them.

"James Dean was *cool*," was all he would say, in response to friends' questions and wisecracks.

That week, he brought me along to visit Dean's old walk-up, in Midtown, and stood beatifically in the little foyer, like a pilgrim in a shrine. Afterward, he related to me with satisfaction certain parallels he had discovered between him and the actor—that, for instance, Dean, too, had been an Indiana kid.

He persuaded a few of us to go with him one night to a Greenwich Village revival house to see *Rebel Without a Cause*, which he sat through wearing his red jacket.

It is still not entirely clear to me what prompted Tim's intense admiration for Dean. But I and others did sense at this time, as we had not before, a disquiet within our friend—some vaguely troubled place he kept unreachable behind his protective layers of James Dean cool. Sometimes, prompted by some indefinite feeling of concern, I asked him about his state of mind, his feelings, how it was going, but I got nowhere. You couldn't get within a mile of that place without getting knocked on your back by a grin and put-down. Quite possibly, he kept that place hidden even from himself. Our friendship from the start had been limited to a bantering camaraderie, and he never allowed it to become more intimate.

It may have been, in part, that troubled place inside him which had responded to Dean. Tim would later admire others like Dean who had become cultural symbols of rebellion and self-destruction—Billie Holliday, Brian Jones, Keith Richards, Johnny Thunders (the drug-and-alcohol abusing singer and guitarist for the New York Dolls and the Heartbreakers, who died in 1991, just shy of age 40). But the special intensity of his attachment to Dean was not repeated. Tim's veneration for the actor was, of course, merely an adolescent phase, but it may have been rooted in a recognition of, and affection for, a truly kindred spirit—a young, rebellious performer who was self-contained, yet deeply troubled; solitary, yet craved attention.

And as M&A's resident James Dean, he certainly drew attention. Girls suddenly began to flirt with him. Among the girls who noticed Tim was a Junior, Carrie Hamilton.

Within M&A's miniature Constantinople, Carrie was a punk. She wore fishnet stockings, had short, platinum hair, and sang with a band called the Whorelords. She also had a sardonic world view that matched Tim's, and being two years older, she freely criticized us and lectured about music or fashion or whatever the topic of the day was. She took us under her wing, led us forward, educated us, expanded our horizons while we hung around outside the school building.

"Why do you wear *beige*?" she once derided Tim, gesturing to his chinos (worn in emulation of the chinos that Dean wore as Cal Trask in *East of Eden*).

"What's wrong with beige?" Tim countered with his put-on, arch tone. "I *like* beige. It's a fine color."

"Beige is the dullest color there is. Wear black or red or any other color but beige."

We abandoned beige.

One day, I realized, through some subtle physical closeness or an exchange of glances while they leaned against a parked car, that they had become romantically linked during some interval that I had been away, perhaps at class. Their intimacy excluded me, and for the first time since I had known Tim—that is, for the first time since I was ten years old—I was socially flying solo. I was unprepared for this sudden change of situation, and was tentative and uncertain among our friends. With his James Dean jacket, his cigarettes, and now his romance with Carrie, Tim was advancing more deeply into adolescence while I watched.

One sunny afternoon, while I was alone on the sidewalk outside the school, I glimpsed Tim and Carrie lying together under a distant tree in St. Nicholas Park, Carrie's platinum hair resting on the shoulder of Tim's red jacket while he smoked a cigarette. I was envious of my friend's romance, even while the image was amusing, as though two New York teenagers had wandered into a Gainsborough landscape.

But Tim's relationship with Carrie lasted only a few weeks and, I learned, was not what it had seemed.

"He wasn't reaching out to me in any way, though at first I thought he was pursuing me, being flirtatious," Carrie told me decades later, over beers at a bar near Union Square (I was startled, despite myself, that her hair was brown and she wasn't sixteen). "I was being the aggressor, and I guess he didn't know how to handle it—maybe he was too young. I remember that day when we lay under the tree, I wanted to be close with him, but he was so distant. Finally, after a few weeks, I stopped trying, because he was so resistant. There was something so remote about him. He struck me as being a tortured soul."

◈

Tim's impersonation of James Dean ended as abruptly as it began, about six months later.

After school one cold fall afternoon during our sophomore year, we went to one of the forlorn thrift shops near Canal Street to buy winter coats. I set aside the bulky parka my mother had bought for me (which Tim always disparaged as making me resemble a Jewish Eskimo) and replaced it with a more grown-up coat: a World War II Belgian greatcoat, the sort of old military coat worn by many of our friends. It was green wool, heavy enough to withstand polar winters, with a high collar and shoulder epaulettes, and a double row of shining brass buttons engraved with Belgian lions. Tim chose a Naval officer's bridge coat—a great, sweeping, night-blue, cloak-like affair, which, like mine, had brass buttons and epaulettes. I'm sure we looked silly, like two kids engulfed in our grandfathers' old uniforms, but we certainly *felt* exhilarated and grown-up when we left the shop.

Tim carried home his James Dean jacket folded under his arm, and he wouldn't wear it again. But I noticed, years later, that he'd kept it hanging in his closet; like his admiration for Dean, he never quite abandoned it, even after he'd found other symbols of teenage revolt.

In fact, we both adopted new costumes. Like our friends, we began to dress in black; we discarded our sneakers for wicked-looking, black Beatle boots.

Our new clothes coincided with our exposure to our friends' music—their own music, and the music they listened to. The bands had names that were surreal, vulgar, as shocking as their songs. Until high school, Tim and I had heard only the radio's top-40—the smooth, packaged music of the seventies. Now, we discovered music that was explosive, raging, raw—the music of the Sex Pistols, the Clash, the Ramones, the Heartbreakers, the Dead Boys. And there were the myriad New York bands that had followed in the late seventies, whose songs were released as singles by obscure record labels and sold in little shops in the Village and SoHo.

After school, we trailed our friends to Manny's Music and other shops along Music Row on 49th street, near Times Square, while they checked out electric guitars, basses, drums sets, discussed the makes of amplifiers, or examined exotic accessories like capos and pre-amps, lingered longingly over gleaming Stratocasters, Gretsches, Gibsons. We hung around our friends' apartments while they rehearsed their own music, began to go to the clubs to watch them play on weekends. Tim and I both were drawn to and fascinated

by this new world. It beckoned with a promise of a grown-up, Diony-
sian freedom after our years caged in classrooms. We both bought
electric guitars, although I had no musical ambitions. Tim found a
black, 1968 Gibson, and I picked up a 1958 Harmony hollow-body
guitar. The wood had been cracked and repaired in several places,
and the neck was warped, but it was a fire-engine red, adorned with
chrome gizmos and inlaid mother of pearl—was as ornate, magnificent and antique-looking as a red Cadillac with tail fins. Our friends
taught us musical rudiments, and at Tim's apartment, or on his tar
roof, he and I would swap chord progressions or pick out riffs from
albums. We bought piles of records, listened to everything: the blues
and R&B of Robert Johnson, Elmore James, and Muddy Waters; the
early rock n' roll of Buddy Holly and Gene Vincent; the latest from
the Rolling Stones, and on through the punk and post-punk and New
Wave bands that our friends had revealed. Music was converging on
us from every direction, and Tim seized on it avidly. He had clearly
found his calling.

For Tim, I think, this music was not merely notes and lyrics
playing on a turntable, they were sounds that had found him from
another world—a hazardous night-world that he immediately knew
was where he belonged: the gypsy world of musicians that reached
back to the blues singers who drove the back roads of the Missis-
sippi Delta. It was, I think, as much a teenage boy's darkly romantic
daydream as anyplace real: a vision of early-morning club-stages and
whiskey bottles and shabby hotel rooms and girls that don't care. But it
appeared real enough for Tim. He left behind his ambition of directing
or acting in films and began to pull together his own band from among
our friends. School was suddenly irrelevant. He dropped out of Music
& Art.

◇

We dropped out together.

We spiraled out like a couple of kamikaze pilots: our grades plummeted as we both began cutting all our classes. Along with a handful of other troubled kids, we spent entire days drinking liquor and experimenting with drugs in St. Nicholas Park, hidden from the school by brambles and trees.

I was ambivalent about dropping out. I had wanted to be a painter, had enjoyed art classes, yet I was driven toward self-destruction by teenage angers that were beyond my control or understanding. Tim, though, appeared blithely indifferent to his impending catastrophe. Even at that time, as muddled as I was, I found his indifference to dropping out and his reckless use of drugs and alcohol shocking and disturbing. It was during those months that I first experienced the foreboding that would grow over the years, an apprehension that Tim was sauntering off alone down a treacherous road. His James Dean infatuation had appeared amusing, if a bit unsettling, but this was serious. Our friends talked and dressed and sang rebelliously but few of them were really dropping out and none were quite so cavalier about drink and drugs: sometimes when we met he would flash his broad grin and tell me that he had just taken some new drug—amphetamines, barbiturates, even LSD.

Sitting in the park, we would see the students emerge during the midday lunch periods and then recede again, like tides. And each hour, each class that went by, I struggled over whether to stay with Tim or return to classes. Increasingly, I chose to remain outside. Sometimes we left the park, and kids we barely knew brought us to their homes, while their parents were at work. While our classmates toiled in classrooms, Tim and I stumbled among elegantly furnished, book-lined apartments on the Upper West Side, artists' lofts in SoHo, antique-cluttered townhouses in the Village, cramped railroad-apartments in the East Village with broken windows and hissing radiators. We spent one snowy day ambling around an empty Bronx Zoo.

Through various subterfuges, we had concealed from our parents our absences from school until it was too late for anything to be done.

With a report card looming that I knew would be disastrous (I would end up with an "F" for Math, Science and Languages and a "D"—which I'm sure I didn't deserve—in English and Art), I followed Tim that fall to another school he had heard about, the New York Metropolitan Campus High School, rather than repeat my sophomore year at M&A.

"MetCam" was a refuge for teenagers who were unwilling or unable to successfully complete high school in the city's public and private schools. Traditional classes were offered, but students mostly worked at offices, theaters, artists' studios, and other places for academic credit. MetCam provided enough freedom from the classroom to allow Tim and me to stick it out for two more years and receive our diplomas. But after the prestige and promise of Music & Art, I was miserable at MetCam, which was housed in a dreary red-brick building downtown. Tim remained impervious to the change. His real life was with the band he had recently formed, and at the clubs in the early hours. He was merely marking time at school.

Once we entered Metcam, we saw each other only on weekends, and in retrospect it seems that it was probably at this time that we began to drift apart.

◇

I later learned the fact that Tim and his mother had not known when he was a teenager: that there was a ghastly, even eerie, history of alcoholism running through his father's family: Tim's great-grandfather and grandfather both died from alcoholism at the same age, twenty-nine, and Tim's own father, Michael McNally, came a hair's breadth from dying of alcoholism at twenty-eight, the age that Tim passed away, before going sober.

The precise causal relationship between heredity and alcoholism remains unclear, but in Tim's case, the strong pull of genetics on destiny was indicated not only by his family's history of alcoholism but also anecdotally, in an e-mail I received from his mother in response to my request for information about her son's death:

> *His father had a moody attitude and dressed in black and wanted to be an artist, had this James Dean slouch—and his son was just like him, even though he hadn't met Michael till he was 14. Everything about them was identical—the aloofness, the slouch, the clothes. When they did meet, they went to movies and they had a very good relationship. They were so much alike in style and temperament without ever having known each other that it was uncanny.*

Tim's father, who is now a martial arts instructor, and who remains, like Tim's mother, deeply grieved by their son's death, told me that he, too, was taken aback by how much his son, as a teenager, resembled him, despite their years apart during Tim's childhood: "I would see myself in him constantly when I visited—in the way he moved, his facial expression, the way he walked, in his sarcastic comments, which I had also indulged in when I was young—he was so similar to me."

Tim concealed his heavy drinking from his parents for years, and his father did not think it necessary to reveal to Tim or Jayne his family's history of alcoholism until near the end of Tim's life, when he was clearly an alcoholic himself.

"I was never aware of how serious Tim's problem was," he wrote me. "We spent a lot of time together and in those years I never saw him drunk nor did I ever see him drinking. I debated with myself about telling him about my father, for fear it might be a self-fulfilling prophecy. My mother said that my father had always said he would die when he was 29 because his father had died at that age—and so he did."

On Tim's mother's side, his grandfather was depressive and suffered a series of nervous breakdowns. It would appear that Tim inherited, along with his bohemian temperament and artistic talent, a predilection for depression and alcoholism. (There also were musical antecedents among Tim's family: his mother's father was an Irish tenor, who sang professionally and as a soloist in church; his maternal grandmother played the organ. Tim's father's cousin, Rick Derringer, of the band the McCoys, hit No. 1 on the pop charts in 1965 with "Hang on Sloopy," dethroning the Beatles' "Yesterday.")

Still, our genetic heritage cannot wholly predict our lives and it cannot entirely explain Tim's descent, just as it cannot fully account for why his father, unlike his own father and grandfather, did turn back from the edge of alcoholic death as a young man.

Tim probably had been quite affected as a boy by his unstable family environment, and perhaps that caused him to develop his defensive fortress of cool detachment. For me, at least, his interior remained unreachable, seemed hidden behind a labyrinth of battle trenches. His mother's relationship with Michael McNally, Tim's biological father, at art school, was brief. A few years after Tim's birth, she married another artist, and took his surname, Vanderperk, but they were divorced when Tim was ten, and his step-father was not part of their lives afterward.

Remembering the period after her divorce, Tim's mother said she was intensely angry and depressed for a year:

I think Tim was so deeply affected by my distance that he

*never could really trust again. He said during one of his good
times that it all felt very fragile, that it could turn back to
pain and loneliness at any point. Sadly, it did.*

Tim's uncertain sense of his identity may have been reflected in
his use of surnames. Born with the name Jordan, he used through his
school years the name Vanderperk, and afterward he used the names
Jordan or NcNally. I remember him saying to me, at the end of our teen
years, that he was going to call himself Jordan or McNally, but hadn't
decided which.

I am certain, too, that the circumstances of Tim's adolescence in
New York were a key factor in his death, robbed him of precious years
to grow up before being so exposed to alcohol.

The downtown New York of thirty years ago, and our particular
friends, of course, also cannot be entirely blamed; teenagers, whether
in New York or anywhere else, will find ways to drink and use drugs.
And for all of those, like Tim, who become alcoholics, so many others
in the same circumstances do not.

Yet in the city and era in which we came of age, the getting of
everything was too easy, and many in our crowd too freely indulged.
New York, with all of its vices, was flung open to us when we were still
barely out of childhood. The drinking age was eighteen—it would not
be raised to twenty-one until 1986—but the law was flagrantly disre-
garded everywhere. Starting at barely fifteen—many of us appeared
younger—Tim and I and our friends went to any bar or club that we
chose, at any hour, and not once, in my memory, during the next three
years, when we attained our majority, were we turned away at a door,
nor were our IDs ever checked. (We never needed the fake ID-cards
we had made in Times Square.)

The first bar Tim and I entered was the Four Winds Tavern, on St.
Mark's Place, on a blustery day in 1979. The Four Winds was a deep,

low-ceilinged place with dark wood everywhere, like a medieval inn, behind heavy wood doors a few steps below the sidewalk. In the afternoon it had only a few neighborhood drunks bent over the counter. I remember standing with Tim and a few friends outside the doors and then our relief, after we entered, when the bartender wordlessly served us several pitchers of beer. We then got wildly drunk at one of the back tables. At twilight, we dispersed outside. Tim stumbled onto the bus. I staggered home and passed out in my bed, my homework assignments forgotten in my book bag.

I don't recall how we chose the Four Winds as our first bar, but we got drunk there regularly after school, and then we began going to dives nearby, for variety. We simply showed up at their counters, a group of smooth-faced kids in outlandish outfits, smoking cigarettes, ordered whatever we liked and were served without questions.

It was not only bars and clubs: we bought bottles of whiskey at liquor shops and drank from them openly on stoops or the streets; we got beer at grocery stores along with cigarettes, years before we boys were even shaving.

My memories of our weekends are admittedly colored by nostalgia for the camaraderie and excitement, but also by anger—anger at the rogues' gallery that allowed us such freedom: the bartenders who served us, the bouncers who didn't check our IDs, the waitresses who brought trays of beers, the young professionals and artists who let us kids crash their parties and gave us drugs. We were allowed to roam, unconstrained, through the nightlife of one of the wildest cities on Earth. There was an atmosphere during the weekends those years, in my memory, of Hogarthian revelry.

Downtown was resurgent with all the arts, but our particular New York—oddly for a group of art students—was centered almost entirely on music in the clubs. We didn't go to experimental plays at little theaters or visit the burgeoning galleries below Houston Street. Our New

York, our downtown, was narrow, cacophonous, dangerous, squalid. It lacked many of the redeeming qualities of previous generations: the intellectual intensity of the bohemians and beats, the communal joy of the folkies and, later, hippies. We soaked in the nihilistic rebellion of the punk and post-punk bands in the clubs.

Manhattan's elegance had been largely destroyed by the turbulence of the late sixties and the fiscal crisis of the seventies, from which it was just starting to emerge. New York was a rougher, grittier city, the city of the burning Bronx and the bankrupt Koch administration, the city before SoHo and Tribeca and Alphabet City were fully gentrified. Times Square was still a perilous strip that jutted up from the Underworld. The subways were a graffiti-covered, gang-swarmed, rail-screeching nightmare. Soaring crime seemed like a permanent plague: our high-school years began shortly after the Son of Sam murders had panicked the city, and were marked by the emergence of the Guardian Angels vigilante group and the headline-making abduction of a boy named Etan Patz on his way to school in the Village; we graduated not long before a mild-looking subway passenger named Bernhard Goetz shot four young men he thought were going to mug him.

For us Music & Art students, our city was bounded by Greek diners in the West Village, Polish diners and dive bars in the East Village, and cheap Chinese restaurants. In the summers we drank on tenement stoops or on friends' tar roofs.

Most of those nights have been reduced to a jumble of images: standing bleary-eyed in kitchens strewn with empty bottles; waiting with friends on freezing subway platforms at ungodly hours and at ungodly stations for the train to take us all—*somewhere;* walking homeward in the early hours through the crumbling tenements of the Lower East Side, lonely and sleepless, with a headache and ringing ears.

But always there were the clubs. We listened, over the years, to hundreds of bands, and many nights I spent listening to friends' bands, including Tim's. For the most part, I enjoyed the music and the scene, especially at CBGB. I liked its cozy, dingy atmosphere—a long, dark, narrow place below the old Palace flophouse on the Bowery, with warped, creaking floor boards and walls covered with bands' flyers and graffiti and a tiny, black stage lodged awkwardly in a back corner. And when some song hit me exactly right, it was a three-minute revelation, a brief visit to bliss. And when some blasting chord-progression summoned my angers from their deep place, I was provided a few moments of emotional release. But more often, I was bored listening to the slashing guitars and thundering drums, and shouted, incomprehensible lyrics. Then, the nights dragged on interminably. And while our friends moved about, or while I waited for them to play their sets, I might find myself sitting at a table, a little drunk, surrounded by sinister characters in leather jackets, and wondering what on earth I was doing there. On nights like these, visiting these dives was, for me, like spelunking in Hell: a tour of hot, beer-reeking caverns, where deafening music ambushed you at the door. The scenes were sometimes whirlwinds of chaos and fury, the bands screaming, the dancing crowds surging under spinning, colored lights or in deep-shadowed darkness. I wouldn't have been surprised to see a couple of satyrs stroll by. But Tim was not ambivalent. He was at home. He would lean back beside me at a table, low and relaxed in a rickety chair, wearing his dark overcoat, drinking a vodka and tonic, a cigarette burning absently in his fingers, as he watched the bands and occasionally cracked a glib remark.

Alcohol was only a start of our nights. We shared cocaine in the club bathrooms, passed around bowls of hash in vacant lots, and, often enough, some of us ended up vomiting in a gutter or an alley, or passing out in a taxi. We were in way over our heads. We had to discover our limits, and that took quite some time for many of us. Tim was the only fatality among our friends, but he was not the only casualty. When I met with our group years later at the bars, more than a few of them no longer touched alcohol, had spent years struggling with alcohol and substance abuse issues. I had left for college at eighteen, but many of them, like Tim, had continued to play the clubs and tour the bars and parties deep into their twenties, and some had lost their way. One friend, who lived in pre-gentrified SoHo, recalled:

> It was such a wild, thrilling time, but also sometimes quite scary and sordid, and it's been difficult to explain to friends I met subsequently who grew up in small suburban towns with intact families and proper parental boundaries. It's amazing how much freedom we had. I don't think my parents tried all that hard to control me, but I doubt whether they'd have been very successful if they had.

I believe only a few of our friends had curfews, and they were routinely ignored. There were not yet mobile phones with which our parents could tether us. We were bright, middle-class students, and our parents trusted us—if misguidedly—to behave responsibly. Many of our parents had liberal child-rearing views, had been hippies or radicals, and now were touring the same nightspots that we were. Some were preoccupied with their own lives or, like Tim's mother, had finally abandoned attempts to control their children. A large number, like my own parents, had been divorced and remarried and their children managed to evade detection of their worst excesses by playing off of parents who were divided into two often hostile households, linked by limited communication.

In truth, much of what we did was rather innocent, even quaint. We sang quite a lot. I remember walking late one night with a few others inside an enormous cardboard refrigerator-box we'd found in a lot on Houston Street, and singing at the top of our lungs, like an inebriated, many-throated beast. In taxis, we attempted barbershop-quartet harmonies for songs like "By The Light of the Silvery Moon."

We usually ended up in the small hours at a diner—generally it was Homer's, in the West Village—with plates of eggs and cups of coffee. Homer's became like a second home. Its large windows faced the red-brick Jefferson Market Library across the street, with its pointed clock tower, and beyond lay the broad, busy intersection of Greenwich and Sixth.

I don't recall that we were ever hushed by a waiter or bounced from Homer's, though, God knows, many nights we should have been—we were drunk or drugged or giddy with exhaustion; we shouted, argued, threw our food, made a mess of our tables, and passed around liquor bottles from the pockets of our overcoats. Our endless cigarettes raised clouds of smoke that now seem unbelievable from the vantage point of today's fiercely smokeless city. And we were certainly a motley crew—the boys in leather, the girls with mascaraed eyes bleary with exhaustion and drink. There were electric guitars and basses lying in cases under the tables. We would arrive after being at some club with the ink-stamps from the door still on the backs of our hands, smudged and fading with perspiration of the night's progress.

But I think our diner talk served as a crucial emotional stabi-lizer—a place to pause and digest, along with meals and bad coffee, our shared experiences as babes wandering that nighttime circus. In the early hours we would regroup, reconnect, sober up before going home. And at those diners we were, in a sense, already halfway home: there was something homey and wholesome about them, after the darkness of the outside city, with their bright chandeliers and Greek waiters bringing food and coffee like indulgent uncles. And Tim was always among us, always out to the very end, a quiet yet vital presence, slouched with a watchful, sly smile, his face pale, his hair tousled, and a cigarette burning in his fingers.

And at some point, we might notice through the windows that the sky was getting light, and if we were at Homer's, as we so often were, we would see the dawn coming over the clock tower of the Jefferson Market Library and the pigeons circling over the roofs of empty Greenwich Avenue, and then we'd know it was finally time to go home, or to a friend's apartment nearby, finally time to lay down our aching, weary heads and sleep.

II.

AMONG THOSE I MET WITH DURING THE WEEKS AFTER I LEARNED OF TIM'S DEATH was Vincent Metzo, who had been beside me in the photograph Tim had snapped at the rehearsal studio that night decades before, and which Tim's mother had included in her letter. Vincent had known Tim well, had been lead singer with his own band and is now a school administrator. I shared with him the photo of the two of us in the tenement cellar, and he studied it, smiled, and we discussed the old days.

"I still can't believe what happened to Tim," he remarked suddenly, with feeling. "It's a waste of so much talent. He was a year or two older than I was at high school. And he was by far the coolest guy around he had those black boots and those good looks. He had such charisma. And he was an incredibly talented songwriter —that a guy in his early twenties wrote those lyrics is amazing to me."

Yes, of course: Tim's music. Now I wanted to listen to his lyrics again, for what they might reveal. Fortunately, JZ Barrell had, a few years before, created a compact disc of fifteen of the Lustres' songs. A week after I met with Vincent Metzo, JZ gave me a copy of the CD and explained, in an e-mail, his delicate audio archeology:

> With the exception of three tunes it was all performed live,
> recorded to now-ancient cassettes, and was only compiled,

with the help of digital forensics, for history reasons, just to
have the tunes documented. Without the benefit of produc-
tion and vocal overdubs. The only sources I had were tapes of
rehearsals, live shows and maybe one or two of the most primi-
tive 4-track recordings. But in context of some of the top bands
25 years later, I think we were ahead of the curve. The music
can be juvenile and amateur in places, but if we'd had real
production value we might've really been contenders.

The CD thrust me, just as Jayne Jordan's letter and snapshots had, back into the past with a sort of horrific shock. A press of a "Play" button and in a half-second I was flung from my forties back to age sixteen, from my law office back to the East Village rehearsal cellar, with Tim and the band harmonizing as teenagers.

Listening to the CD, I discovered that I still remembered every lyric, every guitar riff, every vocal harmony, every drum solo.

◇

After recuperating from the jolt of hearing Tim's voice again, I listened more carefully to the songs, which now, with my knowledge of Tim's death, were infused with sadness.

His subjects revolve around sex and romance, the themes that have always preoccupied young men and rock bands. But musically, the songs somehow manage to combine an aggressive, raw drive with an irresist-ibly catchy tunefulness, even lyricism, with subtle vocal harmonies and double leads reminiscent of Lennon and McCartney, and inven-tive instrumentals performed with professionalism. The songs are lean, yet packed with intricate intros, verses, bridges, choruses, codas. Each track is distinct and memorable, but identifiable as a Lustres' song, and I thought they held together well as a group. I was impressed.

Truc, as a singer, Tim lacked a beautiful voice and had a narrow range, straining to hit some high and low notes, even making allowances for the circumstances of JZ's recordings. And he sometimes sounds self-conscious. But his singing certainly served the Lustres' purpose: he could effectively belt out his savage songs.

Tim's lyrics, like his personality, were hard, funny, prickly, incisive, and at times vulgar to the point of obscene. Even when his lyrics are not especially noteworthy, they are never stale or amateurish. Intentionally or not, he stretched or ignored the structural conventions of rock songs, threw in off-rhymes, changed the rhyme scheme of verses within songs, or even, abruptly, in the middle of a song, dispensed with a rhyme scheme entirely. Yet the songs always work. He and bassist James Noonan,

Song lyrics written by Tim Jordan.

who co-wrote a number of songs and contributed his own, shared in abundance the invaluable ability to recognize the sort of common phrases and simple riffs that make a song commercial and catchy, and the song titles reflect this: "Walking On Eggshells," "Don't Be A Stranger," "What A Day," "Try Too Hard," "Running My Way."

That song, "Running My Way," about a girl who's been put in her place, approaches a threadbare theme that's been covered by the

Rolling Stones ("Under my Thumb") among myriad other bands, but Tim's words and music combine to make his version of the old story thoroughly his own:

> *When I first met her she was cold,*
> *she didn't want to know me*
> *now the girl just can't say no*
>
> *When I used to call her up she'd laugh,*
> *she'd tell me don't waste her time*
> *But now she'll have to stand on line.*

Tim's originality also emerged in his fearless use of the mundane experiences of teenagers in New York, where social life depends not on cars (the subject of so many rock songs) but on mass transit. In "Take the Bus" he wrote of going home frustrated after a visit with a girlfriend:

> *I never really know what to expect when I see you,*
> *I got a token in my pocket, so I don't care,*
> *The only stimulation I can get is drinking too much;*
> *We have so little in common, I think I'll take the bus*
> *At least it's going somewhere*

The reference to drinking in this song is one of the few that appear in Tim's songs.

Listening to the CD—I listened with headphones for a couple of weeks while on subways, walking between appointments, at home, at my office—I began to notice something new: the tight limits to Tim's themes. Most of the songs are rock-outs describing anger and frustration about a failure of communication in some romantic situation with

James Noonan (left) and Tim Jordan performing at Danceteria, 1983.

nameless girls. Other songs are adolescent pull-aparts of friends or
lovers:

> *I know you're thinking you're the one the world was made for*
> *Your nose is sticking up so high it must be painful*

> *You're not a vagrant but you're pissing in my hall*
> *You know you're just a rich kid who always had it all*

There are no songs about politics or social issues. No heart-felt
ballads. No mention of the actual word "love." No lyrics that clearly
express tenderness or romantic yearning. They are as smirkily hard
and as arrogant as Tim was himself. While this makes for avoidance of
clichés, it also confines the songs to a slender range of subjects.

Closing the final song on the CD, "We're only Friends," which was
recorded live at CBGB, Martin Blazy shouts to the raucous crowd that
long-ago night with a sort of grandiosity: *"Thank you very much! We
are the Lustres!"* What poignant hope and ambition Martin's shout
now seemed to hold. The band rehearsed twice each week and played

gigs regularly, perhaps, in all, two-dozen performances before the band dissolved. Yet, if such high expectations and years of hard work had been pinned to their dreams of success, why did Tim's band-mates decide to pack up their instruments and abandon everything? I wasn't surprised to learn that Tim's drinking was the main cause.

◇

In the fall of 1983, I, like many of our friends, went off to college. But the Lustres kept at it. James Noonan worked at a Midtown product-design company (he eventually moved to Texas and entered the market research field); JZ held various jobs. Martin had taken a clerical position at a knitwear company, which put him on a path to a long career in textile production. But Tim didn't look for a job or go to college: he lived at home, increasingly drank vodka, and pressed on with the band, the sole vehicle for his great aspirations. Now, though, the situation had changed. JZ recalled:

> We were playing weeknight gigs—not weekends—we had
> no manager, and there were no high-school crowds to fill the
> tables and no college set, since none of us were in college but
> working odd jobs, except Tim, who didn't work. That period
> was hellatious.

Tim's escalating drinking had become evident to his band-mates by this time. It not only affected the band's rehearsals but also performances, where he'd slip up on his guitar or botch lyrics. This caused friction among the band members. I remember sitting around at their rehearsals when I returned to New York for holidays, and hearing James Noonan and the others impatiently berate Tim for drinking.

The Lustres: James Noonan, Tim Jordan, JZ Barrell, Martin Blazy.

DON'T
LACK
LUSTRES

march 20	CBGB
march 25	INROADS w/ Sly Society
april 3	SNAFU
april 7	the DIVE w/ Fun With Your Mother
april 15	R.T. FIREFLY

"When a person is that bad off, it's just so difficult," James recalled when we met recently. "Tim couldn't remember lyrics, he was making us look bad on stage, and I thought, 'this is not going to work.'"

Tim's alcoholism became "a major problem," JZ agreed. Martin Blazy described the situation at that time in an e-mail:

I think there was so much frustration because we expected so much from each other. Toward the end, Tim was drinking pretty hard and you could see some anger issues starting to surface. We weren't close, so I do not know the demons he was facing. But I got impatient, and all my friends were telling me to play with as many bands as possible, so I left.

JZ wrote to me of his perception, at this time, of the band's future:

I suddenly saw things very clearly. We had to be more aggressive in getting the band exposure. Tim was ambivalent, as though life should hand him a record contract on a silver platter, because he was so cool. We had a very bad meeting at a diner on St. Mark's Place one day, and that was about the end of it. I left the band and joined another. It's unfortunate about the Lustres, because Tim "had the goods"—he really could have done it—he wrote brilliant lyrics: "You're not a vagrant but you're pissing in my hall"—what a brilliant punk-rock lyric. But he was trying to be so cool, thinking the world would come to him on his terms. But he died waiting.

Tim's alcoholism, the band's failure to establish itself quickly enough beyond the New York clubs, and prolonged dissention over how to press ahead finally combined to pull apart the Lustres. Tim's band disintegrated around him. It had lasted, from start to end, five years. When I tallied the number, a strange stillness settled on me: the word 'Lustre,' derives from the Latin *Lustrum*, signifying a period of five years.

◇

Whether Tim and the Lustres would have been commercially successful had they stuck it out a little longer is, of course, an imponderable. The band was only one of hundreds of strong bands that played the New York clubs in the eighties. As it is, the Lustres left little for posterity:

a few copies of a bootleg-quality CD; a few scissor-and-paste street-flyers advertising the band's performances, created by Tim; a series of ads in the back pages of the *Village Voice*, preserved on microfilm. Their stage performances, held long before the proliferation of video cameras, were never taped, and were photographed only a few times. The band's music itself has been mute in audio storage since the Lustres' final gig, more than twenty years ago. The night Tim walked off the stage for the last time with the Lustres was the end of his brief career. Today, it is almost as though Tim's band, propelled for half a decade by its members' huge ambitions and endless musical tinkering in that tenement cellar studio in the East Village, had never existed, had never had any impact beyond its members.

JZ mused wryly over a cocktail: "The Lustres played in the forest and nobody heard."

III.

In the carnival atmosphere of our high-school weekends, Tim's excessive drinking had largely gone unnoticed. It was only when we were on the cusp of adulthood, as many of us prepared to leave for college, or, later, when we got together with Tim while we were visiting home during holidays, that for many of us it became evident, as it had to his band-mates, that Tim's drinking had gotten out of control.

His mother wrote me that she had supported Tim's career choice but that she, too, was unaware of his drinking problem until later:

> I was really happy for Tim and proud when he formed a band.
> I was thrilled watching them perform a couple of times. I think
> I was so relieved he had found a niche that I tried not to look
> at the emerging problems. I believed in his talent and in his
> dreams. I knew he was prone to depression but I did not know
> he was prone to alcoholism. I was naïve and knew nothing
> about this disease. He didn't drink at home and I didn't seem
> to know all that was going on outside our doors. Or I didn't
> want to know.

Tim was not a loud or boisterous drunk, and often seemed sober or nearly so. But he became clumsy, forgetful. He'd stumble when leaving a chair, or forget he had a cigarette burning in an ashtray and light another, or a glass of vodka would slip from his fingers and shatter on the floor. His humor, once so sharp, sometimes seemed simply crude, his comments on our lives at college made him seem as though he were living in another world. We noticed signs that he was not quite sober even early in the evenings, indicating he had already been drinking, alone. He appeared increasingly haggard, disheveled. He was now working odd jobs—never holding one for long—hoping to form a new band.

It was at about this time that his only serious girlfriend, Liz Reinstein, left him.

Liz was probably the most important person to Tim during his life. They met when he was eighteen and she was sixteen, one night on the sidewalk in front of a club, Armageddon. They dated for about two years, until his drinking became unbearable for her, though they kept in touch afterward for a few years. After high school, she attended college, then law school.

I remembered Liz as a pretty, dark-haired, smart and cheerful teenager, but I did not remember her clearly, since by the time she and Tim were dating, my friendship with him had become strained and then I was away at college. But I wanted to speak with her about her relationship with Tim, what she knew of his last years. I eventually found she was in England, where she and her husband, a social worker, live with their three daughters. She shared her thoughts about Tim in an e-mail, which indicated to me that Tim had opened up to her and revealed a gentleness he had kept hidden from male friends, and it also encapsulated much of what so many of us thought and felt about our friend's self-abuse:

> Tim was always incredibly sweet to me. Early on, we'd
> agreed to get married when I turned twenty-six, and I think
> the last time I spoke to him was when I was nearly twenty-
> six, and he called to remind me of our agreement. I'm pretty
> sure that at that time he told me he'd been given medical
> advice that if he didn't stop drinking he would die. I always
> thought that Tim was incredibly smart and talented and
> I wanted to help him to stop drinking and get his life
> together, but he seemed completely impervious to my efforts,
> or anybody else's. It was very sad and frustrating to watch
> him waste all of his talent.

Many of my memories relate to Tim's later deterioration and the frustration of trying to get him to sort himself out. It irritated me that he thought it was fine for him to carry on the way he did, drinking and not doing anything with his life. I really cared about him but any effort I made to help him was always fruitless because he didn't think that anything was wrong. He'd always laugh off my concerns.

I remember his swagger, his arrogance and sarcastic comments, as well as his habit of using archaic phrases. He certainly had an aloofness about him and a sort of leonine self-possession. But overall, I remember him as being very gentle, and in my memory his sarcasm was only meant to be witty, or perhaps self-protective, but never cruel. I always felt he was very patient and caring towards me, and at that time in my life I think I was quite vulnerable. Tim wrote me a letter which he left outside my door the Thanksgiving after I started college. We'd been broken up for a while, and he wanted to get back together. I remember it being a really beautiful, touching letter. I think he said it was the only letter he'd ever written.

Many of our friends also said that their most vivid memories of Tim were sad vignettes from these years after high school, when the corrosion from his drinking had become evident, and that Tim's eventual death had left them not only with sadness but also with frustration and anger at his apparently cheerful disregard for his self-destruction.

I, too, had such memories from this period. One of the last occasions I saw Tim was when I was home from college and I visited him at a dingy apartment he was sharing with a friend, Mike Lumer, in Park Slope. It was early Sunday morning when I arrived, and I found him reclining on a dirty sofa, wearing his usual outfit of black Levi's and rumpled oxford shirt, reading the *Village Voice*, his electric guitar resting against the wall and a tall glass of vodka standing on the table. When I reprimanded him for his drinking, he told me, as always, to lay off. "I know what I'm doing—you just mind your own *beeswax*, mister," and he grinned at me, amused by the quaint phrase, the type of silly old expression that he'd loved since we were kids. I remember walking in the bright daylight back to the subway with the lingering image of my friend in that sunless room, alone and drinking vodka, and my feeling of terrible helplessness, of foreboding. And his grin—that maddening grin—left me wondering, on the subway back to Manhattan, whether he was unaware of his addiction, was aware of it but thought he could manage it, or whether he was embracing it as a depressive's way of slow suicide.

Mike Lumer, who is now a lawyer in Manhattan, told me that he had to kick Tim out, after enduring months of erratic behavior, culminating when Tim, in a stupor, urinated on the living-room floor.

"I don't think he was cognizant of what he was doing," said Lumer. "But there's a limit to what a person can put up with in a roommate. I couldn't help him, and I also couldn't just watch him destroy himself."

He spoke to Tim about his drinking but "he had such a veneer he had built up about himself. You couldn't get anything out of him. He would smile at me and he didn't deny that he drank too much. He just said he was happiest when he was drunk and what did I care about it, anyway. You can't reach someone who doesn't want to be reached. It was very difficult to be friends with Tim—it's difficult to be friends with someone who is trying to kill himself."

Lumer added that Tim wasn't "particularly bothered" by the decision to kick him out. "He shrugged it off, just like he shrugged everything off."

Not long afterward, I finally severed the faint ghost of what remained of my friendship with Tim, which brought us, with unnerving appropriateness, full circle, back to the Four Winds Tavern, to the very same table where we'd sat at our first visit there, when we were fifteen years old.

Tim needled everyone, but had become icy with me, fired particularly nasty insults, and I resented it. I may have reminded him of his awkward, pre-adolescent years; or he may have simply felt we had less in common, as he moved deeper into the music world while I began to think of myself more as a writer. Perhaps my own surliness, which had strained my other friendships to the breaking point, made me too difficult a companion. But in any case, we had little holding us together anymore. I realized this clearly one night when I was visiting New York during my second year at college. Tim and I had been sharing the table at the Four Winds with a few friends and we had decided to see a band at a club. Tim refused to lend me a few dollars to join them. It seemed purely mean-spirited on his part, and it was clear to me our friendship was at an end. I rose from the table and launched into a harangue, primarily at Tim, who glanced around at the others, deriding me with a sneer. I then cursed everyone at the table and stormed out of the bar. It would be six years before I would hear from Tim and we'd meet at the Delphi Diner.

◇

Tim went adrift after his friends, his girlfriend, and former band-mates dispersed. He briefly had another girlfriend after Liz, but the relationship hadn't meant much to him.

Over the next few years, Tim was hospitalized for pneumonia, suicide attempts (at one point, he swallowed an overdose of pills) and alcoholic hepatitis. He was diagnosed as bipolar but was never treated.

His mother told me that she only belatedly took steps to get him help. She looks back in shocked dismay that she had paid for him to attend bartending school, which he completed in September, 1986. He got what would have been a plum job—as a bartender at the Central Park Boathouse—but he was quickly fired. "He made a stupid error and was so sorry about it," his mother recalled. "He had been really enthused about the job."

When an apartment across the hall from his mother's flat became vacant, Tim moved there. He paid rent and bills through disability insurance and other government programs—although much of his income went to vodka. When Tim died, his mother found an eviction notice: he had run up a back rent debt of $2,500.

Tim periodically would stop drinking, sometimes for weeks or even months, but would suffer Grand Mal seizures—violent spasms, potentially fatal, induced by withdrawal.

In the late eighties, he voluntarily entered an alcoholism-treatment program but returned to drinking when he got out. James Noonan recalled that he had hoped to rejoin with Tim in a band, but realized it would be impossible: "He wasn't the same person anymore."

Tim entered counseling with his mother and her young son from her second marriage, Cody. But Tim was skirting death almost every day—he was struck by a car, and the cigarettes he smoked burned through his notebook pages or his bed-sheets while he slept.

Tim's father visited him at the hospital during one of his illnesses, and told me that his son had seemed embarrassed by his condition, sad and subdued: "He'd lost that quality he'd used to have—that gumption."

He wrote Tim a letter, in which he revealed his family's history of alcoholism and also his own struggle:

> *I understand you are still trying to self-destruct. When I*
> *was your age I was very much in the same state of mind. As*
> *I approached my 29th year, I was certain I too would die*

young…I found myself laying on the kitchen floor of my dirty
little Lower East Side apartment. It was Monday morning, the
sun was trying to come through the filthy window. I had been
on a binge, drinking for several days, I didn't remember where
I had been or with whom, my pockets were turned inside out,
the door to the hall stood open. I rolled over and asked the
ceiling "Please help me." The ceiling didn't answer, but from
within came an answer, "God helps those who help them-
selves."… That morning I made the choice to live…

Tim's father, lying at the edge of the precipice, had summoned
the strength to pull back, to renounce the fate seemingly dictated by
heredity, and now he was beckoning his son to do the same. But Tim
was apparently beyond reach. Isolated, without a job or a band, he
talked to his mother wistfully of the past, gloried in his days with
the Lustres, relived old stories—and continued drinking. He had
kept himself remote from everyone, as Carrie Hamilton had felt all
those years ago when he had withdrawn from her proffer of intimacy.
But now he was driven by his isolation and depression to reach out to
others. Sadly, he had disintegrated too far for friendship.

JZ Barrell recalled that he saw Tim at this juncture: "One night he
came by, unannounced, with his guitar, while I was rehearsing with
my new band. He was such a mess, he was drunk and had weird scabs
on his face. We all knew him, except for the one girl in the band, who
had no idea who this guy was. I remember he fell down once. And
it was just embarrassing. Finally, we just wanted him to leave." JZ
paused. "That may have been the last time I saw him."

◇

Although Tim may no longer have been capable of collaborating on songs, he did continue to write lyrics and compose music until he died. He played guitar, taught himself to play keyboard, and made recordings of his songs in his apartment. He wrote and played his music by the window, the wall behind him covered with old Lustres flyers. The window overlooked the traffic of First Avenue, but I suspect, after reading the lyrics he wrote at this time, that his vision was turned within, at some inner abyss.

His music had undergone a drastic change. On loose notebook pages and on the pages of an old-fashioned Composition Book— salvaged by his mother, which still have the cigarette burns and vodka stains of almost twenty years ago—he filled the lined sheets with poignant lyrics that reveal his feelings of isolation, regret, frustration, vulnerability and longing, all of which had been absent from his earlier lyrics.

There is, on one page, a single, untitled verse, in which he describes not only remorse for his years of self-destruction, which he knows have obliterated his ability to achieve his earlier ambitions—but also his torpor, which he realizes is preventing him from altering his course:

Think I'll shower for an hour
I feel so unclean
Feel so much regret and guilt
When I think of what I've seen
Vow to change my ways tomorrow
What do I have today
Just a shower and shave
And promise that's never fulfilled

While his Lustres songs had focused on the difficulties of communication with friends and lovers, they were sung from that lofty perch

Tim had staked out for himself since he was a boy: songs about spurning a girl, or of some amorous triumph—hard-edged songs that spewed scorn and derision for others' shortcomings. Now, his lyrics, while still describing failures of communication, explored the quandary from the side he had once ignored or ridiculed: the needy party, the person who is desperate, lonely. In "Something I Can Use," Tim, in a complete reversal, is pleading for the intimacy of another:

> *There is so much I could ask you for*
> *I need answers and so much more*
> *You give me something that I really need*
> *Please don't make me get on my knees*

It is impossible to know whether Tim's lyrics are truly confessional or are the fictions of a songwriter, or some mixture of both—he may still have had some remnants of his old ambitions shaping his writing. But the words quiver on the page, amid the cigarette burns and vodka stains, with such an intensity of emotion, describe such autobiographical situations, that it is hard for me to doubt these songs served as his personal diary. Several of the songs completely abandon any rhyme scheme, read more like free-form poetry—or like entries jotted by a hopeless young alcoholic in a private journal shortly before his death.

◈

It was at about this time in his life that Tim had startled me with his phone call and invited my wife and me to the Delphi Diner.

That night, after we paid the bill, Tim asked us: "Hey, do you have plans? Why don't you come on back to my place for a while? We can have a beer."

I hesitated. I did not want to see Tim further that night. I had sensed that everything about him was off-kilter somehow, from his skewed eyeglasses and rumpled clothing to his conversation, which seemed sophomoric and unreal; everything was going dreadfully wrong for him, and it shocked, saddened, and embarrassed me in front of my wife.

Tim noticed my hesitation and prodded us—"Come on over for a while, we'll have just one beer"—and his neediness, which I had never seen before, utterly unnerved me.

"Let's go visit," my wife nudged me.

As we walked, Tim smiled, leaned close to me, then nodded his head toward my wife and whispered, *"Very nice!"* with a wink. I remember being touched, thinking it was the kindest thing he had ever said to me—even if it wasn't quite directed at me, except by reflection.

We followed Tim up the six flights of stairs to the little apartment where he lived down the hall from his mother and four-year-old step-brother. It was the first time I had climbed those old stairs in years, and as I followed Tim up, I found it confusing and sad, yet oddly comforting. His apartment was dimly lit, strewn with clothing, a disaster. We sat in the mess and talked awhile, drinking beer from bottles. He was still smoking constantly. I said, finally, "Tim, you've got to stop the drinking."

"Oh, Christ, not that again. I'm fine—I'm in better shape than you," he scoffed, with his old arrogance. He nodded toward a couple of barbells. "I lift sets of those weights everyday."

And then, suddenly, he reached out and gently punched my arm and said with his broad smile, "Hey, do you remember Mr. Durko in home-room, and how we used to draw him?"

I was surprised at the question. "Sure, I remember."

"I still have one of our pictures of him somewhere, I think." He turned to my wife, laughing: "We used to have a home-room teacher named Mr. Durko, and we used to draw pictures of him—"

But I was so embarrassed by my friend in front of my wife that I was only thinking of how quickly we could leave.

It was only after I learned of his death that I realized it was the only occasion that Tim had reminisced with me about anything.

◇

Tim had applied to become a police officer in the months before he died, his mother told me, and at first this information astonished me, given Tim's fiercely anti-authoritarian personality. But his wit was driven, I always thought, by an inner violence: he had always been fascinated with armaments and martial arts, going back to his collection of model tanks, soldiers, and Far Eastern weapons. Still, he also had, as a boy, related to the heroes in his comic books—the saviors. "He always thought he was a 'good guy,'" his mother said. "I think his idea of becoming a police officer came from the idea of being a superhero."

In his last months, she said, Tim was struggling to shake his depression, to finally alter his course, and his decision to become a police officer was an attempt to pursue a practical path that could lead him beyond the dead-end where his music had taken him.

"Tim tried so hard during the last months to get sober," she said. "He wanted to live so badly by this time. He was really turning a corner, was making plans for the future again, he had lightened up, and he wanted so much to live."

On a Monday evening in September, 1992, his mother returned home and climbed the stairs to her apartment, and noticed that the newspaper she had left that morning by the door of Tim's flat was untouched, and she knew something was wrong, although all that weekend, Tim had not taken a drink. She let herself into Tim's apartment, and found the

French doors to the bedroom were closed. Afraid to open them, she asked a neighbor for help. He discovered Tim inside.

The autopsy could not determine a final cause of death, though Tim had no alcohol or drugs in his body. He had cirrhosis of the liver and some brain dysfunction, indicating he may have suffered a seizure. The autopsy also found cerebral atrophy—shrinkage of the brain—a term that struck me as gruesomely horrible, and especially so for Tim Jordan, who had always been so sharp-witted, so smart. The term seemed like a final symbol of all of the long decay that had beset him and made him unrecognizable to me.

Tim had spent the last evening before he died with Cody and his mother. They had watched the old comedy film *Father of the Bride* on television. His mother wrote me: "He cried as I held him and told him life would get better."

◈

The memorial service, at Bethany Church, on upper First Avenue, was attended by Liz Reinstein and a few of Tim's old friends, on a rainy Manhattan evening. I had been out of touch with everyone for so many years that no one thought to invite me. The day of the memorial service, I was in classes at law school downtown.

Tim was cremated, and his ashes are buried with his mother's family, in the small town of Howe, Indiana.

After Tim died, his mother said, she received in the mail an envelope from the New York Police Department containing his test results: a nearly perfect score on the written exam. But he hadn't taken the physical.

◈

Tim left behind grieving parents and a six-year-old brother who would grow up with only vague memories of him.

During the following years, Jayne told me, her son's death led her to "become a better parent" for Cody, who, when we met, I found was an impressive, soft-spoken, considerate, and intelligent young man, a top student and athlete in college, who never drank. He certainly was far more mature than Tim and I were at that age. In many ways, Cody appeared the opposite of his brother.

For him, Tim's death remains a flashing warning about the dangers of addiction. But Tim's life—rebellious, cool, adventurous, self-directed—serves as another sort of example: a corrective, Cody believes, for his own perfectionism, his drive for conventional success and approbation. He said that Tim's song lyrics now often return as words from an older brother, reminding him to try another perspective on his life. Cody reflected:

> One lesson I'm still learning comes from the song "You Try Too Hard." While Tim performed this song when he was younger than I am now, for me it's a casual suggestion from an older brother who's been through it all: You try too hard. Every time I hear it I'm cooler, I'm saved by some increment. For me, Tim's words, which come from a young man who was tormented by personal demons, are ironically Zen-like. It's as if he had attained enlightenment and just didn't know it. It might have been just another song for him—ostensibly, perhaps, about a girl—but for me, it's a lesson.

> Some of the best role models are the ones that are gone, for they are perfectly preserved. Tim will always look as cool as he does in his picture. Despite how affected and constructed his persona might have seemed at times to those around him,

to me it looks effortless. It is a coolness I have never felt in myself. Punk rock was, to a large extent, about rebellion and making a career out of the disapproval of others. Tim was a part of that counter-culture in his music and clothing and attitude. I have always wanted to make the authority figures in my life proud and impress friends and strangers alike. Their approval helped shape my opinion of myself. My image of Tim and his ethos help me depend less on others for happiness.

In turn, Cody unwittingly had a powerful influence on Tim— reminded him, too, of another view of life. Jayne said their time together provided Tim with a greater sense of family, someone with whom he could regain a piece of childhood's wonder, playfulness, and hope:

They loved each other's company, when Tim was not drinking. Cody seemed to give Tim a focus, a reason to try to gather himself again. Before he died, he was drinking less and spending more time with Cody. He made him a wonderful model train track, and a boat and airplane out of balsa wood. And I know that having a brother brought Tim and me much closer together. We were much better able to talk of his alcoholism and my successes and failings as a parent. The door was opened through this new little brother. I carry a great sadness that will never leave me, but at the same time, I carry great joy from the good things in my life.

Still, beyond his family, Tim, like his band, left behind so little: scattered old friends and girlfriends who, during a hectic work day, prompted by some incident, might think once in a while of his fading image.

Today, too, much of Tim's New York has vanished: CBGB: Gone. Max's Kansas City: gone. The Ritz: Gone. Danceteria: Gone. Manny's Music: gone. Even Homer's diner is gone.

One night last year, at a bar with a few of our old friends, the wife of one of our group, who had never met Tim but had heard tales about him over the years, smiled when we were introduced, and said: "So, you're the friend of the mythical Tim!" At that moment, I think, I finally realized that Tim had died. I had met someone in our group who had never known Tim, and of course never would. He, like so much of his city, was gone, and now would continue to recede into the past as the world moved on.

That night, it also struck me that perhaps that word mythical—with its connotation of events so ancient that factual truth is beyond retrieval, of a protagonist who embarks on a solitary and perilous journey freighted with riddles—is an appropriate adjective for Tim Jordan and his descent into alcoholism, his wandering amid the perils of the New York clubs in a distant age, and his leadership of a band he had unwittingly bestowed with a name that seemed to carry a cosmic timetable for its own destruction.

◇

I am walking through St. Mark's Place in February twilight, surrounded by neon, buffeted by cross-tides of kids with tattoos, piercings, dyed hair, jostled by tourists, students, artists. I am heading for the Lustres' old rehearsal studio—just to have a look.

I had missed Tim's memorial and funeral service, and I had a need now, after months of piecing together his life, for some sort of closure. When those near to us die, they take with them a piece of our own lives, and I felt as though a great chunk of youth had been gouged out and buried with my friend in Indiana. But Indiana is halfway across the country, so this quick subway trip downtown would have to suffice, at least for a while.

I had thought that if I accumulated enough facts, if I pieced together all the parts of Tim's life, I would understand his death. But his passing remains for me as unfathomable as his grin. The meaning of that grin still eludes me, seems as inscrutable as a Greek stage-mask. Tim had always kept himself remote behind that grin, beyond reach. I still wonder, as I had after I visited him that Sunday morning at his Brooklyn apartment, whether that grin was an alcoholic's denial of his addiction—a self-protective scoff at our concern—or a cheerfully fatalistic acknowledgement of his drinking problem. Later, the grin had, apparently, faded; Tim had become a person I had not known and could not quite imagine—isolated, suicidal, needy. Although his endless drinking had made his early death seem inevitable, was the source of my years of foreboding, he also had always appeared so cheerful, tough-minded, self-possessed. I could not reconcile the young man I knew with the suicidal young man I had not known. Had depression and addiction driven him, at last, to the death he had sought? Or had he finally, like his father at the same age, seen death up-close and been determined to get sober and begin a new life—except that his body just gave out? I will never know. I can only say farewell.

I find St. Mark's Place even gaudier, more carnival-like than I remembered—tiny shops, bistros, tattoo parlors, and souvenir stands seem to have sprung up in every conceivable cranny among the tenements.

I push on, and pause at the Four Winds Tavern. It has survived, although it is now hemmed-in by the outdoor tables of a trendy looking Middle-Eastern cafe. As I stand at the trash-strewn steps that lead down to the bar's wood doors, I see the ghostly images of my younger self, of Tim and others, walking inside. I follow and peer through the window and see that the murky interior is just the same—the long bar, the wood booths in the back where we sat. I notice, taped on the window of the door is a sign that warns:

NO I.D.
NO ENTRY!
NO EXCEPTIONS

I reflect again on how, when we entered this bar for the first time that afternoon, at age fifteen, the bartender had served us overflowing pitchers of beer until we were blind drunk. When we passed through these doors, we unwittingly crossed the threshold from childhood into adolescence, crossed into that raucous, nightclubbing, free-for-all city, when CBGB and other clubs became like second homes and entire weekends would slide by in a blur of parties, alcohol, and drugs. Tim's passage through these doors was like a crash through a skylight, the beginning of a tragic descent.

I move on, turn right at the corner of Second Avenue and head downtown. I'm in search of a grocery. The store used to display on the sidewalk rows of flowers, boxes of fruits and vegetables, which partly concealed the rusted iron doors in the pavement that led down to the tenement's cellar and the band's rehearsal studio. Those nights we would heave open those doors and then Tim and James and JZ would carefully hoist their instruments in their cases down the metal stairs and we would descend into the dank, narrow, subterranean passage, lit by bare bulbs.

I find that the grocery is still there, and then I see the closed iron doors in the sidewalk. I stop, gaze down at them dumbly, as at a tombstone. Beneath, live the shades of my youth, of my old comrades, of a friend who is no longer here.

6. The Hotel 17 Revisited

6 The Hotel 17 Revisited

Youth is, after all, just a moment, but it is the moment, the spark, that you always carry in your heart.

—Raisa M. Gorbachev

NEARLY THREE DECADES HAVE PASSED SINCE THAT WINTER MORNING WHEN I WAS seventeen and I first noticed her among the late-comers that crowded into our school library for some long-forgotten speech by our principal—nearly three decades since I was bewitched by her face and everything changed for me.

I was sitting, when I saw her, with several other students by a row of tall windows, and I was shifting uncomfortably on a wooden chair that had been wedged too close to a fierce, ancient radiator. I was idly watching the students as they pressed through the door, encumbered with coats and knapsacks, their faces flushed from the cold, all of them slightly breathless from the four flights of stairs they had climbed. As they entered, each glanced tentatively, expectantly around the dim, milling room, its shelves overflowing with books, its walls festooned with maps, notices, and calendars. But I somehow hadn't noticed when she'd entered; she appeared suddenly, standing a few yards away, at the front of the crowd of students.

Her coat was still buttoned and she was still wearing her wool gloves. A colorful scarf was flung around her neck, and her high collar was turned up. But it was her hair that seized my attention—it was dyed a fiery gold-red, was cut short, and shone proudly in the drab

140

assembly. Her gray eyes, which seemed lit with a private enjoyment as she looked at the principal speaking at the head of the room, were dramatically accentuated with mascara. Her lips were painted a lush scarlet. I watched as she whispered with the students around her, breaking now and then into a smile at someone's hushed joke.

As I gazed at her flaming hair and lively eyes, her smiles, her colorful scarf, and upturned collar—everything suggested a bohemian, theatrical, sparkling intelligence that immediately enthralled me. Her vibrancy separated her from the others in the room. The pale winter sunlight flooding through the windows seemed to illuminate her with a special radiance.

The principal's speech wandered interminably, though I heard none of it. His words were reduced to distant droning, for I had instantly fallen headlong for this girl and had resolved to approach her: if I allowed her to vanish, I knew my regret would be unbearable.

When the principal concluded his speech, to desultory applause, she joined the other students as they converged on the door. I pressed through the crowd until I was behind her, and made a remark about the speech that, thankfully, when I heard myself, resembled an amusing observation.

She was startled by being addressed, and glanced back quickly over her shoulder. And then her gray eyes found mine, her lips parted in a smile, and she made some agreeable reply that I barely heard. But her expression indicated such a friendly candor that my anxiety dissolved, and we began to chat easily as we went down the stairs. As it happened, we both had nothing to do for a while, so I invited her to a diner across the street, where I went for coffee in the mornings.

The diner was small and worn, with only a few rickety, Formica tables and a short counter. I remember we sat at a table in the center of the room and ordered coffee; I remember my disbelief and delight that she was sitting with me; I remember the cold-fogged windows, the glare of fluorescent lights, the hectic clatter of dishes; I remember her knit-wool gloves resting by her coffee cup; and I remember she said that she was reading a novel by John Steinbeck— *"I read The Grapes of Wrath and I decided I would read everything he ever wrote,"* and she smiled, amused by her own statement—and then the film of memory snaps, the mind's projector-spools whirl, the screen goes white, and the rest of that morning is lost, maddeningly, into Time's oblivion. Nor can I remember the early hours that morning before I saw her. But that moment when I first glimpsed this girl's face, a moment that led to my first romance, has remained in memory with the vividness of an old Kodachrome slide removed from a box and found unfaded by years. That morning, in that school library, gazing on that girl's face, I fell in love for the first time— passionately, completely.

◇

Her name was Rebecca. She lived with her mother, a music teacher, and her brother in one of those massive, ornate, pre-war apartment buildings on the Upper West Side. Her father, who lived separately, was a professor of French literature.

My first impression of Rebecca had been quite accurate: she was determined to go her own way, to be a performer, a musician—not a classical pianist like her mother, but with a band.

We were, at that intersection of our lives, in extraordinarily similar positions: we were both seventeen, had both dropped out of prestigious high schools and were now attending an "alternative" school in Greenwich Village, where students who had rejected traditional school, or had flunked out, worked at places of business throughout the city for academic credit toward a diploma. We were both rebelling against convention, were resolved to be Artists: I would be a writer, like my parents. My parents, like Rebecca's, were separated, were intellectuals. My father, like Rebecca's, had taught literature. It was, perhaps, foreseeable that we would be drawn together.

A day or two after we met at the library, late on a cold, overcast afternoon, we were strolling along a path in Washington Square Park when, unable to contain my ardor, I stopped in mid-sentence, pulled her awkwardly, urgently toward me, and pressed my lips down to hers. She'd been surprised, but then her arms rose and drew me close, and I spun away to some rapturous place I'd never known. When I returned, I saw her eyes gazing into mine, close and glowing.

We walked, then, along the path, and she slid her arm in mine, our gloved hands clasped. We were together now in magical way that we hadn't been only minutes before, exhilarated by the start of this adventure we had just begun, which would bring us somewhere we couldn't know.

We went to the Astor Riviera Cafe, at that time a new diner, and sat by a window that faced the darkening expanse of Astor Place. We drank cups of watery coffee, our cold fingers intertwined—a bridge between two giddy young souls. She smiled mischievously: *"Well, come on, play footsie with me!"* and kicked my leg under the table, squeezing my hand with hers. Her eyes held mine, as sharply watchful and beautiful as a falcon's beneath stray strands of her flaming hair. Yet at the tables around us, the patrons seemed somehow oblivious to the young man who was plunging, stunned and ecstatic, a few feet away, through one of life's greatest thresholds, into First Love.

◇

Images of those winter weeks we spent together resurface, despite my better judgment, as a Hollywood romantic montage: we held hands and talked of Art and Adventure at Homer's Restaurant, a Greek diner in the Village near our school; wandered the twilit, crooked Village streets arm-in-arm; had drinks at tiny bars in Chelsea; strolled among the empty paths and bare trees of Washington Square Park.

Joan Didion writes in an essay of "the way you love the first person who ever touches you and never love anyone quite that way again." Rebecca was the first person who touched me. There was something so audacious and worldly and bohemian about her that enchanted me, and she surprised and delighted me with an endearing, whimsical humor. I intuited, from her easy familiarity with me, that she was far more experienced than I was in romance, and this fascinated, even while it also vaguely troubled me.

I can dredge from memory only a few words from our intimate hours, but I clearly remember the *feeling*, which I believe was, as least initially, mutual, of a sort of gushing euphoria. She was, for me, simply the most beautiful girl in the world, a Helen to be endlessly gazed at across a Formica table at Homer's diner. Everything connected with her had suddenly become luminous, like objects touched by the Divine—her wool gloves on the table, her scarf, the rings she wore, her apartment building uptown, even her name, which before I'd met her had been ordinary, now seemed so perfect, seemed to capture her windswept beauty as no other name could have.

Yet, all this—this cathedral-gazing wonder at this girl's loveliness, this mysterious elation I experienced just walking with her and holding her hand, this ineffable tenderness mingled with carnal desire—disturbed and frightened me. I had no rule over these strange emotions. They were within me, and yet they were *not* me, were alien forces that had invaded and were ransacking my heart. These feelings were, in part, merely budding adult desires that had lain concealed, awaiting only Rebecca's kiss to be released. But my confusion and turmoil also stemmed from another source—the unlikely circumstances of my life that winter.

I was, in fact, living two completely separate half-lives that I could not reconcile. One half of my life—my school, my friends, my weekend visits to my father and step-mother at their apartment in the Village—was so similar to Rebecca's, as middle-class Manhattan teenagers. But the other half of my life, on the Lower East Side, on Avenue C, where I lived with my mother and step-father, was utterly different. Everything there was *hard*—the unrelieved landscape of wreckage and vacant lots and stripped cars, the swinging sticks of the gangs when they robbed me, their savage faces. And the hardness of Avenue C had led me to become bitterly hard, as that slum had hardened the black and Latino kids there. By the time I was seventeen, I had unwittingly come to despise any sign of weakness—fear, tenderness, gentleness—in myself and others.

My rage at our life there had led me to a ruinous act that I'd witnessed myself perform over several months but could not prevent or understand—I flunked out of Music & Art High School. Now, that winter, I was trapped in clerical jobs arranged by our "alternative" school, was largely cut off from my friends—those few I hadn't driven away with my sullen anger. I saw them only on weekends, which were spent at parties and clubs. I chased oblivion in drink and drugs to ease my loneliness and anger before returning in the early hours to our housing development.

My life was careening out of control, and yet, despite everything, I was prone to dreamy ecstasies, for underneath the rage and hardness, my nature was romantic and bookish. I was impatient to leave high school, was quiveringly eager to leap into Life. I imagined writing novels in a garret in Paris, exploring jungles, voyaging to Tahiti.

And then I'd met Rebecca.

Although I had dated other girls, none had held me so in thrall: our artistic ambitions, our rebellion, our wanderlust, our humor—everything, it seemed—was aligned. We were two of a kind who had found one another. And so, when I'd kissed Rebecca in Washington Square Park, all my long, terrible isolation on the Lower East Side, all my shameful, hidden gentleness, and all my undiscovered adult passion and romantic yearnings surged exultantly forth and unleashed an inner mayhem and panic.

And there was another cause for my turmoil when I was with Rebecca: Avenue C followed me everywhere. When we walked the quiet, residential streets of the Village, I was secretly anxious that by holding her hand I would appear unguarded, a mark for the gangs that haunted my mind: On Avenue C, I walked with my hands clenched in my pockets, prepared to fight or run at any instant. It was not so easy, after so many years, to simply hold a girl's hand on the street. But we had nowhere else to go, except diners like Homer's. We would have no privacy at her mother's apartment, far uptown, or at my father's small apartment. And I would rather die than bring Rebecca to our housing development among the tenements and crime. So I kept my relationship with Rebecca secret. I endured those winter weeks of joys and sorrows alone.

◇

A week or two after we had met, we were walking the side streets around Sheridan Square as twilight darkened the Village. We had lingered over coffee at Homer's as long as we could, and now were again wandering in the bitter January wind. We were weary, cold, and longed for somewhere warm and private. I led her through a quiet lane and inside the dingy vestibule of a small apartment building with Greek columns flanking the entrance. Inside, Rebecca smiled at me expectantly, her face pale beneath the bare fluorescent bulb, and we wordlessly embraced, bundled in our coats and gloves, and I pressed her against the peeling, green paint of the dirty wall and kissed her, and her arms reached up around my neck. Adults came and went through the door, letting in the freezing air, but they left us alone, and outside the door's small window the streetlights came on and passersby hurried along, returning home from work.

I don't know how long we embraced in that vestibule—maybe twenty minutes, maybe less—and I don't remember a word we spoke, as I don't recall so much of our time together, but I do recall the icy touch of Rebecca's cheek against my lips, the delicate scent of her hair, her gray eyes, so close, shining steadily into mine. And I remember our delight at simply being alone together. In that drab vestibule, in that Village lane, Rebecca and I shared an emotional intimacy that I could not have imagined only a few weeks before. I was starved for her—for the feel of her body against me, for her lips, her whispers, her smiles—but my ravenousness was mingled with frustration, because we could not remain together. We had, always, to return home to our parents, to separate.

That evening, we forestalled as long as we could the moment when we had to leave, but finally Rebecca said she had to go home. We left the vestibule and rejoined the darkening city. At the Sheridan Square subway entrance we kissed goodbye and I watched her trot lightly down the stairs, a bag slung over her shoulder, and then she was out of sight. I headed toward Avenue C, cold, haggard, happy, and already suffering the ache of blissful loneliness.

During the following weeks, images of Rebecca constantly flickered in my mind, provoking what, no doubt, appeared to others as merely teenage absent-mindedness, but which was, in fact, a state of unbearable, joyous agony, while I tried to perform my clerical duties at the offices where I worked. I arranged to meet her at every opportunity that our schedules allowed, no matter how brief or inconvenient for me. I rang her on the phone as often as I could. At night, while I lay in bed, her face floated in the darkness and I saw her image with longing and wonder, and cherished fragments of our conversations as we had walked the streets and parks—conversations that have since gone silent for me, but that, I know, revolved around literature and music, and our dreams for when we would be released from school and our families, and we would at last launch our adult lives.

Then one night, all my emotional confusions subsided into a perfect calm, a certainty that I loved Rebecca. I knew that I now wished, as I never had before, only to make *another* person happy, to make *her* happy. I wished only to help her make her way in the world, wherever it might lead.

◇

One stormy evening, Rebecca invited me to a performance to be given by her mother. It was a piano and flute recital at Carnegie Recital Hall, a snug auditorium tucked within the Carnegie Hall building, with chandeliers, classical decorations, dark heavy curtains, velvet seats. The hall was crowded and the audience filed in carrying wet coats and umbrellas. We sat in the front row. The great, gleaming, black piano loomed above us on the stage. Rebecca sat on my left, intently watching and listening. She wore forest-green tights and scuffed, leather boots, pointed like an elf's. Her left hand held the program card and her right hand held mine gently, as the music of Bach, Brahms, and Mozart flowed over us.

Later, riding up Broadway in a taxi to her mother's apartment, we drew together in a shared impulse and the shops' colored neon lights shone through the rain-slashed windows and passed across her face. We left the taxi, ran through the downpour across the tiny, triangular park across from her apartment building. The lobby was bright and grand, with marble and mirrors. An aged elevator brought us to her apartment. Rebecca unlocked and opened the door, and led me directly to her darkened bedroom, and there we made love.

I went home that night standing in the soggy throng of the hurtling Broadway subway, lost in an ecstasy that, if harnessed, might have lifted that train to the heavens. And yet, my joy was, as it had been in that lane off Sheridan Square, made somewhat bitter by our forced parting: I felt like a grown man in love with a woman but unable to lie the night with her. As teenagers, still bound to our families and school, our lovemaking had to be stolen furtively.

I don't remember if I ever, in fact, told Rebecca that I loved her, although I believe that I did; nor do I recall whether she ever said she loved me. But we almost immediately began discussing dropping out of high school, getting jobs waiting on tables and moving into a cheap hotel, where I would write my novel and she would pursue her music. Someday, I said, we would run off to Paris, Rome, or Tahiti. It was I who broached this quixotic plan, but she had agreed, with a thoughtful, daring smile and a defiant light in her eyes which made me love her even more wildly. I wanted to sweep her into the future with all the madcap romance of Christopher Marlowe's lines:

> *Come live with me, and be my love,*
> *And we will all the pleasures prove*

And together, we did visit a few shabby hotel rooms, sat on the beds and excitedly worked out plans. One afternoon, we sat holding hands on a bed in a room in the Hotel 17, near Gramercy Park, discussing it all breathlessly. The Hotel 17 was a once-elegant apartment building that had decayed into a "single room occupancy" hotel with a front desk protected by a Plexiglas wall. The desk clerk led us through a dim corridor. The carpet was dirty, the air was musty. He unlocked a door to a room and left us alone. As we sat holding hands on the

edge of the bed, which was covered with a white spread, we calculated how much money we'd need from our restaurant jobs to cover our bills, yet no matter how we shuffled the numbers, our income kept falling short. Nearly faint with excitement, I squeezed Rebecca's hands and gallantly assured her that I would find a way. All my dreams for a life devoted to Art, Adventure, and Love were miraculously becoming real as we sat in that room, and I would not let them slip away.

Our plan to live at the Hotel 17, while unlikely in retrospect, was at the time, at least as I remember it, undertaken by us both seriously. Though we may not have spoken the word "marriage," I craved to bind my life irrevocably with hers, daydreamed about making a life together at that seedy hotel like a young man dreaming of a cottage for his wife with a white picket fence. My proposal of our living together was, for all practical purposes, the equivalent of a marriage proposal, and her assent, I believed, was her acceptance.

◇

And then she ended it.

The chronological order of events has devolved into a jumble. But, however it all unfolded, Rebecca, with flabbergasting abruptness, severed our relationship.

We met one morning on the sidewalk in front of school, and when I went to kiss her cheek, she drew back slightly.

"But, *why*?" I asked, as a frozen dread sank into me.

Rebecca looked downward, a few strands of her fiery hair fell forward across her cheek, and she shook her head. "*I don't know. It isn't right,*" was all she would say, or all that I remember her saying at this distance of years. In disbelief, I sought more from her, but she would not, or could not, provide an explanation. Finally, she said she had to go and started away toward the school. And as I watched her walk across the courtyard and disappear through the school door, some part of me died with each step she took.

I leaned weakly against the high iron fence, as though I had awoke from a drugged sleep, repeating the scene endlessly in my mind. I searched for meaning in her enigmatic words, her shake of her head. *What* wasn't right? *Why* wasn't it right? *When* had everything changed so suddenly?

I believe, though I have no memory of such a scene, that I attempted to speak again with her. I passed her several times during subsequent weeks outside school when she was with other students, but her glance was uneasy, and she did not acknowledge me. Then, one day, as I was nearing the steps that led up to the school courtyard, I saw her come walking down, holding hands with a slender, pale boy with scruffy clothes and flowing, brown hair. Rebecca averted her eyes as she passed, and I fell apart inside.

Had she left me for this boy? Or had she met him afterward? Well, with her cryptic silence she certainly had hung me out to dry. For the first time, I realized that in the world beyond Avenue C—in this baffling, exhilarating adult world I was entering, of women and the matters of the heart—here too, I could suffer from helplessness and pain. Instead of those street kids' swinging blows and curses, I now was being laid flat, and just as hard, by a lovely teenage girl turning her cheek away just an inch. There were a million things I wanted to tell her, a million questions I longed to ask, but I knew pursuing her would be futile.

The following months, my torment only gradually began to mend amid the distractions of school, work, friends and family. A year later, I was enrolled in college halfway across the country.

◇

I met Rebecca once more. It was in the early spring of 1989—about seven years had passed. I was twenty-four and had recently returned to New York. I had been in relationships with girls in college and afterward in Chicago, and had not thought about Rebecca. But one evening at my father's apartment in the Village, where I was living until I could afford my own place, I discovered my black pocket-phonebook, which I had kept in a manila envelope with other papers in a closet. On one page, I noticed Rebecca's name and phone number jotted in black ink. An old, desolate stillness returned.

I hesitated. Then, apprehensively, I picked up the receiver and dialed her home, waited while the line rang. Her mother answered. I introduced myself as an old friend of Rebecca's and asked if I might speak with her.

"Oh, Rebecca doesn't live here anymore," her mother replied in a friendly way, and it occurred to me, with a surprising feeling of loss, that perhaps she was no longer in New York.

"She lives downtown now," her mother went on. "I can give you her phone number." She told me Rebecca had an apartment in Midtown, on the West Side, an area that I knew would mean a walk-up in Hell's Kitchen.

I called Rebecca at her apartment. After several rings, she answered.

"Hi, Rebecca," I said.

She, of course, remembered me: during an initial second or two of dense silence, I could feel through the receiver as she quickly searched memory to place my name, as she moved to recognition then surprise, then wariness. She said, slowly, carefully, in a tone neither friendly nor unfriendly: *"Oh, hello…"*

We exchanged a few pleasantries and then I asked if she would like to meet that evening. She already had plans, but when I suggested coffee the next day, she cautiously agreed. I suggested we meet at Homer's, from sentimentality and also because it was the only place that came to mind. Again, in the brief silence on the receiver, I felt her remembering it all and closing up, and she demurred with discomfort: *"No…not there…"* And her avoidance of that diner told me everything: that she had left me forever behind, that our meeting would have no possibility of a return to how we had been. And while I had not phoned Rebecca with a conscious intent to renew our relationship, had only thought—if I had thought anything at all—that we might resume as friends, her reply saddened me, was like a door being gently closed.

Instead, we arranged, at her suggestion, to meet on a corner of East Twenty-Third Street the next morning. She would be going to a rehearsal session and we would meet beforehand.

I arrived early. I remember I was dressed up like a schoolboy on a first date, in new wool trousers and new shoes. The morning was sunny but cold. I waited a long time beside a phone booth. Our agreed-on meeting time passed. Then I saw her approaching among the crowds. She was dressed strikingly, all in black, and carried a black guitar case. Her hair, too, was black, a rich, night-black, and was cut straight above her strong, dark brows, her light-gray eyes. When I glimpsed her black hair as she approached, I was startled and unnerved: I had held her image as a seventeen-year-old, fiery-haired girl intact for seven years, and now, suddenly, I saw, in her black hair, that all those years *had* passed, that she had been living a life I knew nothing about.

She set her guitar case on the ground. We greeted each other with subdued, strained smiles. As we talked, I perceived with dismay that she was uncomfortable, remote, guarded. She appeared thinner than I had remembered, even fragile. Her eyes avoided mine.

I suggested we walk to a diner I had noticed nearby, but she said she could spend a only few minutes there on the corner, she had to be at her rehearsal session. I affected nonchalance, concealed my surprise, my deep disappointment.

We chatted a few minutes longer, and her pale, theatrical beauty remained as captivating as before. But her words now seemed timid, her laugh uncertain, and this was so uncharacteristic of the girl I had known, as though something had happened to her, had robbed her of her confidence. At one point, though, when I reminded her, with a smile, of the Hotel 17, her own smile suddenly broadened and her eyes met mine and she remarked: *"Oh! Say, you know, I lived at the Hotel 17 for a while."*

It is the only shard of our conversation that morning that I still can hear her speaking—perhaps because it was the only moment when her smile seemed relaxed and genuine, when her voice rang with a friendly, unguarded tone, as though she was speaking with me, at last, as an old friend. Her words also carried an endearing hint of amusement at her own life—the same amusement she had shown the first day we met, at the diner, when she'd told me she'd read every book by John Steinbeck—as though she was regarding her actions as the silly whims of a younger person.

But then she glanced at her watch—she had to leave. Clearly, she wanted to go. I could not refrain, once again, from asking: *Why?* But again, she merely shook her head, looking away.

"I was so crazy about you, you know," I heard myself saying, and felt myself falling in love with her again, as though if I told her what she had meant to me all those years before, she would reconsider every-thing. She smiled uneasily. We said goodbye, and I watched her walk away, as I had watched her walk away that morning in front of our high school seven years before, and then the crowds closed around her.

◇

During the following years, which led from that day on that street corner at the threshold of our adulthood, through the maturity of our twenties and thirties, and then into early middle-age, Rebecca rarely crossed my mind. I fell in love with my wife, became a father of two children, pursued a career. But if I happened to meet a woman with her name, or glimpsed a woman who resembled her on an airplane or in the subway, an indefinite sadness would descend on me momentarily. Neverthe-less, I doubt that those scattered seconds that I thought of Rebecca amounted to three consecutive minutes during those decades.

Then, about two years ago, during a period when I had been reflecting on the past and had been reconnecting with old friends, I thought of Rebecca: what had become of her? What place had she carved out for herself in the world? She, too, would be in her forties. Had she married? Did she have children? Was she living in New York, the suburbs, Europe? Had she gone to college and gotten an office job, after all?

I checked the Internet. I had hardly typed her name on my computer when a half-dozen photographs of Rebecca were framed in a frieze on the screen: she was now, unsurprisingly, a cabaret singer and musician in New York. Before I knew what had hit me, I saw her chal-lenging gray eyes, which I thought I had forgotten but which were so familiar; I saw her dramatic, scarlet lips, the precise curve of which, I

realized, I still knew so well; I saw her hands on her guitar and realized I *even remembered the contours of her fingers.*

The photographs were those of a professional performer, and she
appeared quite different in each. She moved from a torn T-shirt and
fishnet stockings, to long, old-fashioned skirts, to some look that was
unclassifiable. Her face hadn't changed much. But I discovered that
she had adorned her arms with tattoos, and the tattoos unsettled me.
Just as her unexpectedly black hair had reminded me on that street
corner that seven years had gone since we had last met, the tattoos
now brought home that all those subsequent years had passed, and
had led us in very different directions.

There had been newspaper and magazine articles about her, and
I read that she had rejected college, had instead gone to Europe
and played guitar, lived with Gypsies, returned to New York and
played in the streets, the subways, the clubs. She had put out a few
CDs of her songs, which she wrote and composed. She was living
in a walk-up in the East Village. I had the impression, for some
reason I couldn't put my finger on, that she hadn't married or had
children. Her life seemed to have been exactly what it had promised, so enticingly to me, back when we were seventeen—bohemian,
footloose—while mine had been more conventional. When she had
been living with Gypsies in Spain and playing for change in the New
York subways, I had been in college and then working as a reporter
in Chicago.

Our paths never should have crossed again, or at least not so easily.
But through the Internet, I found myself, in only a few seconds, not only
seeing her face startlingly close, but also listening to her singing what
seemed like a private serenade at my office through the speakers of my
computer. Her voice, the lyrics of her songs, still held the passion and
whimsical humor I remembered. A piece of a forgotten conversation
floated up from a day, not long after we met, when I visited Rebecca at

her apartment, and noticed an acoustic guitar resting against the wall of her untidy bedroom.

"Oh, do you play?" I had asked, as we sat on her bed. Yes, she said.

Did she want to be a musician? To play professionally?

"Yes, I'd like to," she had replied with an endearingly modest shrug. *"...Someday..."*

So, now it was someday—had, in fact, been someday for many, many years. She had achieved her ambition long ago. And here she was, now in her forties, her sharp gray eyes gazing right through me.

I dashed off a brief e-mail to Rebecca, saying I had been thinking of her, had seen her on the Internet, and hoped she was well and would she like to meet for a cup of coffee and catch up.

And that was that.

But the rest of the day, I kept reliving those ancient scenes that I had not thought of for so long. I reflected, for the first time in decades, on how Rebecca had inexplicably severed our relationship, and I endured again the bewildered agony, as though she had calmly slashed off some part of me without explanation and simply walked away. I was sunk in the past, roaming among adolescent images, griefs, and joys that refused to disperse, that clouded my mind like a fairy spell in the bedtime stories I read to my children. And, foolishly, I sent Rebecca another e-mail, telling her all of it—the old pain, the old story. I felt impelled to tell her that I had finally realized she had been, if inadvertently, a central player in the story of my youth. And I wanted her to help me understand who she had been then, what had happened all those years ago. God knows, that letter must have startled and upset her—I might as well have swung a wrecking ball through her window.

I deeply loved my wife and our children, had a rewarding career, a full life. My job at a corporate law firm, while not what I had intended when I was a young man who dreamed of writing novels, was comfortable. I wanted only a cup of coffee with Rebecca, to gain some understanding about a painful and mysterious episode of my adolescence. Still, I was uneasy about my actions, and one evening I told my wife, while she was reading the newspaper in bed. She listened, nodded thoughtfully, asked a few pointed questions, then, wisely, and with a certain condescension, as though speaking to the teenager I had regressed to, said she would leave it to me to work it out, and went back to her newspaper.

◇

I knew that my forceful reaction to seeing Rebecca's face and hearing her voice was, at best, questionable. Yet, compelled by memory, as though by a palpable force, I went to revisit our old places, after escaping discreetly from my office during a couple of slow days, to make quick tours. I sensed that I was searching for something, but was unclear what it was.

I rode the subway to the apartment building on the Upper West Side where Rebecca had lived with her mother, lingered by the entrance and watched myself, at age seventeen, that rainy night, getting out of the taxi with Rebecca and running through those doors. I went into the opulent lobby, which I recognized right away, and watched myself cross the marble floor with her to the elevator.

I left and sat on a bench in the tiny park across the street. At one end, there was a bronze statue of a reclining woman in classical robes, gazing meditatively into a fountain beneath her. The statue was titled "Memory." I couldn't help but smile wryly at the two of us lost together in the past. But then, a new memory surprised me: I was with Rebecca one afternoon, walking by this park, and in my happiness I impulsively leapt onto the statue, but Rebecca had been embarrassed at my antic, and protested, *"No, don't do that, stop, please."* I had dropped to the ground and walked beside her again. And yet, something was disturbing about that memory—I realized now that I had been aware, though only obscurely, that Rebecca had, at that moment, perceived me differently, as a *boy*, and that she had, in her mind, stepped back some very slight yet significant distance. And I had held her closer as we walked and tried to coax reassurance from her, which I didn't quite receive. She had seemed preoccupied, slightly annoyed.

Sitting now in the park, I reflected, with rising dismay and embarrassment, that there had been, perhaps, other indications of Rebecca's distance that I had perceived during those weeks but had not quite admitted to myself. I recalled the tattoos on Rebecca's arms in the photographs, and how they had unsettled me, and suddenly, I knew why: it was not only that they indicated the time that had passed—the tattoos also confirmed something that a part of me had intuited when we were seventeen: that Rebecca was, in fact, more fearless than I was about venturing forth into the artist's life, the gypsy's life, a life unfettered by social conventions and traditional career ambitions; that she would say Yes, where I would halt. And those winter weeks when I knew Rebecca, she was poised, as I was, to leave childhood and home, along with high school, and to embark, at last, on her journey into this adult, uncharted life, and—perhaps— she had realized that I would not follow her all the way.

And I remembered now, too, that even though Rebecca had appeared to share my happiness when we were together, she also, disconcertingly, seemed content when we were apart. I rang her up on the phone almost every evening, but now I realized that she had seldom rang for me. I arranged with her to meet, but she never did seem to quite share my urgency. She had many friends, and I knew she spent time with them, too. But perhaps she was seeing another boy—perhaps that brown-haired boy I had seen her with on the school steps—without my knowledge during those weeks. I had, after all, also intuited that she had been with many boys. Maybe she never did quite share my utter seriousness about our relationship—and yet, I also remembered the affection that lit her eyes when we were together, and I knew she had earnestly been prepared to leave her home, drop out of school and live with me at the Hotel 17. It was all becoming more puzzling, rather than clearer, as additional details returned during my sojourn among the old places.

On another day, I strolled through Washington Square Park, lingered along the path where we had first kissed and my teenage heart had soared. I retraced our route toward the Astor Riviera Café, where we had gone afterward. But the diner had become a Starbucks and the sleek decor had transformed the place too thoroughly to allow for any connection with the past.

I found, too, that Homer's was gone, was now an upscale restaurant.

◇

A week or so later, on a bright, spring morning, I went to find the lane near Sheridan Square where we had escaped the cold that evening. I didn't remember the name of the street, but I remembered roughly where it was, and that the doorway had columns on either side. I scanned houses, crossed intersections, uncertain if the lane had been here, or perhaps there; and then I turned a corner and looked down a short, narrow street, lined mostly with brownstones. It was hardly distinguishable from a half-dozen other streets I had passed through, yet somehow each detail suddenly fitted neatly together, and memory whispered: *here.* Halfway down the street, I saw, as I was certain I would, the apartment building, the entrance flanked by columns. I opened the door, went slowly into the vestibule. And, again, memory told me that this was the place I had sought. Still, I had remembered it so differently—the walls were covered with wood paneling, while I had remembered a wall of peeling green paint. A decorative light fixture hung from the ceiling, while I had remembered a bare, fluorescent bulb. Was memory distorting the past? Or had the landlord simply made changes to this vestibule over the many years? As I stood in this cramped nothing of a place, where Rebecca and I had embraced so passionately that winter evening when we were teenagers, I was overcome by melancholy wonder at my own middle-age and at the sudden immediacy of being back. I ran my fingers along the wall where we had stood—and then the door banged open and an old woman in a housedress carrying plastic shopping bags burst in, scattering memories like startled birds. She glared up at me suspiciously from a crumpled face.

"What do you want?" She demanded. "Do you live here?"

"I'm just leaving," I smiled and went outside.

◊

Our old school. It was housed in an enormous, 19th century, brick-and-stone building. I had not been back since I had graduated, twenty-five years before.

I expected to be rebuffed at the entrance by a guard, but when I tried a door, it opened to an empty building—it was, apparently, a school holiday. I slipped inside.

I climbed stairs, searched empty corridors. The walls were covered with student murals and bulletin boards pinned with notices and class schedules. I poked into classrooms, climbed more stairs. Everything appeared only faintly recognizable—was it possible I attended this school for two years?

On the fourth floor, I turned a corner and saw a wooden door, partly ajar, on which hung a sign: "LIBRARY."

I stepped forward, almost fearfully, and peered inside. It was a long, rectangular room, cluttered with books, tables, chairs, desks. *Yes*, memory again whispered.

The room was exactly as I had remembered—the same bookshelves along the walls, the same desks and wastebaskets and file cabinets. Everything was preserved with a timeless stillness, a perfect silence, as though this room had been awaiting my return, as though only hours had passed, not twenty-five years. The only change was that there were now computers resting on several of the wood tables. I went inside and walked to where I had sat that morning by the row of tall windows. I found there the same old puffing radiator—it was still too hot—and I sat on a chair—perhaps the same chair I had sat on that long ago morning. I remained awhile beside the radiator, in the shadowy silence that somehow was not even ruptured by the distant shouts of kids kicking a soccer ball in the playing fields across the street. The lights were off, and cold sunlight poured in through the windows, just as it had that day. I half-expected the calendar on the wall to read "1982," and to see the students begin crowding through the door for the principal's speech. I looked at the place where Rebecca had stood amid the assembly, smiling with the students beside her, bundled in her coat, scarf, and gloves, her hair dyed fiery orange, her lips painted scarlet, her cheeks burned by the cold.

When I left the building through the courtyard, I lingered on the pavement where Rebecca had broken off our relationship and saw the concrete steps where she had come down holding the hand of the brown-haired boy.

I crossed the street and was saddened to discover that the diner where we went for coffee that first afternoon was now a vacant lot. Or was it? I couldn't tell any longer where on that street the diner had been. And what was its name?

As I headed toward the subway to return to my office, I tried to retrieve more from the past. I walked by pizzerias, cafes, newsstands, but memory was proving tantalizingly elusive. Images flashed then vanished, emerged from depths, then fled back into darkness before quite taking shape.

At a coffee shop on Sixth Avenue, I paused and watched waiters through the windows as they carried trays among crowded tables. I recalled that I had passed this coffee shop with my brother one afternoon, a year or two after my last meeting with Rebecca, and as we had walked by, I had thought to myself, with a secret, fleeting sadness, that I had been here with her. But now, as I stood there, I could no longer actually remember being there with Rebecca; I could only, at this distance of years, remember that *I had once had a memory of that still earlier memory which itself had disintegrated.*

How long ago it all was! As I hung around these places, I felt like Keats's knight who falls for a "fairy's child," is assured by her "I love thee true," before she promptly leaves him high and dry on a cold hillside, "alone and palely loitering," wondering where she had gone. It struck me that Rebecca had been for me as enchanting and elusive as Keats's fairy. There was a maddening unreality about it all. Had there really been by our school a vanished diner, or was I imagining it? Had Rebecca and I really gone to the Astor Riviera Café? Had the Astor Riviera Café existed at all? Had there really been a recital and a rainy taxi ride? Had we really visited the Hotel 17, and how did I know we had embraced in that vestibule? So many, many years had passed. Had there been such passion, such a perfect romance, or was I imagining this, too? How long had it lasted? Weeks? Months? If it weren't for Rebecca's name jotted in my old phonebook—my only relic—I would have doubted I had ever even *known* her.

But as it turned out, I finally received bitter confirmation on that matter: ten days after I had written my second e-mail to Rebecca, I received a reply.

She wrote, after a civil greeting, that my e-mails had disturbed her, and, with controlled anger burning through the electronic words, she said that if I had not dumped on her such an emotional mess, she "might have considered having a cup of coffee," as I had suggested—though she did not understand what I had a need to discuss. She concluded:

The teenage years were particularly messy and fucked up, and
if I hurt you in any way, I most sincerely apologize.
All the best of luck to you.
Rebecca

If I hurt you in any way! My God! Could she be so merciless? Or so uncomprehending? Or had my unsought, wild confession terrified and enraged her past caring? Well, it was plain that there would be no final meeting, no way for me to confirm the truth of those memories, to learn who she had been during those weeks when we were teenagers, or why she had broken away. She would remain a mystery. So, twenty-five years later, she did it again: hung me out to dry without explanations. But instead of the quiet reticence of an adolescent girl, this was the slamming of a door by a middle-aged woman.

I wrote an apology, told her that the last thing I ever wanted was to harass her, that I had been moved by old memories, had only sought to have coffee with her, and I hoped she would accept my apology and reconsider.

She didn't reply—and, as it turned out, I didn't hear from her again.

But over the following weeks, her angry rebuff—and my own intense yet obscure emotions—had deeply shaken me. Why was I fixated on a winter of three decades before?

◇

When I entered the Hotel 17, I discovered it had been completely renovated. The tiny lobby had a self-consciously noirish, 1940s atmosphere. The Plexiglas wall that had once protected the front desk had been removed, and the desk itself appeared to have been moved back from the entrance. The hotel, no longer a decrepit single-room occupancy, had become fashionable among musicians and artists, popular with tourists.

I said to the desk clerk: "I remember the front desk was nearer to the door."

The clerk, a slim man in his forties with long blond hair, was surprised at my remark, but nodded and said that, yes, the desk had been moved, and the Plexiglas wall taken down. "The hotel has been renovated several times. Did you stay here? It must have been a long time ago."

"I didn't stay here," I replied. "I almost did. I visited one day, back in 1982."

"*Nineteen-eighty two?* Well, that *is* a long time ago. I've been here since the mid-nineties. It's changed a lot since."

"Can I see one of the rooms?"

"Sure. Any room in particular?"

"No. I'd just like to look at a room."

He led me down a hall, unlocked a door. I entered a small room and sat on the edge of the bed in my coat. The room needed airing, but it was clean and far more pleasant than the putrid little room I recalled. Somewhere in this hotel, perhaps on this bed, Rebecca and I had once excitedly discussed how we would wait on café tables and live for Art, Adventure, and Love. In my mind, I relived the scene, watched that half-comic young man as he spouted fanciful, doomed plans to that flaming-haired girl, earnestly clasping her hands. I watched him with mingled amusement, affection and wonder—his smooth face, his thick, dark curls, his eyes burning with youthful fervor.

I leaned back against the headboard and stretched my legs on the bed. And I thought back to a long-ago winter, when Art was still a radiant grail, when the distant places still shone with enchantment—when a kiss in the park was still as breathtakingly new as the world itself.

7. Bringing Up Baby

7
Bringing Up Baby

The vast mass of humanity ... have never doubted and never will doubt
that courage is splendid, that fidelity is noble, that distressed ladies
should be rescued, and vanquished enemies spared.

—G.K. Chesterton

ONE NIGHT, JUST AFTER I HAD RETURNED TO NEW YORK AT
the end of my freshman year at college, my nose was broken in the
street—a giant of a derelict spun around and smashed my face so hard
that my nose was completely shattered. My face, as I saw in a hand-
mirror in the hospital emergency room, was suddenly unrecognizable,
twisted, grotesque—an African mask, a Picasso portrait. I could feel
with my fingers that the bones had crumbled away, and what remained
of my nose was sliding around freely, as though on ice. Blood was
splattered all over my clothes, my hair, my hands. I might have been
a war casualty.

The blow wrought such damage because the derelict had worn
brass knuckles—they'd flashed just before I was hurled backward,
blinded by white explosions.

The blow had come out of nowhere. The derelict, who in memory is
seven feet tall and wearing rags, had been shuffling in front of me as
I walked with a friend on crowded Sixth Avenue, then simply whirled
around and knocked me to Jupiter. He hadn't demanded money, nor
did he swing again. He towered over me as I sat with blood gushing

from my face, circled by a crowd, and beckoned me to fight with outstretched arms. *"C'mon! C'mon an' fight!"* When I staggered away, leaning on my friend, this giant merely watched. The incident was not only senseless, but also ironic, because during all the years I was growing up on the Lower East Side, I had often faced gangs wielding sticks, chains, knives, but I had managed to escape to college without being seriously hurt. Moreover, this attack had occurred not in our slum but in the residential West Village, on well-lit Sixth Avenue, on a Saturday night.

The next afternoon I lay beneath the covers in my bedroom in our housing development above the tenements of Avenue C with gauze bandages wrapped around my face, watching the 1938 screwball comedy *Bringing Up Baby*. The absurd story and the silly banter of Cary Grant and Katharine Hepburn helped stave off my rage and despair. The plot, which circles around the reassembly of bones—specifically, the bones of a Brontosaurus skeleton—was, in retrospect, strangely appropriate. Grant is cast as a bumbling paleontologist seeking the last missing bone for the dinosaur skeleton, and through a series of absurdities gets mixed up with an eccentric heiress (Hepburn), and a leopard named Baby. Of course, all turns out well at the end: Grant finds both the bone and true love with Hepburn.

For a week, while waiting for the bandages to be removed, I watched such antique movies. I had been warned to be extremely careful, and I moved as though my face was as delicate as a Ming Dynasty vase— and, in fact, my bones had been so violently shattered it was something of a miracle they could be reset. I certainly couldn't go outside. Our neighborhood had improved since I was younger but for a white boy to go around with a bandaged face would be asking to be attacked by the gangs, as a joke. So, imprisoned by my wound and our slum, I saw dozens of movies as I drowsed in and out of sleep, lulled by painkillers, although I remember only *Bringing Up Baby*.

I had intended to remain in New York only a week or two, to visit family and friends before returning to college for the rest of the summer, where I would work on campus to earn spending money. But now my plans were as shattered as my face.

◇

My situation—trapped in my old bedroom watching movies—was an eerie reversion to a part of my life that I had only recently and desperately escaped when I'd left for college. I had spent so many years in that room watching movies, and for the same reasons that I was watching them now: my terror of our drug-infested slum, my isolating anger toward my mother and step-father for living there, and also, later, for their apparent distance from my adolescent woes. For fifteen years, the tenements had stretched away outside our windows, a labyrinth too vast to escape, too perilous to endure. But I had found a temporary route out: the static-plagued television picture that led to Hollywood's vanished back lots. Hollywood provided a refuge, a parallel black-and-white world flickering within our television where I could forget the terrors below and my conflicted home.

I had watched films, or rather, clung to them with a sort of desperation, amid the familiar night-sounds of our street—the interminable drunken arguments outside Marvin's bar, the heroin dealers' gunfights, the explosions set off by arsonists. And, sometimes, I looked down and watched a drug deal or a knife duel under the streetlights before returning to *Gold Diggers of 1933*, or *Stage Door* or *Angels with Dirty Faces* or *Gunga Din*. The separation from reality was never quite complete, reality inevitably intruded. At certain moments, Hollywood's elegance clashed strikingly with the dire poverty—perhaps while watching, framed in the small screen, Astaire and Rogers in black-tie and evening gown twirling through some magnificent, art-deco set to the harmonies of Irving Berlin, I would simultaneously see framed in my window the tar roofs and laundry-strung clothes-lines. At other moments, reality and fiction all-too-neatly echoed each other: the gangsters' Tommy guns roared on the screen while from our street came the *tok tok tok* of pistols and the *boom-boom* of sawed-off shotguns; or the bickering of drunken couples in a fictional nightclub mingled with drunken Spanish arguments on the stoops; or the fires of blitzed London burned while an arson-bombed building glowed across our street and sirens shrieked. And I remember how, as the sky lightened outside the windows, I saw another sunrise, over the black-and-white farms of New Hampshire, in *The Devil and Daniel Webster,* and was momentarily confused by the crowing of a rooster—it was the morning cry of the bird our Latino neighbors kept for cockfighting.

◊

Those years on Avenue C, during weekends when I wasn't visiting my father and step-mother at their Village apartment, I remember the dreadful feeling—just as I recalled it bitterly while lying in bed that summer—of being caged in our apartment on sunny afternoons, with the ruinous tenements outside and the wreckage of the vacant lots, while the small television screen glimmered with *Tarzan* or *Stage-coach* or *San Francisco.*

Later, in adolescence, movies provided a refuge not only from the menace of Avenue C, but also from the bleakness of the downtown clubs, parties, and bars. At clubs, in the dark, hot squalor, some band would scream hatred, blasting jagged sound until my ears rang. Many of my friends were as confused and angry as I was and could offer little real companionship. I felt as alone with them as I did at home. My parents abandoned curfews and punishments, which I defied. I stag-gered home in the small hours from nights of music, alcohol, drugs, girls, and found a movie on TV, seeking to dissolve away into it, until I could sleep. I once watched, gratefully, *Love Laughs at Andy Hardy*.

Certain films—*The Grapes of Wrath, I am a Fugitive From a Chain Gang, The Best Years of Our Lives*—were serious representations of the world, and could be respected. But what kept me fastened to the hundreds of inane productions—the dramas that ended in impossible, tearful reunions, the corny musicals—films like *Love Laughs at Andy Hardy*? I was living in one of New York's worst slums, attending the city's bruising public schools, was later roaming one of the most nihilistic, decadent nightlifes on earth. In our neighborhood, I would have been the only kid who, at hearing the word "heroin" spoken, would have thought it referred to a Hollywood starlet, not a narcotic. Why didn't I reject such Hollywood confections as I had rejected my children's books?

I remember when I was no more than nine, my brother and I found a woman's purse in the shadowy caverns of a condemned factory we had been exploring. The purse appeared empty, but then I found hidden in the lining a wedding ring, identification papers, and three crisp ten-dollar bills. We decided, after some debate, to bring the purse to the police. At the precinct station, an officer made a few phone calls and then told us, with what now seems surprising bluntness, that the purse belonged to an elderly woman who had been severely beaten, and was on a ventilator in a hospital. A short time later, the husband—a gray-haired man in a hat and raincoat—came for the purse. He spoke with the police then left, after offering only the most desultory thanks to us for returning it, leaving us standing in that station, thinking we should have kept the money.

Such incidents told me that not only were the kids in the streets and public schools senselessly brutal, but so was the adult world: there were, all too often, no changes of heart, no happy endings; the bludgeoned woman would lie on a ventilator at fade-out, and the villain would escape—without even getting the paltry amount of cash he'd beaten his victim for. The husband would be ungrateful. Where was the sense in all this?

The films I watched did not squarely address any of my world, yet I did not reject them, I embraced them. While millions of people have enjoyed Hollywood comedies, dramas, and musicals for their entertaining plots, songs, and cozy nostalgia, I lived in them with passionate intensity and gratitude. Certainly, movies provided a diversion and, superficially, an idealized world that offered escape. The escapist impulse manifested itself not only in my engrossment in the plots, but also in a dreamy yearning to be in some enchanted, distant spot within the soft, soothing grays of the Hollywood sound-stages—a table at an elegant nightclub, or a dirt road winding away through the hills. It was the same impulse that led me to linger over landscapes reproduced in the big art books on our shelves—a blue-hazed village in the background of a renaissance portrait, a thatched hut in a Breughel scene. I would be transported from Avenue C. I remember looking at the Constable painting *The Cornfield*, studying a single, distant tree in the fields and wishing I could laze beneath it. In the same way, I studied the backgrounds of Hollywood sets, longing to leap inside.

But when I drifted off into those sets, I often, by some habitually morose turn of mind, bumped back into reality. I was horrified and fascinated by the idea that all of the "extras"—the distant figure glimpsed stepping off a streetcar—really just a blurred suit and hat—or the young woman crossing a street—were probably long gone. Such thoughts would take me crashing back from timeless illusion with the realization that the actors were in a closed-off sound stage while outside was a bright Los Angeles afternoon in, say, 1936, and after the scene they would get in their autos and drive off to their pools. And I would lose the dream and would be back again on Avenue C.

I didn't realize it, but movies also provided me with a sense of history that I didn't get from school books, with their stories of hillbillies, the Civil War, the Depression, World War II. I learned about Lincoln, Louis Pasteur, Lou Gehrig. I saw Buicks, propeller airplanes, early radios, crank telephones, sleeping cars. And I first experienced beauty in the faces of starlets, as glowing and idealized as the sets around them.

In my teens, the tales of the Jungle, the Arctic, and the Sea stoked my desire to write adventure novels and led me to the Peruvian Amazon. I dreamed, too, of embarking on a bohemian life, partly inspired by Hollywood's portrayals of Greenwich Village and Montmartre: a life of picturesque garrets and cafes.

However, far more important than any of this—the diversion, the escape into a fantasy world, the glimpses of beauty and smatterings of history, the furnishing of unreal ambitions—films provided a part of the world that was missing for me: that part that is sane and decent and where there *are* happy endings. Whether I was in prohibition Chicago, or the Yukon or the South, or a 1930s drugstore or the Stork Club or Shanghai, I was, in any case, some place else—some place *safe*, some place *sane*. It was this place that kept me before that television screen.

◇

Hollywood films were often narrow and hypocritical, not to mention racist, sexist and jingoistic, but within their limits, and beneath the contrived plots, lovable character actors, and clichés, they did present a legitimate world view—that human beings, while often untruthful, brutal, and selfish, are, ultimately, good and decent; that while there is tragedy, it is redeemed by justice, both human and divine. They presented this view constrained by the residual 19th century idea, enforced by the Hays Code of 1932, that in representing evil, sex, drug-use, or violence—all that was considered *vulgar* and *morbid*—one should not descend to that level.

Old Hollywood's world *is* the real world, albeit a narrow piece—but for me it was the crucial missing piece. It was an invaluable corrective to the equally limited, converse reality I faced each day in a fractured home in a savage slum.

In those films, I was seeking, like many in the audiences during the Great Depression and World War II who first saw them, not only something so superficial, simplistic, and fear-driven as "escapism" from the real world, but also that which was far more needed and, in a sense, its courageous opposite: a *re-entry* into the real world, a reassurance, a reminder, from another, better part of the world, that it, too, existed—a reassurance perhaps similar to that provided by religion. Just as Hollywood once offered audiences in movie palaces reassurance that sanity existed amid economic hardship and war, the same movies, decades later, on the small screen in our housing development, provided reassurance for a desperately isolated, sad, and terrified boy, and, later, for a troubled teenager.

I knew, growing up, that most Hollywood plots were ridiculous, that real life could never be as screwy as those screwball comedies. But I also sensed that beneath those plots was a simple and real message.

The actors in those films—Humphrey Bogart, Cary Cooper, Clark Gable, John Wayne, Jean Arthur, Carole Lombard, Rosalind Russell—became as familiar as my own parents and, in fact, became idealized parental figures, who could, in the context of a story, lecture me on right and wrong in a way that I wouldn't accept from my parents or teachers. And all those character actors—Eric Blore, Walter Brennan, Jane Darwell, Margaret Dumont, Alan Hale, Thomas Mitchell, Eugene Pallette, Margaret Wycherly—were my missing, lovable uncles and aunts. Their faces, reappearing in film after film, also became intimately familiar. They brought me up from my youngest years as a sort of adoptive family. And like a family, and the films themselves, they were a moral force: they brought me up to believe that, within our rational and just universe, a man's duty was to do good, confront evil, and save the heroine. And you can't spend years and years watching films like *High Noon* without that message penetrating deep into your being. To this day, thanks in large part to my overdose of Hollywood at a young age, I still believe—or rather, some early, fixed part of me still stubbornly insists, despite all my bitter experience on Avenue C and all my often saddening experience in the world beyond that slum, and all my learning and logic—that life's troubles will, or should, resolve in a happy ending, that good will triumph over evil. And when things don't turn out that way, even now, that part of me is shocked and disappointed.

This world view was surely shaped by these celluloid yarns. I can't imagine that, say, a 19th century American, much less a European, even if fortified with Christian belief, with its emphasis of justice in the next world, would hold quite such an optimistic view.

Still, such films would not have spoken to me if I hadn't possessed a nascent romantic sensibility, a yearning for old-fashioned Romance and Adventure. They lured that out, fostered it. My brother, who was two years younger, and who suffered on Avenue C as much or more than I did, never quite became so attached to those movies.

◆

The first films I saw at theaters were produced in the years after the Hays Code was eliminated, in 1968. I saw many films, without my parents' knowledge, with friends in the dilapidated St. Marks Cinema, in the East Village. Amid all the soothing movies I watched on television, the films shown in that theater were extremely upsetting. Although they offered the same reassuring plots as their earlier counterparts—good still triumphed over evil, the hero still won the girl—the old messages were often buried too deeply for me beneath the splattering gore, the groping, naked bodies, the foul language.

Certainly, there was plenty of violence in Hays Code productions, but it was harmless, almost silly. Those films were genteel, were *gentle*. Even when I was stranded in crossfire in prohibition Chicago or in Dodge City, the battles were so girdled by Old Hollywood's strictures that they were safe in a way that the new films, or the reality outside my window, were not. It was one thing to see a character shot in an old movie—a groan, a hand held to the heart, perhaps a trickle of blood—but it was quite another to see, in a recent movie at the theater, a man's head blown off his body. I had been so often struck by fists and sticks, knew all too well the dazed pain of such blows, that the realistic clashes of the new films made me almost ill. To witness a character have his neck slit open brought back my daily terrors too vividly. The new films were not a refuge or reassurance of sanity, they were, for me, more of the nightmarish part of the world I already knew too well. My real life was already rated R, I desperately wanted G.

But when I was eighteen, my life in New York, as though mimicking those Hays Code productions, did have a "Hollywood ending," when, by a plot-twist that seemed worthy of Capra, I received a letter one morning congratulating me on my acceptance to a college that I had no right to even think of entering based on my academic credentials. I didn't faint clutching the letter, as I should have according to Hollywood convention, and I wasn't roused with a bucket of water in the face. But I did sit down weakly at our lopsided wood table and re-read the letter again and again. I was, in truth, ambivalent toward college, believing that I would be abandoning my dreams of living the life of a bohemian writer. But I decided to go, determined to finally escape

Avenue C and the clerical jobs I'd been mired in since graduating high school.

I rode to the campus on a train, a journey that in memory appears like the montages where the locomotive hurtles the hero forward, superimposed on a sliding map of the United States showing the cities and towns passing by to the rousing strains of a studio orchestra. The back-lot set of my New York slum was promptly scuttled and replaced by a college set, complete with fraternities and sororities, Greek-revival halls, and peopled with a cast of hundreds of kids from farms, small towns, Midwestern cities, and prep schools.

I had finally escaped my New York life—and then, only months later, I had been slammed by a brass-knuckled fist right back to Avenue C, right back into my old bedroom. And now, looking back at myself at eighteen, as I lay in bed those sunny days with a senselessly shattered face, in that slum of futile violence where we inexplicably lived, watching the screwball comedy *Bringing Up Baby*, I can't help but reflect that my world was screwier than the one on the screen, after all.

8. On Chasing After One's Hat

8 On Chasing After One's Hat

...a man could, if he felt rightly in the matter, run after his hat with the manliest ardour and the most sacred joy.

—G.K. Chesterton

We forget all too soon the things we thought we could never forget.

—Joan Didion

MY BROTHER RECENTLY MAILED EIGHT SNAPSHOTS TAKEN DURING A CAMPING TRIP at Bear Mountain State Park, in late 1981, when I was sixteen and he was fourteen. We had gone with a friend of his, Doyle Rojas, a Latino kid from our neighborhood on the Lower East Side.

I hadn't seen the photos since they had been taken, almost three decades before, and hadn't thought of that trip in almost as many years. But when the images unexpectedly appeared that afternoon, I felt immediately a clench deep in the pit of my stomach, a mingling of shock, recognition, and dread, almost fear; an instinctual contraction, swift and self-protective.

That weekend camping trip had occurred during the very darkest period of my adolescence—my personal equivalent of 1932. The Crash of 1929 might be analogous to my earlier plummet from Music & Art High School to an "alternative" school where students worked at offices and other places around the city for academic credit toward a diploma.

The author (wearing a fedora) with his brother during a camping trip in 1981.

That two-year period, from my failure at Music & Art until I left for college, had remained a particularly painful, hazy patch in memory, the details obscured by drink and depression, and over the years I had avoided thinking of that time of my life. Now, those photos threatened to hurl me back, yet I found myself guardedly drawn to them.

The photos were small, square Instamatic shots, the colors faded, the focus blurred from the cheap lens.

My mother and step-father, who had driven us to the state park, had taken a few pictures of the three of us before they left for Manhattan and we started along the trail. The other pictures we had taken of each other during various stages of our trip, all of them posed, except for one candid shot of me beside Doyle, walking on a road.

The trip's climax was our ascent to the peak of a small mountain near the Hudson River, where we paused to take several photos. In one snapshot, taken by Doyle, my brother and I are standing on the scrubby peak toward the end of an overcast afternoon, and I am wearing, incongruously, an old fedora.

The sight of this hat, so prominent in the photograph, unnerved me: I had no memory of it. I puzzled over it. There was something disturbing about seeing that hat so undeniably *there*, yet having no recall of it. I could have described from memory standing beside my brother on that summit at the end of that cold autumn afternoon as Doyle took the picture and, earlier, our arduous ascent. But no matter how I tortured memory, I could not recall the hat. It was dust-brown, worn smooth, and weathered to near-shapelessness, so had likely come from a thrift shop on St. Mark's Place or Canal Street, where I and many of my friends bought used clothes. Did I ever actually wear that hat in the city, in some awkward, adolescent attempt at sartorial style? Perhaps I didn't own that hat, but had borrowed it from Doyle (it certainly wasn't my brother's hat). But no, I am wearing or holding it in the other photos. It must have been mine.

Why would I bring an antique city hat—a *fedora*—camping in the wilderness? But then, all our clothes were inappropriate city clothes, too flimsy to protect against the cold of the woods. We had never been camping, were three city kids wandering the trails of New York State in late fall. Perhaps I wore that hat because I owned no other.

The rediscovery of my fedora spoke, undeniably, of the frightening fallibility of Memory—or, at least, *my* memory. If I had forgotten that fedora, what else had I forgotten of my life then? Recently, I had been revisiting places of my childhood and adolescence, searching memories, trying to make more sense of my past. Now, I wondered: *how many other fedoras had I forgotten?*

Mulling over my hat brought home how our memories, even those most meaningful, lack so many particulars and are preserved in cryptic isolation from contextual events. Memory suddenly seemed a feeble yet rogue faculty, a repository for a jumble of both significant and apparently random images, all riddled with information-gaps, as with my forgotten fedora. If our eyesight were so faulty, we would have been extinct as a species long ago. I can bring to mind, for instance, the clothes my wife and I wore at our wedding, predictably enough, but what did we wear that night we first met twenty years ago, when we talked until dawn at a coffee shop on Second Avenue? And what did we say? What did the closest friend of my adolescence, Tim Jordan, and I *talk* about during a decade spent together at school and parties and clubs? Only a few shards of dialogue remain. One of my clearest adolescent memories is of a moment about a year after our camping trip, when I was sitting beside my girlfriend Rebecca in a room in the seedy old Hotel 17, near Gramercy Park. We were excitedly discussing living together and getting jobs waiting tables, but, in truth, I cannot retrieve a *single word* we spoke. I can still see the tiny room—the dingy white bedspread, the little window behind us—but I no longer can see the color of the walls or the shade of the carpet or shape of the light fixtures or wall moldings. What was the weather outside that window? Where had we met earlier, and where had we gone afterward? The picture of us sitting on that hotel bed remains isolated, stripped of all context, with, no doubt, forgotten fedoras everywhere. And those missing fedoras of memory now jolted me. My few memories of that camping trip also were insubstantial impressions, lacking dialogue, leached of the world's vivid colors—I did not remember, for instance, that the brush on that mountain peak was rust-colored, as it is in the photo, but saw it in my mind as blue-gray, almost colorless.

I wrote to my brother, asking if he remembered the hat and what he could tell me of the trip. He responded, "No, I don't remember the hat," and added:

> *I remember that we started hiking and got to a lean-to and stopped and realized it was freezing and we weren't prepared. So we drank some of the whiskey we brought, which didn't help much. I remember it was pretty naughty to bring whiskey at that age. I remember how taken by surprise we were by the cold and we thought the whiskey would warm us. I don't remember too much else about the trip. I remember fall leaves all around. I think we did a pretty hard uphill hike to the top of that mountain and that's why we were posing rather triumphantly at the top. I don't really remember how many nights we stayed.*

Nearly all of this was news to me. Over the next few days, I went back to those photos, seeking something about myself at that dismal period, and also afraid of what I sought. I lingered over our clothing, our backpacks, the bare trees, the gray, cold sky. Our expressions are weary. In a couple of the photos we smile, in others we don't bother to try. Suddenly, it came back to me that our weariness was not only from hiking in the inescapable cold for several days but from our arguments. My brother and I had quarreled almost continually, though about just what I could not recapture. My brother, like me, was struggling through his own difficult adolescence, two years behind me, and outside that trip our lives had sharply diverged. We seldom spoke any more, and when we did, we argued or even fought. Now, I remembered that when we started our trip, I had looked forward to a conciliation and some respite from my terrible adolescent isolation, but amid the constant arguments, I only felt much older than my brother and his friend, excluded from their camaraderie and still very alone.

Searching the forest trails that led away into the pictures, I remembered that we had gotten lost for some hours and it had been frightening, with the early dark coming on and the deepening cold. We tramped through dense brush, and then, with a sense of relief, we again found the trail—and promptly began to argue over which way to proceed. Abruptly, I also remembered the lean-to and the whiskey my brother had written of, and I even remembered that I, in fact, had bought the small bottle in a neighborhood shop the night before we left. And with the surfacing of each additional memory fragment, I found, mingled with the sadness of that trip, a sort of pleasure at once more discovering a lost bit of my past, a sense of returning to wholeness. My pursuit of that fedora, of that brief, misguided camping trip and of that period of my life provided a surprising elation that came with getting reacquainted with my younger self, which I had too long neglected.

◇

Those camping photographs, with their overwhelming wealth of information, led to a startling immersion in a lost weekend of my youth. Before those photos arrived, I could have recalled almost nothing. Now, in the Instamatic images, I could suddenly study every bare branch of every tree, every button on my coat, every captured cloud in its progress across the sky. My fedora. The pictures provided an almost unbearable clarity, a supernatural rush of bodily visiting the past.

The photographer Lee Friedlander once remarked on the medium's inescapable abundance of extraneous detail, its all-encompassing clarity, when describing one of his pictures:

I only wanted Uncle Vern standing by his new car (a Hudson)
on a clear day. I got him and the car. I also got a bit of Aunt
Mary's laundry, and Beau Jack, the dog, peeing on a fence,
and a row of potted tuberous begonias on the porch and
seventy-eight trees and a million pebbles in the driveway and
more. It's a generous medium, photography.

It's those details—the laundry, the dog, the begonias, the million pebbles, or in my case, my fedora and nearly everything else on that trip—that disappear through memory's crevasses and are brought back so astonishingly through photographs.

When a child looks at its first photographs of its family or itself, you can see the profound puzzlement the picture causes as the child tries to untangle reality and its uncanny image. But children quickly become accustomed to our ubiquitous photos, forget their initial wonder. By the time we are adults, we have long lost our feeling that photography is miraculous, just as we forget that movies or, say, flight or the telephone are miracles. Back in 1981, a few flashes of light fell into a tiny box, a few simple chemicals were mixed in the local drugstore's lab, and—*Voila!*—I am no longer forty-four years old, married with two children, but am once more sixteen, standing on a mountain peak with my brother on a gloomy fall afternoon, wearing a fedora.

We forget not only our wonder at photographs but also that the world once greeted the medium as a wonder. When the daguerreotype appeared in the United States, in 1839, with thirty plates placed on view in New York by Louis Daguerre and others, the show was reviewed by *Knickerbocker* magazine:

We have seen the views taken in Paris by the 'DAGUERREO-
TYPE,' and have no hesitation in avowing, that they are the

most remarkable objects of curiosity and admiration, in the
arts, that we ever beheld. Their exquisite perfection almost
transcends the bounds of sober belief.

When we leaf through an album of family picnics and birthdays, we seldom think of those pages as containing "remarkable objects of curiosity and admiration."

After almost two centuries since the invention of photography, and now in our 21st century glut of computerized mini-devices, I'm not sure we can imagine anymore life before photos, when images lingered only in our flawed, ever-fading memories, when life's events, significant and otherwise, flew past and vanished. Had we taken our camping trip without that Instamatic, it would have been lost to me forever.

Before photography, when only the wealthy could commission portraits, and widespread illiteracy meant that few kept journals, death must have loomed in the human mind as even more terrifyingly absolute. The whirling seasons must have seemed even more relentless, driving our family, friends, neighbors into boxes beneath the dirt. And, too, Death was far more present, stalking with disease, riding accidents, Indians, childbirth hazards. When death arrived, *poof*, you were gone, without even a photograph for your loved ones. A few descriptions or anecdotes might be passed down a generation or two before being lost in the hurry and struggle of the young. And if you survived into your dotage, you might well end up burying your spouse, children, and relatives in lengthening rows outside your window, even while their faces faded beyond recapture. I think of the Kentucky statesman Henry Clay and his wife, Lucretia Hart, who had six daughters and five sons and lost seven of them. All six daughters died before age thirty, and before the daguerreotype appeared in the United States, from diseases such as yellow fever and whooping cough. ("Death, ruthless death, has deprived me of

Six affectionate daughters, all that I ever had..." Clay wrote in his grief.) Clay's son Henry, Jr., was killed during the Mexican-American War, at age thirty-seven.

Abraham Lincoln had no photograph of his mother, who died when he was ten, or of his first romantic love, Ann Rutledge, daughter of a tavern-keeper, whom he courted for about three years in the village of New Salem, Illinois, when he was a poor young man. Ann died at age twenty-two, in 1835, four years before the New York exhibit by Louis Daguerre. (There is a photograph believed to be Ann's mother, Mary Ann Rutledge, taken in about 1870, at the age of about eighty.) Ann fell ill, probably with typhoid fever, and died during the summer. Lincoln, by most accounts, plunged into a profound depression, might have been suicidal. One New Salem resident recalled he would say, "My heart is buried in the grave with that dear girl," and would sit by her grave and read a Bible.

After Lincoln had become president, a friend, Isaac Cogdal, visited him in the White House, and during their reminiscence, asked Lincoln whether he really had loved Ann, as stories around New Salem had it. Lincoln replied:

> *I did really....I loved the woman dearly & sacredly: she was a handsome girl—would have made a good loving wife....I did honestly – & truly love the girl & think often—often of her now.*

So, there is Lincoln at the White House, more than two decades after Ann's death, and nearing the end of his own life, still thinking of her "often"—without a photograph to remember her. How can I imagine this photo-less world of Clay and Lincoln? I wonder if for Lincoln, his times with Ann Rutledge took on an unreal, dreamlike quality, as old memories tend to, if her features and the sound of her voice slowly disintegrated into indistinctness.

For Lincoln, how inadequate would be a neighbor's recollection of Ann, such as this by Mentor Graham, a teacher in New Salem, who described Ann to Lincoln's former law partner, William Herndon, who jotted it all down after Lincoln's death:

> *She was about 20 ys—Eyes blue large, & expressive—fair*
> *complexion—Sandy, or light auburn hair—dark flaxen*
> *hair—about 5-4 in—face rather round—outlines beautiful*
> *—nervous vital Element predominated—good teeth—*
> *Mouth well Made bautiful [sic] medium Chin—weigh about*
> *120-130— hearty & vigorous   Amiuble—Kind . . .*

The author (left) with his brother and Gwen.

I have no tragic Ann Rutledge from my youth, but in childhood I swooned for a little girl named Gwyn (I remember only her first name). I was six or seven years old that August we stayed with her family at their Nova Scotia farm for a week's vacation, and was smitten with her golden hair. In memory, Gwyn had faded to merely a golden blur of a girl. I recalled nothing of her features, her clothes, her voice. But in one surviving snapshot, taken by my step-father, and sent by my brother with the camping photos, she reappears in my life instantaneously: There she is once more, in that picture, sitting beside me, my brother behind us, in a rowboat, and she is holding up a fish that she'd just caught. In the photo you can almost smell the briny reek of the dying fish, feel the sun burning on that lake.

After studying that photo and much prodding, memory brought back not quite an image, but more a *feeling*, of sitting in that rowboat in the hot sun. But I did recall that Gwyn was the only one of us that day who caught a fish (I even recovered the extraneous detail that it was a perch), inspiring my step-father to snap the photo. I have a pensive, even troubled, expression because, I now remembered, I had not caught a fish to impress her.

Had it not been for that photo—which like the camping pictures overwhelmed me, at first, like an unbearably clear apparition—I would never have recalled Gwyn's features and certainly not the clothes she happened to wear that day. Or my own, for that matter. And now I see it all: our shirts, the plastic bag, even the fish itself as it dies.

Although I have the posed picture of Gwyn catching a fish—the sort of moment everyone snaps for the photo album—there are two other occasions I would much prefer to have had preserved: a game of cards she and I played one afternoon while sitting on her living room carpet (was the carpet beige?) and, also, sitting with her on the torn seats of a wrecked, rusted pickup truck marooned in high weeds across the road from her home, at dusk. These scenes would appear insignificant. But they are the only moments that remain from the countless impressions of that week in Nova Scotia—because, I'm sure, it was at those moments that I felt most sharply my longing for that little girl, and some part of me also was awakening to the fact that this feeling was something new and strange and painful and important. But adults would not memorialize with a camera such apparently innocuous games.

Another, unrelated scene, a couple of years later, in Pennsylvania: it's a cold fall day, and my brother, my father, and I have halted on a lawn by a tennis court to study a praying mantis standing in the grass. The insect was clearly dying from the cold, was barely moving, and my brother and I gently touched its long, magnificent, emerald body, with sad fascination. Finally, our father, who was sympathetic, said we had to leave. We did, reluctantly. We asked our father questions about the mantis: would it die? Could we save it by bringing it home?

This encounter lasted only a few minutes and, like my games with Gwyn, was not the sort of event that would be captured by our family camera. But those minutes were, for me, a memorable awakening to the poignant, universal fact of death.

And there are those moments that remain with us even while their significance has become irrecoverably obscure. Three years after our camping trip to Bear Mountain, during my first weeks at college, my girlfriend, Amy, and I went to a Woolworth's with a few friends (now faceless in my mind, remaining only as a vague presence, a sense that she and I were not alone). We were buying odds and ends to furnish our dorm rooms. It was probably a Saturday afternoon. I believe the weather was sunny and warm. I was standing among the store's shelves and racks, holding a couple of towels I had chosen to buy. Amy took them from me, replaced them on a shelf and chose two of heavier cloth (what were their colors?) that were a little more expensive. I believe she said something about their being worth the extra cost. Her gesture was sweet and feminine, but why does my mind cling to those five seconds from that shopping trip, and nothing else of that day? No doubt, judging from my forgotten hat, I am forgetting much of that moment at Woolworth's. I certainly can hear no dialogue, or see what we wore.

Psychology is, of course, our tool for unearthing and explaining the significance of our memories, but certain memories, surely, are merely the result of the mind's automatic, machine-like recording of its surroundings—information-storage gone awry, a quirk in the machine. Perhaps that instant at Woolworth's does stick because it holds unplumbed significance—something about the excitement, the heightened awareness of those first days of college, or the unexpected, intimate, domestic gesture of a girlfriend. But in any case, all that remains is a flash of a Woolworth's in Wisconsin twenty-five years ago. And again, not the sort of moment during which we would halt to pose for the camera—although I would prefer a photo of that moment to all those posed college-yearbook shots.

Unfortunately, we seldom predict that such moments will remain with us forever. We don't press the camera shutter when buying towels, or, usually, write of buying towels in our journals, just as we don't write of what clothing we wear each day, such as a fedora. Many of our enduring memories we never would have bothered to record with a photo or a note in a diary. Our memory, often exasperatingly, retains moments and minutiae of its own choosing, and loses others we would have wished to keep. Our photo albums don't match our internal albums. Perhaps because the epiphanies of our lives seldom occur at weddings or while catching fish or posing for college-yearbook photos.

◇

Photos (or home movies) can bring back the dead as nothing else. But certainly they are not the only entry to our past. The fragrance of a newly mowed lawn still catapults me off to my boyhood summers at our in-laws' big house in Ohio. Sounds, such as that of a friend or loved one's recorded voice, also are extraordinarily powerful.

The written word, of course, predates photography as a way to preserve one's past, and in another age, I might have kept a diary of our camping trip rather than tote a camera. My parents were inveterate journal writers, but I've kept a journal only sporadically, during long journeys abroad or profound life-events, like the births of my children. But even if I had meticulously described our trip, I'm certain that my entries would have lacked the myriad details contained in those Instamatic shots, which brought back that weekend with such impact. My journals, I have found, usually reflect my internal state at a certain time with more immediacy than my external surroundings, while photographs are the opposite, presenting mute, if miraculously perfect, likenesses of ourselves from which we must try to divine our internal states.

In 1839, the same year as the New York daguerreotype exhibition, Nathaniel Hawthorne remarked, in a letter:

> *I wish there was something in the intellectual world analogous [sic] to the Daguerreotype (is that the name of it?) in the visible—something which should print off our deepest, and subtlest, and delicatest thoughts and feelings as minutely as the above-mentioned instrument paints the various aspects of Nature.*

For all our technology, we have not invented such a machine. We still rely, when conveying our thoughts, on a journal, whether written or recorded. But even reading our own words usually fails to submerge us in the emotions that we, apparently, once felt. We read them as we would a letter from a person we used to know. We can sympathize, smile, blush—we can even feel again a faint reverberation of those once-powerful feelings—but we seldom truly relive them in their full intensity. Our emotions, as much as our mental images, fade from memory.

Still, we can glean from photos—such as that of my troubled face in the rowboat with Gwyn—at least hints of our thoughts and feelings when the shutter clicked. And since I kept no journal during our camping trip, I was forced to pursue whatever it was I sought about myself within the frames of those eight snapshots.

As it happened, just as it was my troubled face in that rowboat that led me back to my crush on Gwyn and my forgotten feeling of my failure to impress her with my own catch, it was a similar shot of my troubled face on that camping trip a decade or so later that helped bring me back to myself at that time.

In all the photos of that trip, the three of us are posing for the camera, smiling or staring inscrutably, guardedly, grimly amid our arguments and with our teenage secrets, at the camera, as at an intruder. Only one photo is not posed. In this picture, which might have been an accident of the shutter, I am caught on the trail as I glance back at the camera. And I saw my teenage face, so smooth and pale beneath my mop of brown curls, and my eyes, so dark and desperately sad. And it was my younger self's gaze back at me that began to open memory's doors. I experienced again, for the first time in decades, some of the black infinity of my old pain, my isolation. I felt again some of my old fury at my parents, who had divorced and remarried and seemed preoccupied and distant. I resented them for allowing my brother and me to live in the slums of Alphabet City, surrounded by crime and drugs. I had dropped out of high school in an unwitting act of revenge. I had torn apart my own life and was lost, suicidal. My helpless rage ruptured friendships, drove away girl-friends, exploded in fights.

Looking at that teenager's bleak gaze, I knew once more how I had felt at that moment—how I had locked within me all this, along with all the rest of my seething, desperate teenage inner life—my unrequited loves, my rivalries, my drinking and drug use, my weekend nights at downtown clubs and parties. All was concealed from my parents. I remembered how it was to sit in the gloom of the East Village bars after work and the taste of the vodkas and then the drunken stagger home through the slums and passing out in my bedroom to avoid thinking. To my brother, I could not offer guidance or help because I was myself in need of help and beyond any help.

Yet, surprisingly, even as the old sadness pained me, it was, like my other newly retrieved memories of our camping trip, mingled with a lightness, a pleasure of rediscovery.

◇

But I still, maddeningly, could not recall my fedora. I went so far as to call up Doyle, whom my brother still was friendly with, asking if he remembered that hat ("No, I don't remember it," he said). I wrote to several old friends asking if they could recall me wearing a fedora. None could. It seemed I would not be able to find out about that hat.

But I did remember my sneakers. Why did my hat elude me but my sneakers return? I suspect because the hat was a brief affectation, while I *lived* in those sneakers—those frayed, white, ratty canvas Converse sneakers—that belonged, like us, to the streets, the subways of New York City. And it was then that I registered that not only my sneakers were ratty but all of our clothes—our jeans, our sweaters, our coats—were the drab, shabby clothes of inner-city kids, and appeared so incongruous out in the woods. Those clothes, especially those sneakers, brought back our life on Avenue C: the tenements, the empty lots, the bodegas.

The critic Roland Barthes observed that in photographs it is often a single, inadvertent detail that moves us, that *pierces*, and for reasons that are subjective to the viewer. In that candid photo on that camping trip, in which I am half-turned to the camera, the detail that arrested my attention, that pierced, apart from my own stare, was those sneakers: my life was as ragged as they were.

◇

As I slid the photos back into their envelope, it occurred to me that the camping trip itself could serve as a metaphor for my life at that time—a wandering through the cold wilderness of adolescence, flanked by companions but painfully alone. Or perhaps my hat in that photo of me standing on that blustery mountain peak would be an even more apt metaphor: both that hat and I had been torn from the city, were perched in a dangerous, incongruous place, on the edge of disaster. Like that hat, I was on the verge of being blown into oblivion.

I closed the envelope. And just then, I suddenly remembered my hat. An image of that fedora floated up in my mind: I saw it with perfect clarity, hanging from a nail on my old bedroom wall, above my bureau. Yes, I had kept it there, on a nail where I had once hung a painting— and I remembered now, too, how sometimes, lying on my bed, I'd idly toss the hat at the nail, trying to ring it like a horseshoe on a stake.

The single image of my fedora on my wall was all that I was able to retrieve: I still cannot recall where I acquired it, where I wore it other than that camping trip, or where I parted from it. But at least I am now certain that it had been mine. I have found my hat.

9. A Manhattan Barbarian on the Amazon

9 A Manhattan Barbarian on the Amazon

We must willing to get rid of the life we've planned, so as to have the life that is waiting for us.

—Joseph Campbell

IN FEBRUARY, 1983, WHEN I WAS NEWLY EIGHTEEN, I SWUNG A BACKPACK OVER my shoulder, left my family's apartment in the housing developments of the Lower East Side, and jetted from J.F.K. to the Peruvian city of Iquitos, in the Amazon jungle.

Early that Sunday morning, I had gazed down from my twelfth-story bedroom window at the familiar squalor of Avenue C: the laundry strung across the tenements' airshafts, the sickly trees in expanses of trash and rubble, the men listening to Latino music on transistors while tinkering with car engines. The winds carried the deathly stench of the East River two blocks away. Now, that night, I was 3,000 miles south, below the Equator, in the passenger-seat of a battered little taxi whose gold-toothed driver was hurtling us along a jungle road, past decaying, palm-wood huts. The hot night air was redolent of the earth, of primeval vegetation.

We sped through the shacks huddled against the city, then into the dark, vacant streets and plazas. At my hotel, only a few blocks from the night-concealed Amazon River, I registered at the front desk, called my parents on a telephone that appeared to date from World

War II, with a receiver as heavy and large as a barbell, and brought my backpack numbly up the stairs.

In my room, I turned on the lamp and was startled by sky-blue walls. There was a bed, a desk, a bathroom and little else.

I collapsed on the bed but was unable to sleep. I tried to read.

I had jammed in my backpack, among other items, a canteen, water-purifying pills, tropical army boots, wide-brimmed hat, hammock, packaged camping food, knife, maps, compass, a Spanish-English dictionary, a few changes of clothes and several hundred dollars, half of which I carried as James Cook Travelers Cheques: all the money I had saved by working as an office clerk and in mailrooms since I had graduated high school. Also wedged in my bag were two paperbacks: a collection of Jack London's stories, which I had bought at the St. Mark's Bookshop in the East Village, and my parents' yellowing, mass-market paperback edition of Melville's *Typee*. And I had brought a journal, covered with Persian-red, velvet-like cloth, in which to jot my observations—research for my novel.

My novel would be in the tradition of London, Melville, Joseph Conrad: a literary adventure tale. I was enthralled by their magnificent yarns of gold prospectors, sea storms, castaways, battles with cannibals; fascinated by their themes of Heroism, Honor, Courage; charmed by their bygone world of iron, wood, and canvas.

My romantic view of the Jungle, the Arctic, and the Sea was formed, too, by Hollywood films of those writers' novels, which shone on our black-and-white television in our tower above the tenements: *The Call of the Wild, Moby Dick, Lord Jim.* And I soaked up many other adventure films: *Mutiny on the Bounty, The Four Feathers*, and of course, *King Kong*, which, dating from 1933, was almost as old as some of my authors' novels, and appeared positively ancient, with its sepia images, pith-helmeted adventurers and stilted, old-fashioned dialogue. I found it strange that many of the actors in that film, speaking and moving on the screen before me, had lived even while London, Melville, and Conrad wrote—Conrad had died only nine years earlier, London in 1916, Melville in 1891.

But I was not only attempting to write in the manner of my literary heroes, I was determined to live as grandly: if whaling ships still scudded the seas, I would have signed on one as a deck-hand and leapt off at Tahiti.

My novel, I believed, would deliver me from the poverty and violence of Avenue C, from the dreary prospect of college and office. I would live a glorious, vagabond, writer's life. I would write—between adventures—in the cafes of Paris, savoring bohemia. This wildly unrealistic career plan was particularly inspired by two of my literary gods: Ernest Hemingway, who escaped suburban Chicago to Paris at age twenty-two, and Jack London, who at the same age avoided a laborer's fate in Oakland by writing stories about the Klondike gold rush. Their precedents—I didn't realize theirs was the perilous precedent of genius—proved that one could forge a singular, splendid destiny, if only one had enough talent and worked hard enough. I wrote constantly. I felt that my real life, my destiny, awaited, if only I could reach it.

My parents grudgingly acceded to my plan to go to the Amazon after they realized resistance was futile. To prepare, I studied Spanish in my bedroom in the evenings, read history and travel books, and interrogated a few kindly anthropologists in order to find Indians that were still "uncivilized."

I chose, first, the Jivaro, headhunters of the remote jungles of Ecuador, but I settled on the Shipibo: they were not as distant inland and, while unfortunately not headhunters, they seemed sufficiently savage. My anthropologist acquaintances assured me that the Shipibo had retained much of their indigenous culture. Nevertheless, I would hardly be their first visitor—missionaries had been bringing Bibles to their villages since the 17th century and, in more recent times, Shipibo had been in contact with medical workers, government officials, anthropologists. Shipibo worked as laborers during Peru's 19th century rubber boom and later for agricultural companies. There were more than one hundred Shipibo settlements, whose history reached back a millennium and may have intersected with that of the Incas.

All this I read. But I was not interested in understanding Shipibo culture: the Indians and the Amazon would merely serve as exotic stage scenery for my novel.

And so, late that February night in 1983, I was reading London and Melville in a shabby, sky-blue hotel room a few blocks from the Amazon River, waiting for sleep. Sometime toward dawn, I nodded off.

My eyes opened on a vivid image outside the curtains: a sunlit, yellow building with many green-shuttered windows stood across a narrow street. One of the windows framed a dark, middle-aged woman with a kerchief around her head, leaning on her elbows at a sill, watching the noisy traffic below. I gazed at the yellow wall, the green shutters, and the woman for several seconds before I remembered, with a sort of panicked horror, where I was, and realized the enormity of my recklessness. Afraid to leave the room, I lay in bed and read—oblivious to the absurdity of it—my tales of bold adventurers.

Eventually, prodded by hunger, I set out for breakfast and to have a look at the city. I went first to see the river. At the crumbling riverfront promenade—a remnant of Peru's rubber boom—I squinted through sunglasses at the broad, brown-flowing Amazon. The far shore, about two kilometers away, was a low green line of jungle, dotted with huts, under an immense, empty, blue sky. To the south was the slum of Belem, a shantytown that sprawled crazily down into the water, its tin-roofed hovels perched on stilts. Encircled by jungle, the city was accessible only by the river or by air. With my hands resting on that ruin of a more heroic age, with the Amazon River flowing before me,

I felt excited and terrified, as though I was poised at a distant outpost of civilization, like Marlow at the Company's Central Station in the Belgian Congo. The blinding sun and scorching heat, the dark faces and strange language around me, the sudden proximity of the Amazon itself, the shantytown that reeked sickeningly amid hills of rotting potatoes, all dazzled me. Merriam-Webster perfectly describes my turbulent mind-state that morning:

> *Culture shock: a sense of confusion and uncertainty sometimes with feelings of anxiety that may affect people exposed to an alien culture or environment without adequate preparation.*

◈

The Shipibo village I had chosen was located south of Iquitos, in the jungles of central Peru that surround the big frontier town Pucallpa. And, in fact, the village was not quite on the banks of the Amazon River, but on a lake, Yarinacocha, about four miles north of Pucallpa, and adjacent to the Ucayali River, a major Amazon headwater.

Today, the Shipibo village, named San Francisco, has become something of a travel destination and is included on guided tours along with neighboring communities. This was not the case three decades ago.

At Pucallpa, I hired one of the motorized canoes (known as "*peque-peques*," after the sound of their outboard motors) that ferried passengers across the lake. I had asked one of the two men who ran the canoe if they would take me to San Francisco. The man in the front of the craft smiled toothlessly, nodded vigorously, "*Si!*"

I climbed into the canoe, sat on a plank above an inch of muddy water sluicing around the bottom. I was the only passenger. We started out into the lake in a cloud of gasoline fumes. In my journal, I wrote:

There were huge black birds, like hawks circling only
10–20 feet above the lake, swooping down to only a foot
above the water and 20 feet from the boat. The shores
were solid walls of trees, which grow in the water. In their
leaves were the constant sounds of hundreds of birds,
which were never seen, just behind the first branches…
Several times I spotted 1 or 2 boys in little dugouts fishing
with poles (drop-lines) in little pools just behind the
hanging branches, sitting in the cool shadows, watching
us pass.

We motored on for several miles, then nosed into an inlet. The man at the rear cut the engine, then took up a pole, while the man in front used a short, broad paddle. They guided and pushed the boat through the lush floating plants that carpeted the channel, which led to a cluster of thatched huts in a jungle clearing.

When the canoe halted, I hoisted my backpack and jumped onto the soft, mud bank. I paid the men a few coins—far more money than necessary, I saw, by their surprised and delighted smiles—and they guided the canoe away.

I turned and discovered that about a dozen Shipibo men and women had appeared, and were warily stepping forward to see their visitor. A thrill went through me: I was, at last, at my jungle village.

◇

The group of Shipibo who studied me were slightly built with dark, searching eyes. Their black hair fell straight over their foreheads. The men wore dirty, cheap, Western-style clothing—polyester pants and shirts, shorts, torn T-shirts. The women, though, still wore the Shipibo's traditional, brightly colored skirts and blouses.

In faltering Spanish, I told them I had come to stay at their village. As instructed by the anthropologists, I held out several fish hooks, offered in return for lodging.

A young man stepped forward, took the hooks, examined them and conferred with his young wife, who was holding a child at her hip. In Spanish, he asked me where I came from. I explained I had come from New York City, in the United States, to observe the village. "New York" was meaningless to most of them, though a couple of the men nodded thoughtfully, as though with a vague recognition of the name. The group discussed this information. They may not have heard of New York, but they gradually understood that I had arrived from a large American city. This appeared to both awe and puzzle them. I could see in their eyes the question: why would I want to visit *them*?

The young man continued to inspect the fish hooks, which I had chosen from a glass case at a Manhattan sporting-goods shop. He fingered their points, studied their garish colors and extravagant feathers, and seemed satisfied, impressed and amused. Several men and boys came closer to scrutinize the hooks and passed them around, commenting on them in Shipibo. The young man explained to me that, in exchange for the hooks, I was welcome to stay in his hut, which was a few yards away.

My host's hut, like many in the village, was open on all sides and consisted of just a floor of split palm-wood resting on stilts about one foot above the mud, protected by a roof of dried palm leaves.

I left my backpack in the hut, then took a walk around the village, followed by the group that had gathered. My host, whose Shipibo name was Romillo in Spanish, walked at my side, along with several inquisitive children. I offered the kids balloons—a wonderful rarity, which one anthropologist had advised me would be appreciated. *"Globos! Globos!"* they shouted gleefully, and raced to fetch their brothers and sisters. In an instant, it seemed, every child and adolescent in the village had converged on me, shrieking "Globos! Globos! Globos!" stretching out their hands. In seconds, my plastic bag was empty and the colorful balloons were being blown up and squabbled over. The adults watched the frenzy with indulgent smiles. My anthropologist acquaintance had provided wise counsel—the bag of balloons from the candy store on Fourteenth Street had instantly won the goodwill of the village.

The community consisted of about two dozen huts of varying sizes. The nearby Ucayali River means "Mosquito River" in English, and with good reason: the pests were everywhere. The people in the huts were calmly slapping themselves to be rid of them, as I later saw they did constantly, all day. I glimpsed a line of women walking gracefully with great bowls balanced on their heads. Another group of women went with machetes into the jungle—a dark maw only a few yards from the huts. Roaming the village were chickens and roosters, a few hogs. I passed women nursing infants or cooking meals in metal pots and men sitting in the huts making nets. They all paused to stare at me as I passed with my entourage, and some called out curiously in Shipibo to those around me. I saw several men and boys constructing a large, complex hut with several levels of storage-shelves beneath a partially thatched roof—many homes had at least one such "attic" shelf, crowded with rusted trunks, metal tins, suitcases stuffed with papers.

As the sun descended over the lake, I returned to Romillo's hut and attempted to set up my hammock. I struggled with the ropes and hooks in increasing confusion. In my journal, I noted:

About 15 people watched me set up my hammock the first night at Romillo's house, talking, curious, examining my mosquito netting and rope, until Romillo said he'd set me up with a blanket and cover-cloth beside his own.

Romillo draped a cotton cloth—protection from mosquitoes and insects—over a couple of ropes he had strung above my blanket. Later, he emerged from his own cloth-cover wearing bright-pink polyester pants, cowboy boots and a pink-and-white striped polyester shirt. As he stepped out in this costume, I laughed, which drew from him an offended glance. Apparently, he only wore this outfit on certain evenings, or perhaps he wore it for my benefit, for during the afternoon he had worn only a pair of torn, brown corduroy shorts.

When night fell, Romillo and his wife, Amarilla, and I talked by candlelight in their hut about New York and their village. He asked me about English words and was curious about America. I queried him about missionaries. The Shipibo believed in God, the couple told me, but not the Christian God. We communicated in broken Spanish and hand-gestures while their child slept beneath the cloth. At that time, I held a prejudice against missionaries, and I wrote of our discussion:

The missionaries come here occasionally, and I explained to
him that I disliked missionaries, and he agreed, but almost, I
think, not to offend me. He said he doesn't let the missionaries
in his house (I almost laughed because his house has no walls).

Later that night, the whispers of Romillo and his wife reached me from beneath our cotton nettings—mine was only a foot from theirs. I couldn't understand their words, but it was clear that Romillo's wife was questioning him about my presence there—how long would I stay? Was I to be trusted? And Romillo responded with reassurances. It occurred to me that the pragmatic, intimate whispering of this Shipibo husband and wife was the same sort of pillow-talk I sometimes heard from my parents' bedroom.

◇

During the next few days, I jotted observations and sketches in my journal, snapped photos with my parent's Kodak Instamatic. The village, as I had hoped, had remained relatively isolated. There was no electricity, no running water. There were no bathrooms (you walked a few yards into the jungle). The sole direct connection with the

The author in the Amazon jungle at age eighteen, in 1983.

world beyond Lake Yarinacocha that I could discover was an ancient radio (presumably run on batteries) owned by my host's brother, which received music from Pucallpa. The frenetic Latin rhythms and tinny horns that sounded from that jungle hut were jarringly similar to the Puerto Rican music that blasted from the transistor radios along Avenue C.

The women went barefoot and bare-breasted or wore the Shipibo skirts and blouses adorned with geometric designs. They kept their hair braided or let it fall loosely around their shoulders. They still made traditional pottery. Bowls and jars were decorated with labyrinthine patterns and, disconcertingly, many bowls bore human faces, which stared blankly every which way in clusters. The women painted the bowls with tiny, slender brushes made from their own hair.

The Shipibo's pottery, like the women's traditional clothing, seemed, to an extent, a conscious holdout against the encroachment of outside influences. Despite the village's isolation, there was, in addition to the radio, additional evidence of the world beyond. The people not only spoke Spanish as well as Shipibo, but also could read and write. A few of the men taught Spanish to other Shipibo villages. In each hut was a section of the Bible printed in the Shipibo language, left by missionaries. One old man dug up a yellowed, English-Spanish dictionary and asked me to say certain words aloud. He and several other men repeated the sounds with intense concentration.

They barraged me with questions about America. They were particularly curious about the cost of things: how much had I paid for my shoes, my clothes, my watch, my hammock?

In one couple's hut, the husband, who was about my age, kept on a shelf a disintegrating paperback Western novel. From its cover leapt a lurid painting of cowboys and Indians in bloody combat, the title in bold, crimson Spanish letters.

The glimpse of that paperback, in retrospect, should have served as a warning that I would not find what I was seeking in this village: here was a Shipibo Indian, in the very heart of the Amazon jungle, searching in a novel for diversion from the prosaic pattern of *his* life. Moreover, he was searching in the Wild West of America's 19th century—even as I was seeking the same adventure in some imaginary, 19th century Peru. This young Shipibo man's path and mine were precisely crossed.

◇

But I did soon realize, as had my Shipibo doppelganger, that days in the village followed a prosaic pattern. I wrote:

> *Dawns are usually cloudy & get sunny after an hour or so.*
> *The women start fires with matches and large pieces of wood*
> *and wood-chips. The men stretch and yawn, and Romillo*
> *appears from our hut, utters a cheerful, long and satisfied*

*"OK"—the only English word he knows —and slaps his bare
stomach.*

*The women make pottery with wooden knives and prepare
breakfast with help from the girls. The children play
with a ball or stand around together, the men make fishing
nets with a little wooden hand-tool and a long wooden
stake and work over and over, methodically. Or they go
fishing alone or with their sons. They smile and say "hello"
in Shipibo to each other as they pass and talk a little.
Always there is the never-ending sound of the people slapping
calmly at mosquitoes.*

*In the afternoon the rest of the men go out to fish. In the
evening, the women cook the fish and they eat 1 or 2 hours
before sundown, when they go to sleep. Or they have little fires
and talk awhile or open a can of gas with a wick attached.*

How ordinary! How dull! Where were the blood-drenched ceremonies by firelight to strange gods? Where were the heathen pageants and orgiastic fertility dances?

From Romillo's hut one morning, I ruefully watched women washing clothes in the same narrow channel where I had arrived by canoe. I remembered the garments strung on lines across the tenements at home. In fact, almost everything appeared all too familiar: the preparing and eating of meals, the women nursing infants while chatting like my neighbors gossiping on their tenement stoops.

I became increasingly bad-tempered. Wherever I went, the children asked me for "*globos,*" until I shouted: "*No mas globos! No mas globos!*" Afterward, when I passed, they stared resentfully, even fearfully, and the little ones murmured "*globos...globos.*"

One afternoon, a father and his son, who was about eight years old, invited me to go fishing. The father paddled the dugout, and the boy, wearing only shorts, held a spear tipped with four metal prongs, which he flung with extraordinary accuracy; a pile of small silver fish quickly grew in the canoe. They cheerfully urged me to try. I attempted to spear a fish that they pointed to excitedly, but which I could not see beneath the water, and I missed it with a slow, wobbly throw. The father and son smiled good-naturedly but I sat burning with anger, feeling humiliated.

At sunset, the family cooked the fish in a pot of water on a fire, and they offered me a bowl. I looked at the silver fish floating with staring eyes in the unpurified lake water and didn't bother to hide my disgust. Father, mother and son faced me with hurt expressions. I ignored them and irritably ate packaged food from my backpack. Then I lay down under my netting. I listened to the villagers calmly slapping at the mosquitoes, and talking in Shipibo. It was a long way from *Lord Jim*.

The next morning, I left the village. I had stayed a far shorter time than planned, but I was already impatient to leave. I told my hosts that I was returning to Pucallpa, then waited alone by the water for a *peque-peque* to take me back. Later that day, I set down a few details of my departure:

> I jumped to the little mound of grass and shouted and waved my arms. The peque-peque slowly stopped, turned, and the two men, with an oar and a pole, pushed the canoe through the floating plants. In the boat was an old man, an old Shipibo woman and a young one, who knew each other. The young woman had a baby in a pouch on her back. The boat was a dugout, about 30-40 feet long with an outboard motor. The front steersman, once we pushed off, slept shirtless, lying with his arms folded, his head back, mouth open.

I flew back to New York, twenty pounds thinner, suffering from hundreds of mosquito bites, a wretched sunburn, and a bad case of "chiggers"—a mite larva that burrows under skin.

During the next few weeks, I wrote a collection of short stories, not the novel I had intended. As soon as I had completed them, I realized they were irrecoverable failures—superficial, clichéd adventure tales. I tore them up.

And so, one spring morning I was back at my bedroom window, gazing down at the condemned tenements, the bars, the trash-strewn lots, the bodegas. I was again working as an office clerk and in mail-rooms. The jungle, the village, Romillo and his wife—they already seemed to belong to a dream or to the half-lost past, a silly, adolescent adventure, an elaborate fool's errand I had sent myself on. I was in a state of disbelief after abandoning my manuscripts, as though I had just crawled from a train wreck—and, in a sense, I had: my life had been pitched from its tracks. This was *not* the Plan. Montmartre and Tahiti seemed to be floating further and further beyond reach, a cruel mirage.

In despair, and determined to leave Avenue C and the menial jobs that stretched ahead endlessly, I enrolled for the fall term at a Midwest college. My parents, naturally, approved, but the decision caused me many sleepless nights that summer, prompted a thousand changes of mind: to attend college was to relinquish all my cherished plans for my bohemian, adventurous future. In the small hours, I considered, desperately, working as a deckhand on a freighter to Paris.

In the end, though, I did go to college. And on that campus, as autumn passed into winter, I found, to my surprise, that my remorse increasingly yielded to happiness. I discovered joy in so many unexpected places—in the peace of the cornfields when I walked out alone after a clamorous dinner at commons; in the mornings at the smoky tables of the student union, where the windows overlooked the great lawn, white with the first snows; in the sodden revelries with new friends on Saturday nights; in the ascetic silence of the library on a gloomy Sunday. And then, I found Romance. I fell for a girl in my history class. We took walks along moonlit roads, and I listened rapt as she told me of her girlhood on her family farm. Some nights we bicycled out among the fields and lay in the corn and watched the moon glide slowly across the starry sky.

And in this way, twenty-five years ago, on that campus lost deep among the Midwest cornfields and pig farms, I abandoned my anguished pursuit of storybook exploits and swung onto a true adventure—the journey of my own life.

10. I and the Village

10 and the Village

My forty-year relationship with Greenwich Village sometimes seems as complicated and as fraught with shades of former lives as its networks of old Dutch lanes. I've known these streets, it seems, forever; memories run back to the first years of my marriage, to my teenage years, to my childhood.

Still, I was never entirely sure it was home.

My earliest images of the Village reach back nearly to the start of memory itself, age five, when twice each day I watched as its squares, boutiques, and crowds slid past the dirty windows of the cross-town bus, on my way to and from school.

The school—a Dickensian, granite-and-brick monstrosity that had been converted that year—1970—into a sixties-inspired experimental school—was on Hudson Street, on the western edge of the island. Since my mother and step-father lived on the eastern edge, on Avenue C, my roundtrip journey provided a perch from which to view the entire span of the Village on weekday mornings and afternoons, in fall, winter and spring.

Each day coming home, the bus, the now-defunct M13, would turn sharply right into narrow Greenwich Avenue, pass the Jefferson Market Library with its pointed clock-tower, and, beside it, the Women's House of Detention, forbidding as a Welsh castle, then would cross broad Sixth Avenue and pass the big vertical sign for C.O. BIGELOW'S DRUGS ("EST. 1838"), and the driver would inch the great bus along in the traffic of the main drag, Eighth Street, thronged with NYU students, tourists, hipsters, lined with off-beat boutiques, fast-food joints, bookshops.

For five years, until I entered intermediate school a dozen blocks uptown, in Chelsea, I rode this route twice each weekday. I can still ride it in my mind, block by block. The route, and the order of the bus-stops, and the shops that are gone, still pass with vivid clarity outside those dirty bus windows. Heading further East, the driver would steer us through the abruptly wide expanse of Astor Place, and we would enter the gritty streets of the East Village—here, the boutiques and the crowds were even funkier. The tenements were worn. The bus stopped directly in front of the aged Valencia Hotel, where hookers in miniskirts and fur coats stood by the entrance, along with pimps in velvet hats and platform boots. Then, still further East: we skirted Tompkins Square Park, the border of the slum of Alphabet City (which it was not yet called), and the few remaining passengers would leave the bus before the tenements became mere ruins left by the wrecking ball and arsonists, and the pavements became broken and pot-holed.

The daily journey to and from this region of wreckage lit the Village with a magical glow for me: Avenue C was a war-zone; the Village was beauty, safety, normalcy. In the Village, there were long afternoons playing baseball with classmates in Washington Square Park, and covert expeditions from school to Li-Lac Chocolates around the corner for white-paper bags of jelly beans or chunks of white chocolate. Life in the Village was walking beneath cherry-blossoms in spring and beneath café umbrellas in the summer. It was running in the winter twilight with my brother through lanes of 18th century homes. The Village held the dreamy charm of a scene in a glass paperweight.

Still, the Village also held disturbing ambiguity. I not only attended school there; my father and step-mother lived there, in an apartment overlooking an intersection of Bleecker Street. My brother and I visited them on weekends. And as a boy shuttling between two households, between two irreconcilable worlds, I always felt deeply unsettled, as though on each bus ride I was simultaneously both leaving home and returning home. Were we Village kids visiting the slum, or slum kids visiting the Village?

◇

But if the Village was, for me, both home yet an escape from home, I was hardly alone: this is precisely what its four square miles of lanes and squares had been for its pilgrims for nearly a century. Since the days of president Taft, the Village had beckoned artistic spirits as a place where one could flee one's life and start a new one. It's where Edna St. Vincent Millay arrived in 1917 from Vassar and wrote "My Candle Burns At Both Ends," and where Bob Dylan arrived in 1960 from Minnesota with a guitar.

There was, however, a difference: I didn't choose to live in Bohemia Central; that choice was made for me before I was born, back in the fifties, when my father began visiting the Village from Philadelphia, as a teenager. He later married my mother, also a bohemian writer. After they separated, in the late sixties, my father met my step-mother while visiting the offices of Grove Press, the avant-garde publisher of Henry Miller, Samuel Beckett, and Jean Genet, among many others whose work had not been widely available in America. My step-mother was promoting books such as *The Autobiography of Malcolm X*. Like Millay, she had come to the Village by way of Vassar.

While my step-mother spread the gospel of uncensored literature at arguably the world's most infamous publishing house (its offices, on a corner at University Place, were not far from their apartment), my father wrote books and poetry, edited magazines, taught

A view of the M13 bus route in 1970: The Jefferson Market Library tower is center; the jazz club "Your Father's Mustache" in the foreground.

literature. For him, as for my step-mother and untold others before and since, the move to the Village was not merely a matter of toting one's belongings to another place, it was a life-changing decision, a symbolic gesture.

For me, bohemian life was a birthright. Weekends, my brother and I would sometimes meet our father at a café, where we would find him correcting proofs of a book or editing an article. Or he would bring us to browse at the Eighth Street Bookshop, which we later learned also happened to be a legendary watering hole for the Beats, Auden, E.E. Cummings, Marianne Moore, etc.; or we would go to the old Sandolino Restaurant Café, in a lane off Sheridan Square. Sandolino was a high-ceilinged, noisy hang-out for actors, writers, show-producers, film-makers, with a fully rigged model sailing ship in its window and brick walls decorated with old oars and other maritime relics. The varnished pale-wood tables seemed always loud with jokes and gossip and stories, the air blue with cigarette smoke, and the waitresses joked and talked about their personal lives with customers on the fly between orders.

So, this was adult life: you went to cafes to write. You hung around smoky coffee-houses with artists and performers. You wore whatever clothes you chose. How do you rebel against *this* as a teenager? You either go straight into investment banking or delve so deeply into the caverns of bohemia that even your bohemian parents would—hopefully—be horrified.

But I did not revolt against my bohemian upbringing. I was often angry at my parents and at my life on Avenue C, but I chose to become a painter (my parents were fine with this). Later, I abandoned painting and decided to be a writer (rather like going into the family business, after all). As a teenager and would-be novelist, I would occasionally treat myself to a coffee at the Cafe Figaro, which used to be on the corner of Bleecker and MacDougal streets, a dark, European-style café with a constantly hissing espresso machine, famed as a former gathering place for Jack Kerouac and Co. But as I labored in my notebook, my inspiration was derived not from the beats, but from a bohemia of thirty years earlier across the Atlantic: I had recently read Hemingway's memoir of Paris of the twenties, *A Moveable Feast*, with its nostalgic, lyric descriptions of how he had lived impoverished over a sawmill and wrote in his notebooks at the Closerie des Lilas, and I dreamed of starving in a garret in Paris (my father had spent a year in Paris at age twenty—no rebellion here, either).

I absorbed bohemianism so naturally and thoroughly that it was only when I left for college in the Midwest—with painful ambivalence, mostly just to get out of Avenue C—that I began to perceive that growing up in the Village was considered unusual, even enviable. "That must have been extraordinary!" other students would sometimes say, with widened eyes. "What was it *like*?"

I would reply—seeking to avoid a discussion that could lead into the complexities of my dual households and my life on Avenue C—with a shrug: "It was home."

I still wasn't sure, though, that the Village *had* been home.

◇

Home is as amorphous a concept as love. The law recognizes several types of home—or "domicile," in the dry vocabulary of the bar— "domicile of origin," "domicile of choice," and so forth. Each legal definition has accumulated specific parameters. But there is a domicile that lies beyond law's reach, one that everyone knows is most important: the domicile in one's heart. The place you love. Your childhood town's main street; the corn fields you remember in Iowa; your bungalow in the suburbs. You may not live there now, it may no longer exist as you knew it, you may not even have ever been legally "domiciled" there, but it is where, in your deepest self, you *belong*. No law can describe or even find this place.

Still, it is possible to stretch even this elastic idea of home too far. During the period when I was writing at the Figaro, I would have declared (and occasionally did) that my true home was Paris. To be more precise, Montmartre, circa 1922. The Village was a poor imitation, was where I happened to be at the moment, was not my home or even "domicile," but merely my "residence," as the law would say.

Ten years later, when I finally got to Montmartre, I realized, with a rude shock, that it could never be even a comfortable residence, much less a home. I was not a Francophile; I was entranced by an idealized, early 20th century image of bohemia that happened to be located in France. Paris could never be more than a place to hang my beret. It wasn't where I belonged, wasn't my turf. Those lovely, gray, cobbled streets meant nothing to me. But the Village streets *did* mean something to me. Why didn't I realize it?

The familiar simply could not live up to the ideal. My bohemia, in adolescence, had not been, despite occasional visits to the Figaro, a series of glowing cafes and vistas of picturesque chimney pots—or even nights at the Cedar Tavern or the Whitehorse. It had been a series of dingy clubs in lower Manhattan where bands in leather jackets and with Mohawk haircuts blasted punk music. It had been tacky Greek diners, and dive bars. The aesthetics were all wrong, because the age I lived in was wrong. I was a New York Jewish street kid seeking home in post-World War I Paris. Part of knowing your true home is understanding your identity enough to know where home is *not*.

I also know, now, that Avenue C was never home. It was a nightmare, a plunge into human darkness, a scar. But it was not home. It is, perhaps, best described as my former residence.

◇

When I walk through the Village now, nearly every street holds layers of my history—here is the spot where I waited for the M13 bus; here was Sandolino or the Eighth Street Bookshop; here was the jazz club where I bussed tables one summer; here was Homer's diner where as teenagers we went late at night; here was where my wife and I took long weekend walks when we were in our twenties and lived near Union Square. Past lives here become tangled. This is particularly so because, in contrast to the neighborhood around Avenue C, which is so gentrified I find it unrecognizable, the Village is relatively unchanged, thanks to decades of fierce battles by preservationists. Many places are gone, true, and in the seventies the Village was shabbier and wilder, as was the city itself. The leather-clad crowds that once filled Christopher Street have been decimated by AIDS or have dispersed to other neighborhoods. Many streets have gone upscale, attracting celebrities and the wealthy. Fewer artists can afford to starve in even the tiniest studios: Williamsburg, in Brooklyn, has become the city's symbol of bohemia.

Nevertheless, most of the Village streets and parks remain as I recall them. And the atmosphere still feels different, looser, a little kookier than anywhere else on the island. There are still the NYU students, and kids making their own pilgrimages. And there are still grizzled beatniks and gray-haired flower-children clinging to low-rent apartments and reading the *Voice* through spectacles at cafes, even if they now do so beside venture capitalists reading *The Wall Street Journal*. There are still fathers who carry guitars strapped on their backs while walking their kids to school.

Today, too, the Village still often seems, as it did when I was growing up, less a fabled bohemian enclave than a real village—albeit a somewhat wacky one. This village-like ambiance is most palpable on weekdays, when the streets are emptied of weekend crowds and life returns to its natural pace—a slower pace than that of other Manhattan neighborhoods. It's the pace of people who savor their unlikely niches, who don't follow office hours, who instead are on the schedules of poets, or graduate students, or bats, or worlds in science fiction. But the Chinese laundries, newspaper stands, and groceries on nearly every block are reminders that daily life, even here, goes on with a certain prosaic regularity. Sit in a coffeeshop on a late weekday morning with the lanes outside quiet beneath the trees, and the Village still feels so serene and indolent that you might be in New England.

In the Village, I now find that I am comfortable as I am nowhere else—here, among the brownstones I've known forever, and the coffee-houses that still have pale-wood tables and black-and-white photographs on the walls and waitresses who are "really" dancers, as they were at Sandolino.

We are intimates, the Village and I. We share the sort of incommunicable depth of intimacy that spouses or family members share. Its streets have known me from boyhood, through adolescence, young adulthood and, now, parenthood. And I have known the Village in all its changes of moods, changes of light, changes of fashion through the years.

Although I haven't lived in the Village for more than two decades, my wife and I sometimes bring our son and daughter from uptown to the places I knew in my boyhood, like Washington Square Park, or to visit their grandparents: my father and step-mother still live in the apartment on Bleecker Street.

One recent afternoon, an icy winter day, when we stopped in for a visit, I asked my father, now in his seventies, if he would prefer to live in Florida or some other warm-weather place.

"Well, I don't think so," he replied. "I have more than forty years of history here," he gestured toward frozen Bleecker Street outside the window with a smile. "The Village is my home."

Yes, I understood.

Sources

1. My Sixties

p. 10. Laugh-in/SNL: Brooks, Tim and Marsh, Earle. *Complete Directory to Prime Time Network and Cable TV Shows.* Eighth edition. New York: Random House, 2003.

2. Farewell, Avenue C

p.18. Lyrics for "Avenue C": Lambert, Hendricks & Ross. "Avenue C." *Sing a Song of Basie* (Verve, 1957).

p. 19. Quotes by Edward D. Reuss: *NY Cop Online Magazine.* (www.nycop.com); February, 1999, issue.

p. 31. Hobbes, Thomas (author). MacPherson, Crawford Brough (Editor/introduction). *Leviathan.* New York: Penguin Group USA, 1982.

p. 35. Chambers, Marcia. *The New York Times,* "Going Cold Turkey in Alphabetville," February 19, 1984.

p. 36. Gross, Jane. *The New York Times,* "In The Trenches of a War Against Drugs," January 8, 1986.

p. 38. Colman, Andrew, M. *A Dictionary of Psychology.* New York: Oxford University Press, 2009.

p. 40. Moynihan, Colin. *The New York Times,* "In Images, the Lower East Side of Starker Days," February 18, 2008.

3. The Forest in Grand Central Station

p. 48. Opie, Iona and Peter. *The Classic Fairy Tales*. New York.
Oxford University Press, 1980.

p. 50. Perrault, Charles. *Perrault's Fairy Tales*. Mineola, NY:
Dover. 1969. (Reprinted from *Old Time Stories Told By
Master Charles Perrault* (1921) translated by A.E. Johnson;
verse morals reprinted from *Perrault's Fairy Tale*s (1912),
translated by S.R. Littlewood.)

p. 54. *The New York Times*, "Hunt Goes Into Fifth Day For
Connecticut Child, 7." July 31, 1973.

The Boston Globe: Gaines, Judith. "A Killer Confesses,
Repeatedly." July 9, 1999.

4. Crossing into Poland

p. 58. Baldwin, James. "The Harlem Ghetto." *Notes of a Native
Son*. Boston: Beacon Press, 1955.

p. 63. Lifton, Robert, Jay. *The Broken Connection: On Death
and the Continuity of Life*. Washington, DC: American
Psychiatric Publishing, Inc., 1996. (Quoting Jakov Lind's
autobiography: *Counting My Steps: An Autobiography*. New
York: Macmillan, 1969.)

p. 67. Babel, Isaac. Walter Morison (Translator), Lionel Trilling
(Introduction). *The Collected Stories of Isaac Babel*.
New York: Plume, 1974.

5. Lost Lustre

p. 76. Johnson, Samuel (author). Donald Greene (editor).
"A Rooming House Chronicle." *The Major Works*. New York:
Oxford University Press, 1984.

6. The Hotel 17, Revisited

p. 140. Gorbachev, Raisa. *I Hope: Reminiscences and Reflections.* New York: HarperCollins, 1991.

p. 144. Didion, Joan. "Goodbye To All that." *Slouching Towards Bethlehem.* New York. Farrar, Straus and Giroux, 1990.

P. 149. Marlowe, Christopher. "The Passionate Shepherd to His Love." *Christopher Marlowe, the Complete Poems and Translations.* Orgel, Stephen. New York: Penguin Classics, 2007.

7. Bringing Up Baby

p. 168. Chesterson, G.K. "In Defence of Penny Dreadfuls." *On Lying in Bed and Other Essays.* Editor: Manguel, Alberto. Calgary, Canada: Bayeux Arts, 2000.

8. On Chasing After One's Hat

p. 180. Chesterson, G.K. "On Running After One's Hat." *On Lying in Bed and Other Essays.* Editor: Manguel, Alberto. Calgary, Canada: Bayeux Arts, 2000.

p. 180. Didion, Joan. "On Keeping a Notebook." *Slouching Towards Bethlehem.* New York. Farrar, Straus and Giroux, 1990.

p. 186. Friedlander, Lee. *The Desert Seen.* New York: D.A.P./ Distributed Art Publishers, Inc., 1996.

p. 186. *The Knickerbocker, or New York Monthly Magazine.* New York: Clark and Edson, December, 1839. p.560. Vol. XIV, No. 6.

p. 187. Remini, Robert Vincent. *Henry Clay: Statesman for the Union.* New York: W.W. Norton & Co., 1992.

p. 188. *Herndon's Informants: Letters, Interviews and Statements
About Abraham Lincoln*. Urbana: University of Illinois Press,
1997. Editors: Douglas L. Wilson and Rodney O. Davis.
p. 440.

p. 189. *Herndon's Informants: Letters, Interviews and Statements
About Abraham Lincoln*. Urbana: University of Illinois Press,
1997. Editors: Douglas L. Wilson and Rodney O. Davis.
p. 242.

p. 193. Valenti, Patricia Dunlavy. *Sophia Peabody Hawthorne:
A Life*, Volume 1, 1809-1847. Columbia, Missouri: University
of Missouri Press, 2004.

9. A Manhattan Barbarian on the Amazon

p. 198. Campbell, Joseph (author). Osbon, Diane, K. (editor).
*A Joseph Campbell Companion: Reflections on the Art of
Living*. New York: HarperCollins; first edition, 1992.
(The quote has also been attributed to E. M. Forster.)

Photo credits:

Cover: Photograph by Larissa Gonzalez.

p. 21. Avenue C: Photographs by Marlis Momber.

p. 49. Lower East Side, 1980s: Photograph by Q. Sakamaki.

p. 217. Tenth Street Looking East from Seventh Avenue: Photograph
by Richard Friedman.

Author Photograph: William Grant.

About the Author

Josh Karlen, a native New Yorker, grew up on the Lower East Side and in Greenwich Village. A former journalist, he was a correspondent in the Baltics for United Press International, Radio Free Europe, and other news organizations. He lives in New York City with his wife and two children and is a media relations specialist.

Lost Lustre: A New York Memoir
Josh Karlen

8 X 5
Paper
220 pages
ISBN 13: 9780981932118
October 2010
Tatra Press
Distributed by National Book Network

For media or review enquiries, please contact Chris Sulavik at
Tatra Press, tatrapress@hotmail.com, 845.596.7075

More Advance Praise for Lost Lustre:

"Growing up in the shadow of the Sixties, parented by the Sixties, Josh Karlen fills the space created by the hippie, radical movers and shakers. The story of what it was like to come after, to belong to the past and to make your own present, is impressively and elegantly told in these fine essays."

—Jenny Diski, author of *The Sixties*

"Many of us who remember the New York of the 1970s and 1980s can't put our fingers exactly on what we miss. It isn't the dirty streets, high crime, and poor services but a certain grittiness and, paradoxically, lustre, that went along with simply surviving the Lower East Side or similar neighborhoods that felt simultaneously desolate and exciting. Josh Karlen can and does put his finger on this "lost lustre," as it were, describing now-defunct clubs like CBGB and Danceteria with the same verve he gives to accounts of having his face smashed in by a derelict. One gets the feeling that given the choice of doing it all over again, Karlen would still take the trade of a broken nose, suicides, muggings, etc., for that *je ne sais quoi* that was New York City circa 1980. By the end of the book, you would, too."

—Dalton Conley, author of **Honky**